THE PAPERBACK
BADSHAH

ABHAY NAGARAJAN is the author of the bestselling *Corporate Atyaachaar: The comical journey of an office doormat* (2010) and *The Off-Site Tamasha: A comical tale of team building* (2012), both of which offer a comical, entertaining view on corporate life.

Born in 1983, Abhay did his schooling in Mumbai and Bangalore. He studied commerce at SRCC and followed that up with a Master's degree in Finance (MFC) at Delhi University. Having worked as a financial advisor for a few years, he is now busy exploring his skills as a fiction writer. He currently lives in Bangalore.

THE PAPERBACK
BADSHAH
...The Comical Journey of a '100 Rupee' Author

ABHAY NAGARAJAN

Srishti
PUBLISHERS & DISTRIBUTORS

SRISHTI PUBLISHERS & DISTRIBUTORS
N-16, C. R. Park
New Delhi 110 019
editorial@srishtipublishers.com

First published by
Srishti Publishers & Distributors in 2013

Typeset by EGP at Srishti

As always,
For my loving parents
&
In the memory of my grandfather
Mr. Malayatoor Ramakrishnan
(1927-1997)

ACKNOWLEDGEMENTS

Thanks to:

My mother for reading initial drafts patiently.

My father and my brother Hareesh for reading subsequent drafts and offering valuable suggestions. My brother also took time out of his busy schedule to set up my website (www.abhaynag.com).

My friends: Rajesh, Ajeet, Santosh, Ravi, Anupam, Kunal, Bhomik, Janeet, Ghanu, Nirmal, Meher and Sudheer for their friendship, and interest in my writing.

To the readers of *Corporate Atyaachaar* and *The Off-Site Tamasha*, who gave me their valuable feedback.

My publisher for accepting my work and having it published.

And finally, none of this would have been possible without the blessings of God who made it all happen.

PART 1

CREATIVE INITIATION

ASPIRATION

The world knew him as TB.

The nickname stuck for superstar Indian writer Tilak Bhatia because whenever he would greet his fans, he would cough. A deep throated cough which was usually associated with the dreaded disease, tuberculosis. So enamoured were fans by his deliberate coughing manner, that in such commercial times in which a carefully cultivated image of an author had to be formed to push book sales, his cough was enough to form an instant connect with a reader.

TB was presently in Bangalore to launch his latest book *Hey politician...r u getting a hard-on when the legislative assembly is on?* which earlier in the week had been launched in Delhi followed by another launch in Mumbai. Prior to its release, the book had created a fair bit of pre-release buzz among expectant readers. Initial media reports stated that over two lakh copies had already been pre-ordered online!

Waiting excitedly with other readers for TB's arrival in the bookstore on Residency Road was 25 year old, Raghu

Balakrishnan who had left office early on that Friday evening to be in time for the book launch.

He was a big fan of TB's writing and was quite excited about getting an 'author signed' copy of TB's new book. He also had dreams of his own of becoming a successful published author someday.

If one had to assess TB's meteoric rise since 2006 to become 'THE' name in the Indian publishing world, it was best to start at the beginning.

Media reports had it that TB (born to lower middle class parents who passed away in his youth) left India on a scholarship to pursue his education in the US. He studied at the mother of all schools of excellence-engineering undergrad at MIT and an MBA from Harvard. He then worked at a big league private equity firm for a few years.

A mentor of his at work told him, 'You can either let destiny decide your life or let your passion determine it. I had dreams of becoming a singer. But I let destiny decide my life. But now it is too late. I'm destined to die a number cruncher for a PE market player. You are a youngster. You should have the fire in your belly to take charge of your life.'

TB cried. But also felt inspired.

A few days later, he happened to watch the movie *Swades* on DVD.

He got very emotional seeing SRK's award winning performance. He decided that this was a sign from God for him to return to India and contribute to her development. While he was on the flight back home, TB looked out of his window at the clouds and arrived at a decision. He suddenly felt he had it in him to become a writer. Writing was a passion which he had indulged in during his school days, but since then it had been totally forgotten and put on the backburner. He decided to explore the possibility of bringing about change through his writing. He wanted to write about social issues to further the progress and development in his nation.

Two years on from his return to India, TB's first book was launched.

More than any meaningful contribution to the social change of the nation as he had envisaged, his book certainly ignited heated sexual discussions throughout the nation! His debut work *Why desi men play with their penises and why desi women shuttle in a metro between Mars and Venus* (first published in 2006) offered a fresh, humourous look at the done to death battle between the sexes. The book discussed why men were such bastards and why women occasionally drowned their break up sorrows in feel good haircuts, impulsive shopping outbursts and a generous helping of chocolate and caramel custard!

The book met with a thunderous response from readers across India.

Youngsters in particular (of both sexes) lapped it up with glee like how India's flat track cricketing bullies feasted on opposition bowling attacks on slow Indian pitches.

Published by a local Indian publisher and priced at only seventy five rupees (with later editions at hundred rupees) it was easily affordable and also accessible to readers.

With this book, TB broke most rules of the publishing industry-the title was lengthy, the cover was sexually explicit, the language was reader friendly, the content was raunchy, the manuscript was poorly edited, the grammar was suspect.... yet it went on to become a mainstream success.

Some sections of the media loved this new openness towards sexuality in Indian writing.

Literary critics however were less than happy.

They found the story to be crude, vulgar, frankly cheap and demeaning for readers of a progressive nation. What irked them more was the simple use of English and the use of Hinglish (a combination of Hindi and English) in his writing which seemed to offend their sensibilities given that he was (or claimed to be) of high quality academic pedigree! Their views however did nothing to impact TB's meteoric rise and the unabashed love, affection and the readership which he got from the public especially from the college going youngsters!

TB followed the success of his first book with his second *The desi top performer in the bedroom and boardroom* (first published in 2007) which catapulted him to national stardom. He followed this up with his third book *Enjoying threesomes while preparing for competitive Indian examinations* (first published in 2008) which cemented his position as the 'most popular author' for a college going youngster. His 4th, 5th and 6th books were the *'Hey Indian lady dressed in red '* series which were all published in 2009. The first in the series was *Hey Indian lady dressed in red…will you please come with me to bed?* followed by *Hey Indian lady dressed in red…can you please spank me in bed?* and the final book in the series was *Hey Indian lady dressed in red…can you please teach me mathematics in bed?*

The *'Hey Indian lady dressed in red'* series was hailed in the media as lad-literature (lad-lit) at its finest.

The critics however could take it no more.

Six published books had provided them with enough fodder to rip apart his simple reader friendly writing style.

But this time the issue of criticism was no longer the writing style. The issues raised were different.

The main serious issue raised by critics was that TB offered a skewed representation of human relationships in his books. They also had an issue with the amount of sexual content in his various books especially the '*Hey Indian lady dressed in red*' series.

TB defended his position in various interviews and gave it back to his critics.

He clearly stated that he just wrote stories the way he visualized them in his head and was accountable only to his readers for the final product. He didn't have to be accountable to the self declared moral guardians of society who were in charge of preserving the nation's great tradition and culture.

He also clarified once and for all that he wasn't apologetic about his commercial success.

He was clear that his books belonged to the commercial fiction genre of Indian writing. Not the literary high quality 'beyond comprehension of most' writing. He was fairly certain that he would never ever win a literary award but he would continue to win the hearts of readers who supported him in pushing forward the unstoppable TB juggernaut!

Egged on by his writing success, TB then identified a larger role for himself in the public space through his additional role as a columnist and an opinion maker. The media hailed him as a 'youth icon'. He started to have an opinion on pretty much everything under the sun. Critics bayed for his blood as if he was a fugitive on the run.

He had an opinion on which political party should be in power to how to find your dream lover. He offered sex tips on how men should stay energetic and virile to how grumpy people should learn how to smile. He had a view on how a woman should drape a sari to how an individual should drink bhang and celebrate holi. He had a view on the latest brands of red wine to the Government's shocking, ill defined '32 rupee a day' definition of the poverty line.

TB's incredible success as a writer and subsequently as a youth icon had changed life for everyone. With each passing day since 2006, his success story also gave birth to a number of desi writing clones. These desi clones (mainly from a top tier Indian institution like an IIT or an IIM or both) tried to replicate TB's success story and flooded the Indian commercial fiction market with their stories of campus life, work life, love life which in most cases sadly turned out to be nothing more than autobiographical accounts of their glum, non-happening, boring lives!

Unlike TB's super success, their stories met with limited success.

But the important takeaway from TB's success story was that anyone could be the master of one's own destiny.

There was a market for affordable Indian fiction in spite of the many points of criticism.

And this thought continued to motivate aspiring authors like Raghu Balakrishnan who was anxiously waiting for his hero to arrive for the book launch.

*

TB, the star of the publishing world finally arrived.

The gathering gave him a thunderous rock star kind of reception.

He waved to them.

He then coughed deliberately. His right hand stylishly slanted in at an angle to cover his mouth.

'TB!"TB" ka problem hai kya?' someone from the audience screamed.

The crowd started cheering wildly.

Raghu caught more than a glimpse of his hero.

TB was casually dressed in a black T-shirt and blue denim jeans.

He however looked much shorter in real life than in the photos and the TV appearances in which Raghu had seen him in. He was accompanied onto a makeshift stage by two beefy security guards and a present day Kannada actress who currently had no significant roles to speak of, but was present to launch TB's book in Bangalore officially.

Raghu noticed a large pile of TB's various books and in particular his latest book placed on a table on the stage. He also saw a large projector screen which showed clippings of TB's various television interviews.

On stage, a compère introduced both TB and the actress to the crowd as they happily posed for the cameras. A few minutes later, it was time for the unveiling of TB's book. The actress handed TB the book which was wrapped in a gleaming silver cover with a red ribbon tied across the face of it. With photographers furiously clicking away, TB opened the silver cover and officially launched his book for his Bangalore readers.

TB then began to read excerpts from his book.

The projector screen at the same time displayed the story blurb of his latest book *Hey politician...r u getting a hard-on when the legislative assembly is on?* The book was about a politician who was caught watching a porn clip on his iPad during a state assembly session. The country was shocked. The politician was forced to resign from his post. More than the resignation, what really upset the politician was the fact that the media and the general public was under the erroneous impression that he was watching a XX rated video instead of a XXX rated video! How he fought the media to clarify his stance and how he left the political entertainment industry after bagging a five film contract in the adult entertainment industry formed the remainder of the story.

Half an hour later, the floor was thrown open for a quick audience interaction with TB. Just as the interaction was about to begin, an old man sitting in the corner of the room got up and asked TB a question.

'Why do all your books only have talk about sex and a woman's body parts? No true love or what in your life?'

The crowd suddenly turned silent. Raghu also looked on interestedly.

What a direct question!

'What to do Uncle? I have been in my fair share of relationships. I love women. Seeing them…kuch kuch hota hai suddenly happens for me here,' TB replied, pointing vulgarly at his crotch.

'Is this how you talk to your elders? *Loafer magane,* you should be sent to a coaching centre to learn how to respect women. You have no good Indian values!'

'*Loafer magane*' in Kannada loosely translated to 'son of a loafer' in English. The Kannada actress provided TB with a translation.

'What Uncle! I'm a lover…not a loafer!'

The gathering again laughed loudly. TB was like a politician and this book launch was like his political rally!

'Is this how you talk? You are supposed to be a youth icon! Also what's this nonsense you keep doing by coughing? Don't you know how many people die of tuberculosis in India every year? This coughing action of yours is thoughtless and lacks sensitivity to a serious human condition. You are really shameless!'

'Now Uncle, you are getting rude. I'm no youth icon. That's media created. I'm just a regular human being who coughs.'

The old man kept quiet. He did not want to speak to TB anymore.

Others readers then began asking TB questions on his personal life, his life as a commercially successful author, his literary influences, his views on the Indian publishing industry, whether paperback books would be replaced by e-books among other questions.

TB answered each of the questions patiently.

'Who's your competition in the mass market Indian fiction writing field?' a woman asked TB.

'Competition? With my level of success I have no competition! I'm competition for myself,' he replied confidently.

'Is it true that your *Hey Indian lady dressed in red* series is inspired from real life, from one of your past relationships?'

'Not true at all.'

'Is it true that you don't go to literary festivals because you hate people who act intellectually superior to others?'

'That's not true. I want to go but I never get to go because I'm never ever invited!'

The gathering laughed again.

This was possibly why the masses loved TB.

His confidence, his arrogance, his part megalomania and

his honesty all rolled together in one coughing package was irresistible!

Twenty minutes later, the book launch had officially drawn to an end.

Many fans stood in a queue to get their copy personally autographed by TB.

Raghu also joined the queue with a copy in his hand. The book promised to be a really entertaining read at an affordable price point of just hundred rupees!

His turn arrived.

He shook hands with his idol.

'I'm a big fan,' he told TB.

'Thanks man. What's your name?' TB asked him.

'Raghu Balakrishnan.'

'Enjoy the read,' TB replied, as he autographed Raghu's copy.

Raghu put his mobile on camera mode and gave it to a store attendant to click his photo with TB. He planned to upload the photo on Facebook later. He wondered whether he could take a minute or two more and tell TB about his own plans of writing a book. But he decided against it as the next crazy fan pushed past him to meet TB.

He then stood in a different queue to get the book billed.

He noticed that in his queue, at least ten people had bought the book.

The general impression that reading was a dying habit among the younger generation and that paperbacks were being replaced by e-books in current times was certainly misplaced at least as far as TB's paperbacks were concerned!

He finished billing and came out of the bookstore.

He looked around. There had been a light drizzle which

had thankfully stopped. He tucked the book inside his office laptop bag.

En route to his home in Jayanagar, he thought about his directionless, 'no dreams fulfilled' life.

His day job at Star Financial Planners & Advisors Limited (SFPAL), located on MG Road, was that of a financial advisor cum salesman who sold investment products to retail clients, who rightfully asked about two hundred questions before parting with their hard earned money for the sake of investments.

Having now worked for close to two years, a sense of boredom had set in.

This he realized was not because he was underpaid or overworked or had a horrible boss (Well these factors accounted for about 72% of his dissatisfaction!) but more to do with the fact that he was possibly stuck in the wrong profession. His academic qualifications (a commerce degree from a tier 2 college and a specialization in finance from a tier 2 MBA school, both of which were Bangalore based) suggested an inclination to excel in a career involving numbers and Excel spreadsheets. However deep down he felt his raw skills were more in tune with something more creative. Seeing the flood of mass market commercial fiction novels in the market, he felt a logical extension to display his creativity was possibly through writing.

He had actually made some progress on the writing front.

He had been working on a novel which he had titled as *The Paperback Badshah (The Paperback King)* which he had begun writing infrequently on weekends sometime during his first year at work. Over a period of time till now, he had written about seventy pages of content in a Word document. At this point of time, he was too shy to discuss his story with anyone as the plot line was still work in progress and the various ideas were still being finalized in his head.

But at the heart of the novel was a love story.

Of late, with work getting increasingly hectic and with weekends also being spent largely focusing on work, he just didn't get any free time for himself let alone any free time to write! His novel was pushed to the backburner as week after week just rolled by.

He reached his house which was a ten minute walk from the famous Jayanagar 4th Block shopping complex. During his childhood he had shifted homes across Karnataka as his father had a transferable job as a bank manager in a nationalized bank. However for the last few years, he called his current house 'his home' as his father (who was still in service) was now a senior bank manager at the main branch located in Bangalore itself.

He entered his home.

He waved to his parents who were sitting on a couch in front of the TV in the living room.

His parents waved back to him-their only child, who had conveniently become a permanent fixture of the house (with no signs of moving out after his MBA!) just like the couch and the TV which cozily occupied their respective positions in the living room!

He noticed that his father was explaining something about the state of the Indian economy to his mother. He noticed that his mother was not in the least bit interested. As a full time homemaker, she had finished all her daily home chores and had mentally readied herself for her exciting daily dose of TV but now his father was hell bent on eliminating the excitement with talks about the state of the economy!

He noticed his mother glancing at the wall clock.

And then in the direction of the prayer room!

Maybe she was praying to God that even if her husband was trying to spend quality time with her during her TV time, how about talking about something more romantic with less focus on finance and economics? How about an affectionate hug to show some love after so many years of marriage? Or how about a…."my South Indian loving and caring darling"…how was your day at home? Or even better, how about a platinum or diamond band of love like it was shown in TV commercials which reinforced the modern day consumerist maxim that life is short and material gifts of love, rock?

His thoughts were interrupted when he noticed his father getting up from the couch to attend to his mobile, which was ringing in another room.

He now saw the look of excitement on his mother's face!

With the TV remote in hand, she was now entering the 'zone', a term which sports psychologists and cricket commentators often used to describe a situation in which, a sportsman stayed in the present moment and focused only on the goal in sight by blocking out all external disturbances!

In addition to the term 'zone', Raghu loved to draw a whole lot of other parallels from the game of cricket applicable to real life in his observations and conversations with family and friends. He felt that it was his way of being closely associated with the game he really loved.

A few minutes later, he began having his dinner.

The food was very tasty. He was really thankful to his mother as she was the one who single-handedly took all the initiative on the domestic front and ensured the mechanical yet well coordinated functioning of the 'slightly above middle class' Balakrishnan household.

Suddenly, he saw his father walking towards him.

'Raghu, I heard you went for some book launch today? How was it?' his father asked him.

'Good,' he mumbled back.

'How's work going?'

'Going on.'

'I'm sure you are enjoying it.'

He wanted to reply 'Not really' but instead just kept quiet and gave a wry smile during this father-son moment of dinner bonding!

'Do you want to know about the changes that are happening at the bank? Also what's your view on the current interest rate scenario?'

He started to eat faster.

He didn't want to hear the changes at his father's bank or discuss interest rate changes!

'Actually tell me later. I'm tired.'

He stuffed his mouth with more food.

His father got the hint and walked away, back to the TV room!

TENSION

Monday morning blues.

Raghu yawned. Lying on his bed he stared at the ceiling fan. He was bored of his mechanical life. He felt like he was a chained corporate dog with one leg tied to a corner of his office cubicle. He wondered what life would be like to be a street dog. He would be free. He could schedule his daily itinerary the way he wanted. He could wander aimlessly like a king across the lengthy unexplored passages of Bangalore with no deadlines, tensions or restrictions.

He was however no street dog.

He was a well oiled machine destined to mechanically go through the motions called life. He got up and stretched a bit.

He then had a cup of coffee to energize himself for the day. Then, he went about his morning business. He had a quick breakfast, followed by a quick glance in the mirror to check his hair before finally rushing to work.

He glanced at his watch.

He was running late for the customary 9 a.m. Monday morning sales meeting.

The meeting was important and significant as it was also the first meeting of a new sales month. The previous month had been particularly bad for him. Despite his sincere efforts, the hard work had sadly not translated into meeting the expected revenue numbers.

Finally, he reached his office, Star Financial Planners & Advisors Limited (SFPAL).

He glanced at his watch again. It was 9.10 a.m.

He gently slid into the small conference room.

The Monday morning sales call was already in progress.

His team led by his manager Shekhar were in a huddle, in front of a landline phone which was on speaker mode. They were listening to the Super boss based in Chennai. The Super boss was in charge of the southern region of SFPAL. For each of the teams (there were six in all in the Bangalore office), the Super boss held an individual twenty minute team call on the first day of each month. Raghu's team in this case was the first in line for the 9-9.20 a.m. slot for which Raghu was late.

Shekhar spotted Raghu. He put the call on mute momentarily.

'Good morning, Raghu. Finally the *most important* member of the team has come,' he said sarcastically.

Raghu hung his head in shame. He knew that his manager would blast him later in the day for his non-performance in meeting the previous month's target and also question his punctuality and professionalism.

'…..Guys, the investment climate is getting very grim. As a team, it's not the time to grin…,' the Super boss remarked during the call. Raghu looked around the room as the Super boss spoke about the investment climate. In a corner of the small conference room, he was surprised to see his office friend, Suresh grin to himself. Suresh too had not met his targets for the previous month but seemed pretty cool about it. He was a huge fan of Bollywood movies (Raghu also enjoyed Bollywood movies) and in particular was a diehard fan of superstar Salman Khan. *But he had taken his idol worship a bit too far.* To show his allegiance to the superstar, Suresh was dressed in tight fitting pants and a fitted shirt to give himself a beefy appearance even though he was puny and had no biceps!

He currently sported the actor's hairstyle from the movie *Tere Naam* in which part of the hair fell on the forehead and in front of the eyes which was hugely inappropriate for an office setting! He also wore a loose bracelet on his wrist just like the actor did and had a huge scar near his right eye which he felt very proud of, as he felt it gave him a 'bad boy' image in line with what the media portrayed of the actor!

Raghu also noticed Mohan standing a few feet away.

He had never liked Mohan right from the time they began work together at SFPAL. It was because Mohan for some strange reason had a chip on his shoulder and always felt superior to his peers. Maybe this was his way of trying to get ahead in the rat infested journey called work life.

But one thing which Raghu couldn't find fault with, was Mohan's professional accomplishments. Mohan had been an overachieving salesman month on month at SFPAL across all the teams in the Bangalore office. His impressive results (obtained using a combination of aggressive selling and a fair bit of mis-selling!) made him very popular among the superiors. He in turn reciprocated the love for them (for Shekhar in particular) by engaging full on, in fake butter makhan praise!

Another reason why he was disliked by Raghu and most others in office was because of the amount of monthly incentives and rewards which he kept winning! Raghu during his entire time at SFPAL had never overachieved to win the big incentives like Mohan had. During most months, he brought in revenues which just about matched his monthly cost to the company to justify his presence at work. For the last two months however, he wasn't even able to bring in revenues to match his monthly CTC, which was a cause for concern.

A few minutes later, the morning sales call was coming to an end.

'….So guys, as an organization and as a team, we have to focus our energies on reaching our targets this month,' the Super boss stated.

'Sir, we'll get it done,' Shekhar replied confidently to the Super boss.

'That's great to know. Mohan, are you there?'

'Yes sir. I'm very much here,' Mohan replied.

'How much business are you going to do this month?'

'I'm planning to do at least three times my last month's numbers.'

'Fantastic! If this were to be an exam, I would give you a definite 10 on 10! You deserve all the awards and incentives which you've been winning.'

'Thanks sir. I just want to say one thing. My achievements wouldn't have been possible at all without the confidence, support, encouragement and motivation which Shekhar has given me. He's the one who taught me the importance of hard work, the importance of being well networked and how to do team work effectively.'

'Absolutely! Well done, Shekhar.'

Shekhar thanked the Super boss for his kind words and then smiled at Mohan.

Mohan had further endeared himself to the boss and the Super boss with this deadly Monday morning makhan maska baazi!

'Suresh, Raghu, I want to know your expected business numbers for this month. I do understand that the last couple of months have been tough for both of you. Let's begin with you, Suresh. Target kar payega?'

'Definitely sir! Tension mat lo. Dhandha ho jayega.'

'Really? Can you assure me that there will be no underperformance like last month?'

'Sir, there will be no underperformance. I'm confident of meeting my target. Jab mein ek baar commitment karta hoon to mein khood ki bhi nahi sunta.'

Raghu couldn't believe it! Suresh had used a filmy line from Salman Khan's movie *Wanted* to make his point to the Super boss!

Even Shekhar and Mohan looked surprised.

'Suresh, I hope you are serious or else you might realize that life is certainly not filmy and will instead become very dark and gloomy. Anyway let's check next month to see if you will deliver your committed numbers. Raghu! My underperforming friend! Are you there?' the Super boss asked Raghu.

'I'm very much here, sir.' Raghu replied.

'Same question to you. Will you meet your target this month?'

'Yes sir, I will.'

Raghu explained how he planned to reach his super stiff numbers. He saw Shekhar look at him sceptically.

'So guys, just to conclude, I do understand that the market conditions are tough. But it's high time we flush out all the negativity and target maximum business! Let the fireworks begin big time this month!'

'The committed numbers will surely be delivered this month, sir,' Shekhar said on behalf of the team.

'That's great to know! Guys, as you all know....you are my favourite team in Bangalore. Keep up the good work!'

As per the office grapevine, Raghu knew that the Super boss told each of the teams in Bangalore that they were his favourite team to motivate them! But that didn't seem to dampen Mohan's enthusiasm one bit.

'North, South, East or West, Shekhar's team is the best!' he screamed into the phone and spread his arms by his side like a cricket umpire signalling a wide to show the team's geographical might!

The telephonic call ended.

The team trudged out of the small conference room.

'I want to see you in my cabin in twenty minutes,' Shekhar told Raghu as they walked out of the conference room.

'Sure Shekhar,' he replied. He then walked to his workstation knowing fully well that his manager was surely going to fuck his happiness.

As he waited for the agonizingly long twenty minutes to pass, Raghu thought about the professional relationship he shared with his manager. At best, he could describe the superior-subordinate relationship as uneasy and frosty.

A specific incident from his past contributed to this uneasiness in his view.

The incident had happened just a few weeks after he had

joined SFPAL. It dealt with his alleged lack of focus at work. Shekhar was taking the team through the list of financial products to be sold for the sales month. They were in the office conference room.

'....So guys, as I've explained, I do believe that our products are the best in the business. You should focus on pitching it appropriately to a client, as per the client's needs,' he concluded after fifteen odd minutes.

Suresh, Mohan and Raghu as good subordinates of the team clapped.

As the discussion was about to be wrapped up, Shekhar's phone rang.

'Listen! For the last time I'm asking you, is dental covered in the mediclaim policy mail which you had sent?' he screamed at someone on the phone.

The team kept quiet hearing their manager scream.

'....You idiot! I'm not mental! I'm asking about whether dental is covered. Forget it...I don't want any further discussions with you. You are the one with no brains!' he screamed into the phone again and then cut the call.

Raghu found the 'mental-dental' word play puerile but very entertaining. Instead of smiling to himself in his mind, a smile gently broke across his face.

He suddenly noticed Shekhar glaring at him.

He stopped smiling and looked down at the floor with a serious expression.

'Something seems to have really amused you, Raghu. Want to share it with us?' Shekhar asked him.

'Sorry sir,' he replied. Back then as he was a new recruit, he addressed Shekhar as 'Shekhar sir' or just 'sir'.

'So how many client meetings have you lined up for the day?'

He froze. As luck would have it, that day he didn't have any client meetings!

'No meetings today, sir.'

'What! Please remember, you are a financial salesman and advisor. You shouldn't be wasting time sitting in the office. I want at least 2-3 meetings in a day. I've seen you smile on many occasions in the office. It's time you also do some work. Look at Suresh and Mohan. They're so sincere and dedicated to their work. Learn something from them. You are all of the same age but with different focus, excellence and hunger levels.'

He was really pissed hearing this but just kept quiet.

'Thank you for your kind feedback, sir. I have scheduled two meetings back to back today,' Mohan chipped in, nicely adding to his misery.

'I have three meetings, sir.' Suresh added.

'What a liar!' Raghu thought to himself. Suresh didn't have any meetings. He knew that for a fact!

Shekhar then left the conference room to do some other work.

'Raghu beta, tu to gaya. Tera band bajega. Good luck!' Mohan told him once Shekhar had left. Mohan placed his forefinger in front of his neck and moved it from left to right to demonstrate what he meant.

'I agree with Mohan for a change,' Suresh added.

Raghu was now really tense.

He reflected on what had just happened. He realized that smiling gently during a situation which involved a manager was an act of sacrilege and was potentially damaging to a subordinate's corporate career! An impression about him was formed by Shekhar which would remain in his mind and be used against him during the appraisal time!

Raghu was back in the present.

That impression based on the incident had more or less not been reversed till date!

It was now time for him to go and meet Shekhar for the one on one discussion.

It was time to get blasted.

Taking a deep breath, he entered Shekhar's cabin.

'Welcome Raghu! Dhandha kidhar hai? When are you going to get business? You gave some big talk to the Super boss during the morning call. Will you perform this month or just give some excuses at the end?' Shekhar thundered.

'Shekhar, abbb…abbbbb…,' he muttered. He was at a loss for words. Droplets of sweat began to line up on his forehead. He felt like he was in a *Roadies* interview in which he was face to face with his namesake, the bald angry man-RAGHU!

'What are you mumbling? I'm just not happy. Mohan just cannot keep contributing more than 50% of the team's revenues every single month…..'

Further humiliation took place over the next five to seven minutes.

'So Raghu, I want results. Did you understand the various points I made?' Shekhar asked.

He nodded mechanically. Shekhar had made so many points during his dressing down that he had switched off mentally after the first three! His mind had wandered aimlessly but in full speed like a race car on the awesome F1 circuit in Noida!

'This month, along with Suresh you are going to be under strict observation. This is your PIP month. You know what will happen if you don't perform this month. The job market is tough. People are fighting for jobs…'

He nodded. He understood the veiled threat.

He knew what would happen.

PIP stood for 'performance improvement plan'. It was specifically designed for underperforming financial salesmen. If a drastic improvement was not shown in terms of revenue numbers, the employee would be shown the door. From being a 'significant' human resource at the time of recruitment it would become a case of goodbye and get lost!

'Just one more thing. Super boss in Chennai feels that maybe it's a lack of motivation which is the problem. He has arranged for a motivational sales trainer to come down from Chennai sometime next week to motivate you and the rest of the underperformers across the teams.'

'Sure Shekhar,' he replied.

'Good. Now get back to work and focus on getting some good results. Send Suresh in.'

He left the cabin and while walking towards his workstation, he signalled to Suresh to go to Shekhar's cabin.

He reached his workstation.

His confidence was low. He felt demotivated and felt the pressure. He sat down on his chair and stared into space.

He visualized a scenario.

He wanted a day to come when he could just throw a cover containing various investment cheques given by clients on Shekhar's desk. Initially Shekhar would be stunned by this action of his. He would then go through the contents in the cover and smile. Seeing the huge inflow of business, Shekhar would immediately extend an oily arm of corporate superior-subordinate friendship towards him and remark, 'Raghu, I knew you would do it. You are a born superstar financial salesman! I knew about your potential all along! I knew my encouragement would work!'

'More like your constant demotivating threats!' he would mutter under his breath but would nevertheless feel super happy after receiving all the fake appreciation and attention. Suresh would feel happy for him and genuinely applaud his achievement. Mohan however while noticing the proceedings from outside the cabin, would have a look of total jealousy and insecurity on his face as his position as the team's top performing salesman would be under threat......

He snapped out of the dream scenario.

The fact of the matter was that despite his constant efforts, his decent communication skills, his good client base, his good understanding of the various financial products....he was still not getting the results.

'So what was the problem?' he asked himself.

Was he underperforming at work because motivation was a problem? Was it because he wasn't passionate enough about financial sales? What was he truly passionate about? Writing a book?

At this point in time, he had no definite answers for any of these questions.

Late in the afternoon, he was with Suresh in the office canteen. Sipping coffee and digging into some oily samosas, they were discussing how their respective meeting with Shekhar had gone.

'Will you achieve the numbers you committed this month?' he asked Suresh.

'Let's see. This is just the beginning of the month. I'll evaluate as the month progresses. Till then I will just chill.'

'But aren't you feeling the tension?'

'No dude. I'm not feeling any tension. In sales, you have to do a lot of goli baazi. Talk big, commit big numbers, deliver a bit and act super enthusiastic and cheerful. You should also not feel too tense.'

'I will also try not to be tense. But the next time Shekhar humiliates me, I will give it back to him. I will give him a piece of my mind.'

'Raghu, let it be. No disrespect to you but I think you are a total feku. A total timepass dhongi. A total gas master. You always talk but do nothing. Each time, you do the same drama. The same rona-dhona. The same disco dandiya with your confused thoughts. I have heard it all before.'

'What do you mean?'

'I remember the same time last month also, you told me that you would give Shekhar a piece of your mind. Instead what did you do? You did nothing. You ended up forgetting everything.'

'I guess, you are right. But this time it's going to be different.'

'Why? What will you do?'

'For the last several months, I have been writing a novel which I haven't told you about. I think I will quit my job and write my book full time and get it published and then reapply for a new job.'

'Raghu, this is hilarious!'

'What's so funny?'

'I suddenly just remembered something which you had told me six months ago. You had said that you wanted to become an entrepreneur and start something cool like Facebook or Google and then sell a stake in it for a cool billion or more and then live off the interest accumulation on that money.'

'Yes, I remember.'

'What did you do? You did nothing! I also remember telling you that even I would quit this job and retire and take up farming. Not on Farmville but actual kheti baadi. I would buy a bull, an ox and a goat and grow tomatoes and onions.'

'Make fun. But this time, I'm actually quite serious. I could actually visualize myself as an author when I attended TB's book launch on Friday.'

'Oh. Some new book of his has come out?'

'You are not aware or what? You don't ever read newspapers, do you? You didn't even see the photo I uploaded on Facebook?'

'Dude, you know me. The last book or newspaper I read was in tenth standard. Reading is only for boring people with no social life.'

'Suresh, it's because of fuckers like you, that the intellectual development of our great nation is under threat. Anyway TB's book launch was awesome. His book *Hey politician...r u getting a hard-on when the legislative assembly is on?* is just too good. It's very entertaining.'

'The title does sound interesting. By the way, what's your great book about?'

'I can't tell you. It's a secret.'

'Tell something, dude. At least tell me the title.'

'Ok. All I can reveal at this point is that at the heart of the novel is a love story.'

'Dude, you've never ever had a girlfriend but you are writing a love story! Seriously, this is hilarious!'

'Make fun now. But when the book is published and available in bookstores you will know.'

'Ok man. I'm sorry. But put lots and lots of emotional masala and sex in the book. It will become a superhit.'

'Let me decide as I continue to write.'

Just then, Raghu saw a person from the HR department stick a notice on the notice board in the canteen. The notice read-

"It has been brought to the attention of the admin & HR department of Star Financial Planners & Advisors Limited (SFPAL) that employees are spending a lot of unproductive time in the canteen engaging in unhealthy negative discussions about managers. Such talk needs to be avoided completely."

'Fuck! We can't even talk in peace,' Suresh said, reading the notice. 'I will eat this samosa later. I'll leave for a client meeting now.'

'Who are you meeting?' Raghu asked.

'Mr. Singh.' Mr. Singh, a cardiologist, was one of Suresh's main clients.

'Any good investment inflow expected?'

'I hope so. Two months ago, Mr. Singh broke his right leg and injured his left arm in an accident. Since then, he has been on a wheelchair. So each time I go to meet him for investments, he tells me that till his hands, legs and haddis recover fully and start working 100%, he will not make any investments.'

Raghu chuckled.

It was very insensitive on his part but he needed this haddi humour to keep him going especially after such a stressful day. Such was the nature of financial sales which had reduced his life to focusing on only revenues targets and business inflows.

Returning home in the evening in an auto, Raghu thought about how he had got the idea of writing a book.

During his school and college days, he had never been a voracious reader nor had he written a lot in the form of a diary, blog or a journal.

One day during his initial period at work, he was screamed at by Shekhar for the first time.

While the dressing down took place, he felt a sudden migraine explode on the left side of his head. He then felt a sudden lower back spasm followed by a sudden churn in his stomach. Overall he felt a bit sick. It was his unhappy introduction to the world of deadlines and stiff targets. Thankfully, he had a long weekend coming up which gave him an opportunity to recuperate.

It was during this weekend, while sitting lazily in front of the TV at home, that a sudden bolt of creativity hit him. The dose of the earlier corporate tension led to a story idea which he titled as *The Corporate Coma*. He suddenly thought of himself as some sort of creative artist and he ran excitedly and purposefully from the TV room to his bedroom! He opened a Word document on his laptop to work on his story idea. Three hours later, he had written a four page story which surprised him on account of the number of words he had typed and really amused him on account of the sheer absurdity of the plot! *The Corporate Coma* was a story of a cubicle dweller who on account of the work tension, slips unexpectedly into a deep coma. The cubicle dweller however manages to wake up every alternate day to go to work and gets paid by the company HR for full time!

The following day, he wrote another two page story on the same topic. He titled the new story as *Romancing Roma in a Corporate Coma*. In this story, the same cubicle dweller who is in a coma, falls in love with a hot nurse named Roma. Dressed in only a blue string bikini with a stethoscope around her neck, the nurse helps the cubicle dweller cope with the office stress and nurses him mentally and sexually back to good health.

As the long weekend ended, Raghu felt that writing these two stories had really calmed him down and helped him cope significantly with the stress at work. More importantly, the writing had made him think creatively. Creativity was something he never thought he possessed. It was now an exciting new addition to his modest set of skills.

A few weeks later, on yet another weekend, Raghu encountered another sudden burst of creativity. This latest burst was *significant* as it proved to him that his *Corporate Coma* stories were no 'flash in the pan' occurrences. This time, he was inspired to write a love story which he titled as *The Paperback Badshah*. He chuckled to himself as he had never been in love but was attempting to write a love story!

He started to type some story related ideas in a Word document.

As the days rolled by, he continued working infrequently on his story over the weekends over a one-year period which had resulted in the seventy odd pages of content in the Word document. This progress in his writing, gave him the confidence that the story could be developed further into a full fledged novel.

But did it have the potential to get published someday?

Would yet another love story be of interest to a reader?

He thought about these questions based on the publishing trends which he had read about in various news reports. As per the reports, publishers were flooding the market with 'love story' type novels at price points of 95, 100, 125, 150, 175 and 200 rupees.

The love element in most of these novels fell into one of the following categories- First love, second love, lost love, last love, high school love, college love, married love, extramarital love, fight for love, loss of blood for love, parental opposition to love, public display of affection type love, yearning for love, 'floating madly in the air' type of love, random reflections on love, rainy day reminiscences of love and other permutations and combinations involving love which could make a cynical 'not in fucking love' reader to pull his or her hair out in frustration and for an emotional, sentimental reader to shed a tear or two followed by a silent prayer to God to help them rediscover love and romance in their fast paced lives!

From a publisher's perspective, this genre continued to remain significant as most of these 'love story' type novels went on to become bestsellers. They were on the constant lookout for the next big writing star on the horizon. They weren't even expecting a literary kind of writing star. They were on the lookout for someone in the TB mould who could capture the nation's imagination right from Mumbai's reclamation lands to the deepest, darkest corners of India's hinterland with their tale of love!

As an aspiring author, Raghu too felt that this genre still had plenty to offer to a reader. He however wanted to write *The Paperback Badshah* in a slightly different manner from the existing run of the mill love stories. He wanted to write it in a light, breezy, non preachy manner, with only a view to offer pure timepass entertainment for a reader.

He suddenly realized that he had reached home.

It had been a horrible day at work.

MOTIVATION

'Hello everyone! How are we doing today? What do you know about passion? What do you know about being a winner?' asked the loud booming voice of the motivational sales trainer. 'Oh. By the way, I'm Babu Jagannathan Prasad from Chennai. You guys can call me "Jaguar" if it reminds you of the animal or the sleek car. If you wish you can also call me "BJP", "Jag", "Babs" or "Babu" but please don't call me "Jugs", "Babes" or "Bebo" as I'm certainly not size zero!'

Mr. Prasad laughed at his own remark.

As if on cue, his assistant, sitting by his side played the song '*Bebo mein bebo…*' from the movie *Kambakkht Ishq* on his laptop. Raghu and the rest of the underperforming financial salesman of the SPFAL Bangalore branch grinned mildly. Except for Suresh who was yet to arrive, the rest had arrived on time for the motivational training session which had just begun in a conference room at the IRIS hotel on Brigade Road.

As the session got underway slowly, Mr. Prasad asked everyone to briefly introduce themselves and mention the name of the manager to whom they reported to. As Raghu waited for his turn, he looked at Mr. Prasad rather curiously. There was something about his appearance which was different, entertaining and humour inducing. He had two big boils on his double chin. At the base of the double chin, in between the two boils, a small but significant vestigial growth of loose skin, the size of a small baby penis, hung rather vulgarly. It looked like a telecom tower hanging vertically upside down in isolation!

When Raghu's turn finally came, he introduced himself and also informed Mr. Prasad that he had just received a text message from Suresh which said that he would be reaching the venue in the next few minutes. Mr. Prasad glanced at his watch. He didn't look too happy.

Five to seven minutes passed and there was still no sign of Suresh.

'Ok guys, I have waited enough. Suresh can join in whenever. I'm beginning the session,' Mr Prasad remarked, sounding a little irritated. Everyone decided that it was the right thing to do.

'As individuals in life and in personal relationships, you shouldn't just have a name. You should have an identity to create an impact. Similarly when you meet your various clients, don't just wander aimlessly and enter their homes but instead make a stunning, purposeful, well planned entry!' Mr. Prasad explained.

Just as Mr. Prasad said these words, Suresh barged into the conference room! He was breathless and his appearance was dishevelled. He removed his *Ray-Ban* sunglasses and placed it behind his collar like Salman Khan in *Dabangg*!

'So finally, the great man Suresh has arrived!' Mr. Prasad said sarcastically.

'Yes, I finally managed to come,' Suresh replied, gasping for breath.

'I'm Babu Jagannathan Prasad aka Jaguar, your motivational trainer for the day. I dislike people who are late. It reflects an unprofessional attitude. If a client appointment is fixed for 9 a.m., you cannot saunter in at 9.30 a.m. You have to be on time.'

'I'm late because I overslept.'

'Overslept? Excuses will never get you anywhere in life, my friend. If I can come from Chennai in an early morning flight and be on time, I expect the same from you as well. If I had overslept, the flight would have left without me. Learn to respect a professional's time. To begin with...sleep less. You will still survive!'

Suresh nodded.

'Suresh, I still don't think you are apologetic about your late arrival. What's the apology word you should use right now?'

'What word?'

'What's the word you should say to apologize when you are late? What's the word you will tell your mother if you forget to wish her on her birthday?'

'I'm sorry, mummy?'

'Finally! You said the magic word of apology.'

'Mummy?'

Raghu burst out laughing. So did the rest of the salesman.

'No Suresh. You finally said the word "Sorry." Who do you report to by the way?'

'I report to Shekhar.'

Mr. Prasad made a note.

Suresh found an empty seat next to Raghu and sat next to him.

As the session was finally about to begin, there was another delay. Mr. Prasad got a call on his mobile which he said he had to attend. He excused himself and went out of the conference room.

'I'm sure, just like we report to Shekhar, Mr. Prasad reports to the little lulli hanging from the base of his chin. It's the master of his body. Did he have to buy an extra flight ticket for his lulli while coming from Chennai?' Suresh asked Raghu.

Raghu grinned. Suresh's observations were highly juvenile but very funny! Lulli for the uninitiated was Hindi slang for a penis!

Mr. Prasad returned and resumed the session.

'Remember guys, if you wish to become a big success and enter the record books of your company, you have to first ask yourselves if you are genuinely passionate about financial sales. The only way you can create history for your company is by creating high quality chemistry with each of your clients, every single day for the rest of your professional lives. I'm telling you guys this, because of the environment in which you operate. You are all a part of the competitive corporate world which is shaped in the form of a pyramid. You will notice that non performers are weeded out at every stage as the pyramid tapers at the top. You have to perform or you will perish. You will be able to deliver outstanding results month after month and find true personal happiness only if you truly believe that financial sales is 'The Career' of your life. Think about what I'm saying for a few minutes.'

Everyone present reflected on what Mr. Prasad had just said.

Raghu also thought about it. As per Mr. Prasad's explanation, 'passion' was clearly important for professional excellence and advancement.

'Guys, I need to know if we're all on the same page. I'm going to ask a few of you some questions,' Mr. Prasad said a few minutes later. 'I have a question for you, Raghu.'

'Yes, Mr. Prasad,' Raghu replied. He was suddenly caught unawares like a deer in front of a speeding car's headlights.

'Do you feel wow, awesome, incredible, energetic, excited and happy on a Monday morning before you leave home for work? Does the excitement build up from a Sunday afternoon itself? Think and tell me.'

Raghu thought about it.

Was Mr. Prasad stupid?

There was nothing rosy or happy about a working Monday morning! Saturday evening was the only time in the week when life was actually rosy. The entire Sunday would go in thinking about Monday and the week up ahead. And there was nothing worse than reporting to an irritated Shekhar on a Monday morning.

'Yes, I guess, I do feel excited on a Monday morning.' It was a clear and blatant lie but it was an answer which Mr. Prasad was clearly impressed on hearing!

'That's great to know, Raghu! I would suggest to all of you that you should stand in front of a mirror on a Monday morning and talk to yourselves, before coming to work. Talk to the man in the mirror about the goals you want to achieve for the week,' Mr. Prasad continued. 'So Suresh, the late comer for the day, do you talk to yourself in front of the mirror?'

'Not really, Mr. Prasad. But I occasionally stand in front of a mirror and touch and scratch myself. It activates me for the day,' Suresh replied.

The gathering burst out laughing.

'Thanks for the unwanted personal information. But on a serious note, why do you come to work?'

'I come to work only to earn money. Otherwise I hate the thought of coming to work.'

Mr. Prasad was shocked. Clearly Suresh's answer wasn't what he wanted to hear!

'WHAT? Why? How can that be possible? What about aspects such as the daily excitement of coming to work and the opportunity you get to make a brilliant contribution for your team and company?'

'Mr. Prasad, none of those aspects interest or motivate me while working. Only money motivates me. Every morning while having boiled eggs for breakfast, I think of how I can build a comfortable retirement nest egg for my parents. I also have dreams of buying a new house for my parents which again costs money. I want a girl to love me. But no girl even talks to me as I have no money. So I only think about earning money. But the sad but true fact is that I don't think I will meet any of my goals as I'm earning such a low salary in this company....'

There were loud laughs from the gathering.

'Good to see this financially responsible and mature side of yours, Suresh. But does this work fit in with the goals which you've set for yourself in life?'

'Not really, Mr. Prasad. What I really want from life is a Jaguar.'

'Don't make fun of my nickname, Suresh.'

'No, Mr. Prasad. I'm not making fun of you. My real big dream in life is to own a Jaguar car. In my garage, I also want a Maserati and a Suzuki Hayabuza bike. I also want to sip on some chilled beer on a yacht somewhere along the Mediterranean coast with attractive women and rich industrialists who always seem to enjoy the good times.'

'Suresh! These are high priced, fairly unrealistic monetary goals. Be realistic about the goals which you set for yourself.'

'I know. I got carried away. I'm middle class but my dreams and aspirations are always high class. I guess, I'm born and destined to remain this way. I will just have to keep on working like a machine for the rest of my life whether or not I'm interested in the work I'm doing.'

Suresh made a sad face and looked down.

'C'mon, Suresh. I didn't expect such sadness and negativity from you. Cheer up. Life is beautiful. It's not as bleak as you make it out to be. Blaming destiny and circumstances is the weak approach. Treat struggle as a welcome guest in your life to achieve success.'

'But will my ticket for success ever come?'

'It will come but it might take some time. Be patient and opportunities will automatically arise. When they do arise, you have to be ready to seize them. You can't be late like you were today.'

There was yet another mild chuckle from the gathering.

Raghu noticed that Suresh had a disgusted Mr. Prasad-finish-your-motivational-session-and-get-the-fuck-out-of-here look on his face!

'Guys, I shall now share with all of you, my own personal tale of struggle which eventually led to a lot of success. Maybe my tale might motivate some of you. I have titled my own life story as *Stay Motivated, Stay Foolish*. Being in financial sales or any other type of sales is all about demonstrating inner resilience and spirit. It tests your character every single day. I realized this, when I was a door to door lingerie salesman in Nagpur in the early 1990s.'

'Chaddi salesman! This is hilarious! I'm already feeling better about my own life!' Suresh muttered to Raghu.

'Dude, this is really hilarious!' Raghu replied. 'Plus you know what? The title of his life story sounds suspiciously similar to Steve Jobs's commencement address *Stay Hungry, Stay Foolish* to the students at Stanford University in 2005.'

'Oh. Then that makes him both a chaddi salesman and chaddi title chor.'

Before Mr. Prasad dived into his talk, his assistant showed a photo of a suitcase on his laptop and said, 'Guys, this was Prasad sir's magic suitcase. This was his wonderful companion during his journey of success.'

'More than being a magic suitcase, this looks like a door to door suitcase for chaddi kamasutra,' Suresh told Raghu.

'I agree!' Raghu replied.

'There's this chick Sarika in my colony. I don't know her too well. But she's damn hot. Maybe I'll gift her chaddis from this magic suitcase collection. Maybe she will then fall in love with me.'

Suresh started laughing at his own comment.

Over the next forty odd minutes, Mr. Prasad outlined some of the struggles he faced as a door to door lingerie salesman and the success strategies he used to become an effective salesman. He then spoke about how he made a successful transition from being a lingerie salesman to becoming a motivational trainer!

'So guys, I just want to reiterate a few points which I think will benefit you all….,' Mr. Prasad said as he was nearing the end of his talk.

'Mr. Prasad, may I interrupt you for a minute?' Suresh asked.

'Yes Suresh. What is it?'

'If I may ask, why did you never explore the *andar ki baat hai* requirements for a man as well by selling banians, boxers, frenchies and other types of chaddis?'

The gathering burst out laughing.

'Don't trivialize my efforts, Suresh. The undergarment market for an Indian male was already well set and well positioned. In my case, the opportunity as I explained was in the ladies market.'

'Ok, Mr. Prasad.'

'So guys, getting back to the points I want to reiterate... always remember that being a winner is all about consistency in performance and slowly taking your skill set to the next level. Set your own bar of excellence and achieve it. Just don't exist. Make your presence count! Ask yourself the questions, I posed to Suresh and Raghu earlier as to what motivates you and what drives you in life. I'm sure you will find your answers. Think of yourself as a dream merchant who comes to work daily to execute dreams which will help you realize your true potential and make you a true winner!'

The gathering gave Mr. Prasad a thunderous round of applause.

Raghu thought to himself.

Completing the work-in-progress novel, *The Paperback Badshah* was certainly the dream worth chasing which would allow him to unlock his hidden potential.

'Guys, I want to make one final point before I close this session. In this burning quest for success, you shouldn't forget your family and friends. They will always remain your true support and the force behind your success. Open your arms and your heart to your loved ones. Give them a tight warm hug every single time of the day when you meet them. If you are married, please give only your wife a tight hug. Don't hug your neighbour's wife or any of your ex-girlfriends!'

Mr. Prasad smiled. Everyone in the gathering also chuckled mildly.

'Mr. Prasad, I just have one final question,' Suresh said.

'Shoot Suresh,' Mr. Prasad replied.

'What if I don't achieve sales success after all your tips?'

'My methods are almost foolproof. But in your case, you have to first get rid of your excess negativity. I also conduct "advanced negativity elimination" sessions. You can enrol for it and attend the sessions in Chennai.'

'Ok.'

'So guys, thank you all for your time and may all of you meet your sales targets, month on month while enjoying the overall process.'

Everyone stood up and gave Mr. Prasad a big round of applause. The motivational session had come to an end.

Raghu actually felt quite enriched and charged up post the session.

That evening, he reached home earlier than usual.

His mother opened the door. He gave her a quick five minute update of the day's events. She then walked away to the kitchen to wrap up the dinner preparations before her TV time began. He walked to the fridge and grabbed a bottle of cold water and then sat on the couch in front of the TV in the living room.

Half an hour later, he heard the door bell ring.

He opened the door. His father had arrived from work.

He gave his father a warm, affectionate hug just as Mr. Prasad had recommended.

'Raghu, what the hell are you doing?' his father asked him, as he was caught unawares by this sudden display of affection by his fat son.

Raghu quickly told his father about the motivational session he had attended in which Mr. Prasad had told the salesmen to give their loved ones a tight hug.

'You can't do proper sales but you believe in all this? If the trainer asks you to jump from a building to test your strength or to jump into a well to see how deep it is...will you do it?'

'Just out of curiosity, how high is the building or how deep is the well, you are talking about?'

'Raghu don't test my patience. I've had a rough day at work. Please focus on your work properly and meet your targets.'

As his father walked towards his room, Raghu felt like a total fool. He promised himself, that if he met Mr. Prasad ever again, he would wring his neck for giving such bullshit advice!

4

DECISION

Two weeks later.
Raghu was at home.

He had arrived at an important decision.

He had decided to quit his job to write his book *The Paperback Badshah* full time and see it to completion.

The decision to quit his job had been on his mind for a few months and had gained momentum during the last few weeks. Mr. Prasad's motivational session had also cleared a few of his doubts.

The reasons for quitting were simple.

The main reason was that he had neglected his writing far too long. The dream of writing a book had now become all consuming. The dream which had been relegated to some random corner of his brain was now at the forefront and required execution on a fast track basis.

The ancillary reason was that his work had become increasingly routine, repetitive and very transactional in nature, which didn't offer any outlet for his creative endeavours. He just didn't feel productive or enriched after a hard day's work. Mr. Prasad's words, 'Just don't exist. Make your presence count!' came to his mind. He wanted to break free, even if it was for just a few months and chase this exciting new opportunity which was staring him in the face.

He decided to inform his father about the decision he had taken. He saw his father sitting in the living room reading the newspapers.

Just then, he heard his mother shout from the kitchen.

'The pressure cooker is making a noise...HOOOSHHHH. How will I make rice?'

'What do you mean HOOOSHHHH? That's not even a noise,' he heard his father reply.

'Come fast! I need you here.'

'But I'm busy. I'm reading the paper.'

'Just come. I think the cooker has stopped working.'

His father got up, made an irritated face and then went to the kitchen to attend to the pressure cooker. Meanwhile he walked purposefully to the living room and waited for his father to return.

'No office or what today?' his father asked him, on his return.

'Today is a company holiday. I want to discuss something with you.'

'I knew something was up. You've been very busy and very silent in the last few days.'

'You are right.'

'Are you getting a promotion?'

'No.'

'Then?'

'I'm planning to quit my job.'

'Quitting your job? Are you stupid or what?'

There was sudden silence all around.

His decision had certainly taken his father by surprise!

His father had the jaw-dropping expression of a car driver who had suddenly braked in the nick of time to avoid colliding with a cow on a main road!

'The job market is so competitive. People are fighting for jobs and like a hero you are talking about quitting a job?' his father continued.

'No. I have thought it through. I want to take time off to write a book.'

'What? How come this sudden thought of writing a book?'

'It's not sudden. On weekends over the last year and a bit, I've been working on a book. Writing is something which I'm passionate about. It's a feeling which is coming from my heart. I want to go all out and concentrate on it.'

'Ah! What dialogues! You know what?'

'What?'

'You are an idiot.'

'You really are the ultimate idiot,' his mother also added, who had joined the discussion. She had a look of concern on her face. She had obviously heard most of the resignation related conversation from the kitchen itself.

He was silent.

He thought to himself.

In the movie *3 Idiots* by the time Farhan had made an honest admission to his parents that he couldn't understand engineering and wanted to become a photographer, his father had promised to replace the laptop which he had purchased for him with a high quality camera. Unfortunately, that was a superhit movie. This was life...which was unfolding real time in front of him in which his own parents felt that he was a real idiot.

'Why can't you continue to write on weekends? Why do you want to quit your job?' his father continued.

'I'm not enjoying the job. It's boring. Also I'm always tense. I think now I will also be far happier.'

'Happier? Words like happiness don't exist in our slightly above middle class lives. You have to be dissatisfied and keep on working. Life is full of challenges. Are you trying to run away from challenges? Take work tension as a challenge and fight through the stressful time.'

'I'm not running away from any challenge. In fact, I'm taking on a new challenge of writing my book full time till it is completed.'

'Be practical. Don't be a fool. Learn to balance both. Get up early in the morning and write. Or sit late in the night and write. Do authors quit their regular jobs to write? They don't! Don't they take time out of their busy daily schedules to write?'

'I don't know about others but I don't think I will be able to do justice to either my work or my writing by balancing both. I want to spend the most productive hours of my day on the book.'

'A future recruiter will not look upon this work break favourably. How will you justify it?'

'I haven't thought about all that. All I'm clear about is that I'm passionate about writing this book. I'm sure a recruiter will appreciate someone who has done something different and had the courage to follow his dreams.'

'What's this new thing called "passion" you are talking about? Life is based on perception. Be it for a promotion or for any other aspect of life. That will never change. I'm speaking from experience.'

'Hmm.'

'Take some more time to think about your decision. Get a new job and continue to do this writing or whatever… on weekends. You have to make your existing degrees in commerce and finance work in your favour.'

'Actually, I'm still not clear if finance is the field I wish to pursue my entire life.'

'Raghu! You are 25! Not a directionless 15 year old. How can you not be clear as to what you want to do with your life?'

'I don't know. I still don't have a concrete plan.'

'No plan? At your age, I had a clear plan.'

His father put his hands up in the air in disgust.

He suddenly thought of a juvenile *'no plan?-please have complan'* joke to share with his parents. But he decided to keep the joke to himself. This wasn't the time for it.

'Raghu, in future when you get married, you can't say you are bored or you don't have a plan, can you?' his mother asked him suddenly.

'I guess not,' he replied meekly.

'Which girl will like…let alone marry a soon to be unemployed fellow like him?' his father asked with a smirk on his face.

His mother nodded sadly.

'Ok. Let's assume you are writing full time. How much will you earn from your writing?' his father asked him.

'The money will be much less than what I'm earning right now. But I'm thinking of it like a creative entrepreneur. There will be a bit of initial turbulence. A few ups and downs.'

'What do you mean?'

'What I'm trying to explain is that the cash flow generation at my end will be deferred initially. But I will manage by using the existing resources optimally.'

'I'm still not able to understand anything you are saying,' his mother chipped in.

'Let me explain. Raghu is a confirmed 100% idiot. He will not be earning anything while writing!' his father explained.

'Oh, no....,' his mother gasped.

Silence filled the room.

'So Raghu, the cost of living expenses have gone up considerably. How are you going to pay for the various expenses?' his father asked, a few minutes later.

He was stumped!

This was unexpected.

He had assumed that being an important member of the family, he could quietly sit in his room and write his book without focusing on the 'cost of living tensions' as his father was anyway going to work!

'I will cover my cost of living expenses by dipping into my savings,' he replied eventually.

'Savings? What savings? That same twelve thousand rupees which you have in your bank account? Your savings will not even last for one month. So basically, the bottom line is that you are going to live like an unemployed lump under my roof.'

His father pointed in the general direction of a tube light in the living room.

'Raghu, why do you want to be a hero? Why don't you just keep a regular job and make all of us happy?' his mother asked.

'I'm not trying to be a hero. I'm trying to chase a dream which I've felt strongly about for sometime now.'

He kept quiet for a few minutes and then decided to convince his parents using a different approach. He gave them an example of a person who had achieved modest success in a creative endeavour.

'Remember how happy, supportive and excited you were, when Mehul decided to pursue a career in music?' he asked his father.

Mehul was his father's colleague's son, who had quit a reasonably cushy job in advertising a few years ago to become a full time musician. What impressed Raghu about Mehul's story was that, the sudden burning desire to chase a dream could strike an individual at any moment and at any age. It could make a person forget everything else and focus only on the dream with single-minded devotion and obsession.

'His case is different,' his father replied.

'Why is his case different? So basically if someone else is doing something different, then it's fancy and cool but if I tell you that I'm planning to write a book, then you guys think I'm a fool.'

'Raghu, don't start your rhyming "cool-fool" poetry with us. Let's focus on your decision. For how many months are you planning to write?'

'I will be able to assess the time frame as I go along.'

'What if you don't complete your book?'

'Come on. What kind of question is this?'

'What I mean is…what if you suddenly get bored of writing the book? Then what will you do? Then you will have no job and no book.'

'I will complete it.'

'Let's see. So anyway, what's this great book of yours all about?'

'It's a love story which begins in a campus setting and then the story moves forward from there. I have already written about seventy odd pages in Word.'

He waited for a reaction. Sadly, there wasn't too much of excitement or enthusiasm from his parents.

'I only wish, you had spent the same time learning Excel properly, the most important tool for a finance professional,' his father sighed.

'Hmm.'

'Once you finish writing your book, how are you going to get it published? We don't own a printing press nor do we have any contacts.'

'I will figure out the publication process along the way.'

'Ok. But what if your book is never published? Or if gets published but no one buys the book?'

'You are thinking of too many extreme worst case scenarios. Let me stay in the present. Let me first complete the book.'

'Ok, fine. So I guess, you are pretty clear and firm about your decision.'

'Yes, I am.'

'As someone with years of experience behind me, I can only advise you. The old model of a parent trying to impose their will on a child is over. If you want to ruin your career... it's your choice.'

He nodded silently.

He liked this strategy adopted by his father.

No anger. No fighting. No shouting. No display of emotions. No drama whatsoever.

He looked at his mother.

His father also looked at her.

She was looking in the general direction of the ceiling fan and seemed to be having a quick one on one with God, stationed about two trillion kilometres away.

'God can't help him. I believe in hard work. Having no career focus and only leaving it to prayers has never helped anyone,' his father stated.

His mother nodded.

'But remember Raghu, irrespective of whatever happens, at the end of the day, you are still our son. We'll be supportive of your decision,' she said.

She sounded emotional.

He reciprocated the motherly emotions by making a deliberate *Taare Zameen Par* type sad face!

He was relieved.

The discussion with his parents had gone off fairly well. They were wary of his decision but thankfully the initial resistance had been broken as he had provided them with some clear explanations.

Just after lunch, he called up Suresh to tell him about the decision he had taken.

'Dude, I've got news for you!' he told Suresh, excitedly on the phone.

'What? Yet another plan to take over the world or something?'

'No man. I'm doing it.'

'Doing what?'

'I'm quitting my job to write the book I was telling you about.'

'What! Are you serious? You are actually doing it?'

'Yes.'

'Deadly. Do it for the right reasons. Fuck man…from being a feku master you are actually going to become the control master of your destiny. Good stuff.'

'Thanks dude.'

He quickly summarized the discussion he had had with his parents.

'Raghu, I'm telling you now itself. If your book gets published and is made into a movie someday, I want to play the main lead. Shekhar can be my assistant and Mohan can be the spot boy on the movie set.'

Both of them laughed.

They spoke a bit more and then Suresh hung up.

Later in the evening, Raghu gave his close school friend Nandu (who stayed close to Manipal Hospital on Old Airport Road), a call to seek another opinion on his proposed decision. An always super busy software consultant at work, Nandu was his age but already married for close to three years and had a little son. He respected Nandu's opinions a lot, especially on matters pertaining to the commercial aspects of life.

'So dude, what's going on? How are Kavita and Gopu?' he asked Nandu.

'Life's going on. Kavita and Gopu are fine,' Nandu replied.

'That's great to hear. There's something I wanted to discuss with you.'

'What?'

'I'm planning to resign from my job.'

'Seriously? For what?'

'Yeah, I'm serious. I'm planning to write a book....a love story.'

He again quickly summarized the discussion he had had with his parents.

'Listen Raghu, in life there's a price to pay for every decision,' Nandu said, after hearing the various points.

'What do you mean?' he asked.

'See right now, it's cool that you are chasing a dream and all by writing your book. But say maybe in a year or two, at the time of marriage will it be cool? Will a girl be cool with someone writing books but with no steady job?'

'Good point. But I'm planning to reapply for jobs once I finish writing this book.'

'Yes, you should do that. And you should be clear in which direction you want your career to head. Maybe you can try something related to journalism or content writing. But more importantly right now, you shouldn't waste your time because you will be on a work break. Having said that, remember that this chilled out life may not last forever. So maximize it till you can.'

'That's the plan.'

'Raghu, I'll be honest with you. I'm actually kind of jealous of your soon to be chilled out life. Taking a work break to write a book sounds like so much fun.'

'Dude, relax. You are the one with the big bucks and a well-settled life.'

'That's true. While I'm enjoying married life…there are just too many responsibilities and deadlines.'

'What deadlines?'

'Kavita keeps calling me and asking "Where are you?"'

'Oh. But what's wrong in that? Compromise, sacrifice, taking on responsibility and a loss of freedom is a normal part of marriage. But in return you get someone who cares for you.'

'You fucker…stop giving your stupid relationship gyaan. As it is you are trying to write a love story without ever having been in love…ha ha.'

'Dude, you are underestimating my talent. This is where my imagination comes in. What else is up?'

'Nothing really. Life is just stuck in a complex routine. On weekdays, I'm fucked for at least 14 hours at work and stuck for around 2 hours in the traffic. On an average on the weekends, I spend time with the family, I pay pending bills and buy vegetables. Life has become too fast paced for my liking. I have no fucking time for myself. I think I might crack. I just don't get time even to watch cricket nowadays on TV. Not even India's matches!'

'Oh. Not getting time to watch cricket really sucks. Take a holiday to chill out. Maybe you will feel better.'

'Thanks Raghu. A holiday is on my list. I'll get going now. I've to go do some shopping.'

'Ok dude. Enjoy.'

Raghu hung up.

He felt sad for Nandu but felt happy for himself and thankful to his parents that at this point in time, he could afford to chase a dream without the burden and tension of extra responsibilities. He was also happy that both his friends in his age group felt that his plans were cool. The execution of these plans however rested solely in his hands now.

Later that night before going to bed, he looked at himself in the mirror.

'So Raghu, are you really all set to bid goodbye to a moderately secure life as a financial advisor and ready to embark on an unstructured journey as a writer?' the reflection in the mirror asked him.

Maybe it was his excitable state of mind, but actually standing in front of the mirror provided answers and also clarified many of his other niggling doubts.

He felt like an explorer slowly entering exciting yet unchartered territories.

The journey of writing a book would be difficult and maybe even plagued by moments of self doubt. But this was a journey he wanted to embark on. If the carrot of a cushy corporate lifestyle didn't deter entrepreneurs from taking the plunge, surely the security of a job as a financial advisor needn't deter him from achieving his dream. After all, if he didn't take a chance in his twenties to seize an opportunity, when would he ever do it? If he didn't do it now . . . how would he ever know the extent of his untapped potential?

He had to adopt the mindset of a creative entrepreneur and execute his dream one step at a time.

The first step would be to complete the book, the second to find a publisher to publish the book and the final step would be to promote the book and resume a 'normal' life after the book.

He felt excited.

The only thing left now was to inform Shekhar about his decision and then get cracking.

The next day, he reached office on time to announce his decision.

He walked in to Shekhar's cabin.

Shekhar was on the phone. He was screaming at Miss Rosie who belonged to the operations department. '....Look Rosie, the investment climate isn't rosy. It's your duty to check the investment applications for errors. That's your job...'

He smiled to himself.

Once he was out of SFPAL, he would definitely miss his manager's unintentional yet entertaining one-liners!

'Shekhar, can I come in?' he asked, a few minutes later.

'Come in,' Shekhar replied.

He entered the cabin.

'Raghu, where's the business? You know you are in PIP right? Time is running out....'

'I know, Shekhar. I have come to discuss something else with you.'

'What?'

'I've given it a lot of thought and I've decided that I want to move on from SFPAL. I'm resigning today.'

'What! Why? How come all of a sudden? That too during the peak time of the sales month? It will demotivate the rest of the team. Which company have you got an offer from?'

He briefly explained that he wasn't joining any other company but was planning to write a book. He didn't get into too many specific details but spoke with surprising clarity and confidence. He spoke more confidently than he ever had while peddling investment products to clients!

'....So Shekhar, those were the reasons. Work on one hand and my dream for writing a book have set sail for separate shores. I don't think I can balance both. It's a decision I've taken after much thought, consideration and with a heavy heart.'

He was waiting for Shekhar to take the discussion forward and to ask questions.

Shekhar had a what-the-fuck-is-this-non-performing-employee-talking-about-writing-a-damn-book expression on his face!

After a few minutes, Shekhar finally spoke.

'Raghu, are you sure writing the book is the real reason you want to resign?'

'Yes, it is.'

'Or is the problem with me or with my leadership style?'

'No Shekhar. You've been a good, target oriented leader. As I explained, my resignation is only to take time off to write the book.'

'That's good to hear, Raghu. I've always felt that I've been very approachable as a manager and leader. And you know what?'

'What?'

'I always felt that you are a real hard worker and have the potential to have a successful career here. But I guess you've taken a decision in an altogether different direction.'

'Yes Shekhar, I've taken the decision.'

He was surprised hearing this sudden, unexpected early morning praise from Shekhar! There was nothing better than a resignation announcement to listen to one's own hidden positive qualities which were *never ever* spoken about earlier at work!

'Ok fine, Raghu. Give me a day or two to finalize your notice period. Meanwhile draft your resignation email and send it to me.'

'Sure.'

'Also continue to work sincerely till the end of your notice period. The work shouldn't suffer. I also need to start handing over your clients to Suresh and Mohan.'

'Sure Shekhar.'

A few minutes later, he came out of Shekhar's cabin.

The mission had been accomplished.

Thankfully Shekhar had accepted his resignation with minimum fuss and with a fair degree of understanding. Perhaps if he was resigning and joining a competitor, things would probably have been very different!

He started to walk to his workstation.

He saw Suresh giving him the thumbs up sign. He saw people stare at him as he had been in Shekhar's cabin for close to forty minutes!

He suddenly saw a slimy fox like animal run towards him! *It turned out to be Mohan!*

'Raghu, what was the discussion inside all about? Is it true that you are resigning?'

'Yes. It's true.'

'What happened? What happened?'

'Nothing happened. By repeating "what happened" nothing extra has happened!'

'Oh. So which company are you joining? Bata yaar, kaunsa company? What's the offer? What's your new CTC?'

'I'm not joining anywhere. I'm taking time off to write a book.'

'What?'

Mohan had a quizzical look on his face. He couldn't believe it.

He began asking a number of questions as if he was a prosecutor in charge of busting an insider trading scandal! Raghu answered some of the questions patiently and then walked away to his workstation.

He sat down on his chair and stared into space.

The pressure was off!

Only the notice period now, separated him from plunging full time into his creative endeavour.

*

The notice period was finalized.

Raghu had to serve a three week notice period.

During this time, he began the process of handing over the details of his various clients to the new advisors in charge- Mohan and Suresh.

Before he knew it, his last day at work had arrived.

The Super boss in Chennai sent him an email, which read-
Raghu,

Today as you leave this corporate jungle (here at SFPAL) for an unexplored creative jungle, I wish you the very best of luck. Do stay in touch. Do remember us, if your book sells like hot cakes from Kanyakumari to Kutch! ☺

He replied to the Super boss and thanked him for his kind words.

Suddenly, he started to feel a bit sad. The feeling that his journey at SFPAL was coming to an end had started to sink in. A few minutes later, he got an email which wiped away whatever little sadness he had in his system and instead made him grin.

Shekhar had sent an email marked to the entire team as a follow up to the Super boss's email. It read as follows-

It gives me great pleasure in having worked with Raghu. I wish him all the best for his future endeavours. He is a good human being. He is a hard work. He will be a missed.

He read Shekhar's email again and grinned to himself.

He always knew that Shekhar was intoxicated by the trappings of power which his position as manager gave him but had he consumed low quality liquor while drafting the latter half of the email? Or maybe he was strapped for time like an overworked manager and possibly didn't get time to proofread what he had composed?

With Shekhar, anything seemed possible!

During the early part of the afternoon, Raghu was taken for a 'farewell lunch' by his team to a restaurant on Church Street. Very sweetly, they also gifted him a laptop bag as his farewell gift.

'So Raghu, all set for a life away from work?' Shekhar asked, as the lunch was coming to an end.

'Yes Shekhar. The focus will be on writing. Let us see how it goes,' he replied.

'Remember the doors of SFPAL are always open for you, in case you wish to join back.'

'But which office door will be open for him, Shekhar? The front door, back door or the canteen door?' Suresh interjected.

It was a lame PJ but Raghu couldn't stop laughing.

But on a more serious note, he was clear that he didn't want to work here again and go through the torture willingly. Thanks, but no thanks!

'Raghu, ever since you told me about your decision, it made me think,' Shekhar continued.

'About what, Shekhar?'

'I feel I should use my life experiences to write a book on *"Tips for corporate success"*.'

Suresh coughed. Mohan seemed really curious like always. Raghu wanted to grin but gritted his teeth instead.

Clearly everyone believes that they have at least one blockbuster story to tell during their lifetime!

'So Raghu, once I do decide to start writing, I would like your inputs from time to time,' Shekhar said as he paid the bill.

'Sure Shekhar. I'll be more than happy to help.'

'Even I would like to help! I love reading books especially management books!' Mohan remarked suddenly.

Raghu glanced at Suresh, who smiled. Mohan was back to being an ass licking slimy fox!

It was an entertaining end to the farewell lunch.

Early evening arrived.

Raghu had just finished his HR exit interview which was a mere formality. In under an hour, he would be a free man. He walked to the office canteen to have a final cup of 'office' coffee.

Half an hour later, he glanced at his watch.

It was 5.15 p.m.

It was time to say the final goodbyes and leave.

He met Mohan and exchanged some fake 'All the best and stay in touch' corporate talk. He then walked up to Suresh.

They embraced.

'Ok dude. Good luck with everything,' he told him.

'Raghu, don't forget…if your book is made into a movie, I'm the main lead.'

'I remember.'

He then walked to his workstation and cleared all his personal items. He put the items in the laptop bag which he had been gifted. With the bag in hand, he walked out of the office.

He looked at the SFPAL building one final time.

He now no longer belonged there.

He was now officially out of work.

One phase of his life had come to an end.

An exciting, unstructured creative life awaited him.

PART 2

CREATIVE CONSOLIDATION

TRANSITION

A few days later.
Raghu had just woken up.

He stretched a little and then shouted in the direction of the kitchen for his mother to make a cup of coffee.

He then stared at the wall clock and smiled. It was 9 a.m. It was a Monday morning. But it didn't matter as he was on a sabbatical!

He was a free man! No job. No stress. No manic rush to work. Just a sense of excitement to execute the decision he had taken.

He ambled to the kitchen to pick up the piping hot cup of filter coffee which his mother had prepared. He slowly sipped on it and it vitalized him instantly.

On his way out of the kitchen, he saw his father, who was about to leave for work. He noticed that his father was dressed fairly stylishly in a finely cut dark blue suit.

'So Raghu, all set to start your great "writing"....your great "dream" from today?' his father asked rather sarcastically.

'Yes,' he replied.

'Have a great day at work. Oh. I forgot! You don't work! But I'm excited about my day at work,' his father replied laughing. He opened his briefcase and ensured he had the necessary office documents in place for the day.

Raghu smiled. He got a feeling that this would be first among many father-son conversations linked to his book and unemployment.

An hour later, after having had a heavy breakfast, he picked up the newspapers from the newspaper rack lying in the corner of the living room.

He couldn't recollect the last time (especially on a weekday) when he had read the newspapers slowly and without being in a hurry. While his father read *The Hindu*, he however read a mass market newspaper which focused less on news content and more on advertisements and other bullshit promotional content.

He skimmed through the main paper. It took him less than ten minutes.

He then picked up the promotional supplement of the newspaper for a quick round up of the events and the parties which had taken place in Bangalore over the weekend.

He spotted a picture of the Kannada actress (who had been present at TB's book launch) which was clicked at some charity event to raise funds for orphaned children. The actress was in a short black skirt and a transparent top! The actress's delectable, attention seeking nipples stared at him from the paper! They seemed to have the opinion to express that life was difficult for them in the glamour business!

He flipped the page and glanced through the rest of the supplement.

As he folded the papers and put them back in the newspaper rack, he thought to himself. Would the quality of newspaper items he read also reflect in the quality of writing which he would dish out to a reader?

Would his writing fade away after a quick initial blaze of glory or would it remain for long in a reader's memory?

Would there be any takeaway from his writing for a reader?

Or would *The Paperback Badshah* just be viewed as some frivolous, lacking in depth, timepass writing for a generation on the move, along the lines which he had thought of, right from the beginning?

These complex thoughts drained him.

Suddenly, he started to feel very sleepy.

He had plans of beginning his writing immediately after reading the newspapers. Those plans were now shelved. He walked to his room.

In his room, he first drew the curtains to block the stream of sunlight. He then gently collapsed on his bed for a mid morning nap!

At around three in the afternoon, his mother woke him up.

She told him that she was going to meet a friend of hers who had recently undergone surgery and that she would return only later in the evening.

He nodded groggily.

A few minutes later, he locked the front door and returned to his room, to take another nap. If there was something which gave him as much happiness as a mid morning nap, it had to be an afternoon nap!

The happiness was however short lived as the electricity went off suddenly.

The fan stopped rotating.

His body got stuck to the bed. He tossed uneasily. It had become so hot and surprisingly humid. It was most unlike Bangalore and seemed more like Chennai! He wiped the droplets of sweat which had lined up on his forehead.

A few minutes later, he heard someone banging on the front door.

He opened the door.

An agent of sorts from one of the gas companies (which supplied the gas cylinders) was at the door. Sounding serious like an FBI officer, the agent told him, that he was a gas inspector and had come to check for gas leaks. The inspector showed him a smudged ID card and a sheet of paper in which his home address was listed. The inspector then told him that it was routine inspection which would not take more than a few minutes.

He nodded in understanding and then took the inspector to the kitchen.

The inspector first squatted and checked the gas connection under the stove. The inspector then sniffed around for a gas leak like he was a dog from the bomb detection squad. The inspector finally drummed a few musical beats on the sturdy red-coloured gas cylinder to conclude that everything was fine and in order. Back at the front door, the inspector asked for five hundred rupees as part of the routine inspection charges.

He was surprised at the cost, but went to his room to get the money. He returned and made the payment to the inspector, who gave him an oily smile while pocketing the money.

He then shut the door.

As he was now wide awake, he decided to have his lunch quickly and then finally begin work on his novel.

About twenty minutes later, there was another disturbance.

This time it was the familiar face of the cable operator who had come to collect the payment for the monthly cable bill.

He found the cable operator very irritating.

The operator was a big time *kaam chor* but when it came to collecting money, he was always on time! Whenever there was a hint of rain (which would invariably coincide with an important India cricket match), the entire cable connection would go kaput. When he would frantically try to reach the operator regarding the connection, the operator's mobile would either be switched off or unreachable! If he somehow did manage to get in touch, the operator would give bullshit reasons such as-'Saar...too much rain in Bangalore. Cable wires got wet. Connection went *phusss*' or something like 'Saar...I'm sorry I couldn't pick up your call earlier as my mobile fell in the water and the keypad got locked. But the good news is that while the cable is still not working, my mobile has finally started working.'

With umpteen instances of disrupted cricket matches flooding his mind, he deliberately lied to the operator and told him that he didn't have any money to make an immediate payment. The operator made a sad face and decided to come later in the week.

As the evening set in, he realized that he had done no writing for the day.

He however noted that he had made a smooth transition from office work to domestic household work!

He decided to go watch some TV.

He kept flipping through the various channels as nothing interesting got his attention.

Some time later, he heard the doorbell ring.

This time it was his mother.

She was back after her visit.

Just as she started telling him about her friend's surgery, he interrupted her and told her about the cable operator and the gas inspector who had come.

'Gas inspection?' she asked.

'Yes,' he replied.

'But Muthu, our regular gas cylinder collector never mentioned anything to me about an inspection.'

'Oh. But I paid five hundred rupees to this gas inspector for the inspection!'

'What! Raghu, you should have called me up to check. You can't do anything properly or what?'

'I didn't want to disturb you.'

'Ok. Let me check with Muthu later about this inspection charge.'

As his mother walked off, he again started surfing through the various TV channels.

A repeat episode telecast on a news channel got his attention.

In the episode, the news anchor was in discussion with four studio panellists. As a viewer, he had seen other episodes hosted by this news anchor and totally enjoyed it for the sheer entertainment it offered. Irrespective of what the panellists would comment, state or express, the news anchor would ensure that his opinion was always the most important one!

The topic of discussion this time around was Pakistan foreign minister, Hina Rabbani Khar's maiden visit to India and how it could improve Indo-Pak diplomatic ties. As a political analyst on the panel waxed eloquent on Indo-Pak ties, a visual of the foreign minister came up on screen. In the visual, the minister was holding a Birkin bag in her right hand and her sunglasses were placed on top of her head. Unlike most Indian women politicians who captured limited attention with their obtuse shapes and pre-independence arm length blouses, this foreign minister seemed to capture everyone's attention with her stylish presence!

He focused his attention back on the panel discussion.

He noticed that one panellist seemed pretty pissed off with the autocratic behaviour of the news anchor. The panellist had a look which suggested- 'Why the fuck did you invite me for this stupid panel discussion if you are never going to give me a chance to speak?'

As he smiled to himself, he heard the doorbell ring.

He went and opened the door.

His father had arrived.

'So how many pages did you write today, Mr. Author?' his father asked him rather sarcastically.

'Nothing much,' he replied.

'Raghu, I hope you will not be just sitting at home and wasting your time?'

'Relax. It's just that today I didn't write.'

He did not like this interrogation. He wanted a day to come when his father would somehow be on a panel discussion with the news anchor and be denied a chance to speak! That would be fun!

'Ok. Do whatever. She's an impressive lady,' his father remarked, a few minutes later.

'Who?'

'The foreign minister.'

His father pointed in the direction of the TV screen.

'Yes, she is.'

'She's impressive, just like the woman who had come to the bank today from Sydney.'

'Since when did a bank like yours start having people coming from Sydney?'

'We may be a bureaucratic bank at heart but we are very global in mind and spirit.'

He noticed his father's eyes flicker with excitement.

There was also a perceptible energy shift in his voice. *His father really seemed to have had an interesting day at work.* For a change, he wanted to know more!

He asked his father for details.

His father launched into a detailed description of how the bank was changing with the times and staying relevant by embracing technology and offering clients an online banking platform. In this regard, the woman from Sydney had come down to make a business presentation.

A few minutes had passed and he noticed that his father was still gushing about the 'Sydney woman' like anything and was praising her impressive presence and the fonts which she had used in her presentation! Hilarious!

He was so engrossed listening to his father that he didn't notice that his mother had also joined them.

His father finally paused and looked at the TV. The foreign minister's sartorial style was now being discussed, decoded and deconstructed for the benefit of the television viewer. The earlier visual of the foreign minister with her Birkin bag was on display again. As per one panellist's explanation, such premium end bags were custom made, expensive, had a long waiting time and as a result had immense prestige value for owners all over the world.

'I think even she was carrying a similar kind of bag to our bank today,' his father remarked, talking again about the

'Sydney woman'.

His mother grunted to make her presence felt.

'Do you also want one?'he heard his father ask his mother.

'You are a bank manager. Not an IPL cricketer or a Bollywood superstar! You can afford one for me, only in your dreams!' she exploded.

His father was stumped! He was at a loss for words.

Ah! The fragile ego of a senior bank manager was temporarily hurt.

He was however totally enjoying this! The evening had begun with his father asking him about his unemployment and now had ended with a focus on his father's own employment!

*

A couple of days later.

Raghu was in his room.

He had made the transition into his 'full time' writing avatar. He had just finished cleaning the desk in his room. He placed his laptop and a notebook to jot down some sudden ideas. He opened the window in front of his desk. Sunshine streamed in. He saw a shy squirrel make a friendly guest appearance at his window and then disappear. He rejoiced at the mild breeze enveloping his fat body.

He felt truly artistic.

With a cup of coffee in hand, he went through the Word document on his laptop which contained the content of *The Paperback Badshah* which he had typed till now. In a separate Word document, he typed the main points of the plot which formed the backbone of his story.

The Paperback Badshah is the story of Alok and Alka, who are final year college students. They are in love. A classic, old fashioned Bollywood type case in which Alok is a poor boy and Alka a rich girl. Their union is opposed to by their parents. The trials and tribulations they go through and how they finally manage to gain parental love and acceptance forms the remainder of the story.

Just as he finished reading through the points of the plot which he had typed, his mother barged into his room.

'Raghu! I spoke to Muthu about the gas inspection,' she said.

'Ok. So?' he asked sounding a bit irritated, as his writing had been disrupted.

His mother explained.

The entire gas inspection check had been nothing but a total money-making scam! He had been the latest victim in the colony! Rogues masquerading as gas inspectors had been collecting money from the unsuspecting 'gas leak' fearing public, who were more than willing to pay up as they felt that if their gas connection went unchecked, the cylinder might explode in their face while cooking!

'Thank God, you are safe, Raghu. Things could have been worse. What if in addition to the five hundred rupees, the inspector had beaten you up and robbed us?' his mother asked him as oodles of motherly concern flowed.

She then gave him a hug and walked off.

He was pissed off by his own stupidity. He was nothing but a gullible, unsuspecting dumb fuck who had been conned in the most amateurish scam of the century!

Later in the day, his father came home from work.

His father seemed to be in a jovial mood. His mother had told him for about the third time as to how 'little and gullible Raghu' had been conned by the fake gas inspector but thankfully how 'little and gullible Raghu' was safe!

'How many times do I have to tell you? Nothing would have happened to Raghu. He's a fat hulk. Not a small five year old boy who would have been kidnapped,' his father said.

'Don't talk like that. He's our son. I was worried,' she replied.

'Even if they had robbed him, they wouldn't have found anything. He's unemployed!'

He glared at his father. *Yet another unemployment related comment.*

'Oh wait! I forgot. They could have stolen something very important,' his father said suddenly.

'What? The TV? The fridge?' his mother asked.

'No. They could have stolen Raghu's great book from his laptop. The masterpiece! The bestseller of tomorrow!'

His father started laughing uncontrollably. His mother also burst out laughing. All the love for 'little and gullible Raghu' seemed to have disappeared!

The joke was on him.

He thought to himself.

Make fun…make fun…but what if *The Paperback Badshah* actually became a bestseller someday in the future?

INSPIRATION

One month later.

Raghu was working on his novel.

He had settled into a writing routine which was very different from the routine he had had while working. In this new structured routine, he did the bulk of his intended daily quota of writing in two main time slots- one in the morning (between 6-9 a.m.) and the other post an afternoon nap (between 3-6.30 p.m.).

His lifestyle had also undergone a change.

It had now become a fairly antisocial one, in which he spent a lot of his time in self imposed solitude to mull over various ideas and situations, some of which could eventually become a part of his novel.

After about two hours of nonstop writing, he decided to take a break.

He walked out of his room to the living room to read the mass market newspaper which was lying in the newspaper rack. A few minutes later, an advertisement in one of the supplement pages caught his attention. It was for a day long creative writing workshop aimed at aspiring authors which was going to be held in Bangalore in a few days time. He decided to register for the workshop as it was being conducted by none other than, the well known writer Zarine Begum!

In her late forties, Zarine Begum was quite well known in the Indian literary scene. Armed with a PhD in creative writing, she was known for her high quality, hard hitting style of writing which appeared as opinions in many newspapers and magazines. She was also well known for her vociferous opinion on the 'TB style of writing' which she felt had corroded the overall quality of Indian writing. Unlike TB's incredible commercial success, her high quality writing however had not translated into the big numbers. Her first and only book till date, *The Stressed Indian Woman* (2005) was applauded for its literary merit among the 'literati' but as per some media reports didn't sell more than a thousand copies across India! Her complex story went over an average Indian reader's head just like a bouncer which went over a batsman's head! Apart from her writing, she also conducted writing workshops right through the year for aspiring authors, working executives and for students.

She was however *well known* for a far more interesting reason.

Unverified media reports stated that, it was only when she had mutton biryani for dinner (at her posh home in Banjara Hills, Hyderabad) that the spark of creativity in her was truly ignited. The specific culinary interest opened up her creative faucets in such an incredible manner, that it enabled her to write nonstop, right through the night till the afternoon of the following day without even taking a single toilet break! Latching on to this unusual, punishing writing schedule adopted by her, the media often referred to her as Biryani Begum just as Tilak Bhatia had become TB on account of his cough for the general reading public.

✴

The next day, Raghu reached an office on Cunningham Road to make the payment to register for the writing workshop. While the workshop was going to be held in a hotel on Richmond Road…the payment for the same had to be made only at this designated office on Cunningham Road! Why couldn't the registration be done at the hotel itself? Or online? Was creativity only for the jobless and for those with time on their hands?

En route back home after making the payment, he was passing through MG Road. He decided to give Suresh a call. After moving out of SFPAL, they had not been in touch.

'Hey dude. What's up?' he said.

'Raghu! Long time! How's it going?' Suresh asked.

'Dude, all good at my end. I'm right now on MG Road. Do you want to catch up for lunch?'

'Oh cool. Give me twenty minutes. I'll wrap up some work and come. Can you come to the food court in Garuda Mall?'

'Sounds good. See you there.'

Half an hour later, he was already in the food court when he saw Suresh arrive. He had a broad grin on his face.

'Hey writer, good to see you,' Suresh said.

'Same here, dude.'

'How is your writing going?'

'Going on fairly well. I had just gone to Cunningham Road right now, to register for a writing workshop. How are things at work?'

'The same shit. A couple of funny things though happened in the office after you left.'

'What?'

'Shekhar sent our team an email which read: "Guys, it is time to deliver solid numbers. It is time to get a *peas* of the meat." Then a couple of days later, he sent another email, which read: "Guys, I want more effort. I want a bigger *peace* of the meat."'

'Hilarious.'

'The other funny thing happened when Super boss from Chennai had come to office. He was telling us that we have an impressive suite of investment products to sell for the month. And you know, what Shekhar said?'

'What?'

'In front of everyone he said that it is very important to be *sweet* to clients. Super boss started grinning. Then Shekhar tried to change the topic by talking about the investment products. For one real estate NCD product, he told all of us that there were three main reasons to sell the product. Firstly…, secondly… and then he suddenly stopped. Bejoy, a new guy who joined the team asked, "But Shekhar sir, those are only two reasons. What about the third reason?" Shekhar was super pissed and embarrassed. And this time Super boss laughed loudly.'

'Hilarious. So it looks like work has become a lot of fun?'

'It has its moments. But it's not that great. What about your chilled out life at home? No tension and no sales targets to think about.'

'That's true.'

'Speaking of the devil, look who's calling!'

Suresh pointed at his mobile. It was Shekhar!

Suresh picked up the call. '…Sure Shekhar…I'll get it done.'

'Raghu, let's wrap this lunch quickly. I've to get going. Shekhar has given some urgent work.'

'Sure dude. You go generate business while I'll head home to take a nap.'

*

A couple of days later.

Raghu had reached the hotel on Richmond Road for the start of the day long writing workshop.

Just as he entered the conference room where the workshop was being held, he was given a notebook and a pen by someone from the hotel staff.

He glanced at the gathering inside the room.

The turnout was pretty good. Around forty people had enrolled for the workshop.

He took a seat.

He noticed a loose sheet jutting out of his notebook. The sheet contained the schedule for the day. The workshop was divided into three sessions-

Morning session-The power of observation

Post lunch session-Technical aspects of storytelling

Post tea session-Tackling the writer's block

As he quickly read through all the details mentioned in the sheet, Begum arrived.

'Hello everyone! Welcome to my workshop. Please remember that in the field of creativity, we are all students. We are all gathered here today, for some knowledge accumulation...,' she began. Raghu noticed that she was quite shapely (to put it mildly) in real life. Maybe it was on account of all the night time biryani eating!

After having briefly introduced herself, Begum asked the people assembled to introduce themselves. As the introductions began, Raghu spotted an attractive woman in the row in front of him. She seemed to be in her twenties. She was dressed in a manner which perfectly complemented the 'writing' theme of the workshop. Her tight red T-shirt on the back had quotes from famous authors. Her earrings were designed in the shape of pens which dangled from her ear lobes. Her hand bag was designed in the shape of a book cover! Very creative indeed!

What really got his attention was when the notebook which she was holding in her hand fell to the floor.

She bent to pick it up.

That movement revealed a generous portion of her lower back on which there was a tattoo of a book and the titles of two books! The titles were-*Hey Indian lady dressed in red* and *The desi top performer in the bedroom and boardroom.*

Clearly like him even she was a TB fan!

'Hi everyone! I'm Roma,' she said, when it was her turn for the introduction.

His ears perked up. She had such a sweet voice.

'I'm currently in between jobs. I'm a voracious reader and I hope to write a book someday.'

Everyone clapped as she finished her short introduction.

He was super excited.

They now shared two things in common!

Firstly, they were both TB fans. Secondly, she shared her name with the lead character Roma in his unpublished short story, *Romancing Roma in a Corporate Coma*! Real Roma was however way more attractive than the bikini clad hot nurse, Roma in his short story!

'Hi guys, I'm Raghu. I was a financial advisor. I recently quit my job to work on a book,' he said, when his turn came, a few minutes later.

'Raghu, it's good to know that you are writing a book and that you are no longer a financial advisor. You don't seem like you are capable of advising anyone,' Begum told him as everyone burst out laughing.

He noticed that Roma also turned around and smiled at him.

'I was just joking, Raghu. Hope you didn't get offended,' Begum continued.

'No biryani. I mean...Begum...I mean Zarine...I mean Madam.'

Begum smiled.

'Relax Raghu. Call me Zarine or Begum. In this workshop, there shouldn't be any formalities.'

He nodded.

'Young man, what's your name?' Begum asked the guy, sitting right next to him.

'Hi everyone! I'm David. I currently work as a content writer with an IT firm. I also intend to write a book someday.'

'That's nice to know.'

'Can I ask a question?'

'Sure. Go ahead.'

'Is the biryani story about you true? The one in which you write nonstop in the night after eating a biryani?'

'Thanks for your question, David. I keep getting asked this question a lot, especially during my various workshops. I however feel it's best if I choose not to answer.'

'Why's that, Begum?'

'As a writer, I feel a reader should only have an opinion on the quality, tone, plot and style of my writing and not on the media buzz surrounding how I go about my writing.'

David nodded understandingly. He made a note of something in his notebook.

A few interesting thoughts suddenly came to Raghu's mind.

If Begum actually didn't want this attention, then why couldn't she just issue a one time clarification? Why was she keeping the speculative interest going? Was it a case that she didn't dislike *but actually liked* the attention and wanted to keep it going by not clarifying?

A few minutes later, the workshop finally began.

'Class, I want to begin this session by telling you all, that a good writer is one who finds interesting ideas from the most mundane situations and settings. Always remember that observation is a key element in the process of writing,' Begum began. 'To get things started, I want all of you to step out of this room and observe life outside this hotel. Come back after half an hour with what your feel is your best observation. Make a note of it in your notebook.'

Raghu walked out of the hotel along with the rest of the class.

He walked along the footpath on the side of the busy main road to record his observations. He observed the traffic, the noxious fumes coming out of vehicles, a set of low hanging electricity wires which were ready to kill someone and the footpath itself ,which was more like a death path as it was fully ready to give way below his feet!

As he recorded these mundane observations, he spotted a garment shop selling college street wear. Outside the shop, a shop assistant was changing the clothes on a lady mannequin from Indian wear to western wear. After finishing the task, the assistant gently spanked the mannequin on its backside! The delight and happiness on the assistant's face was equivalent to the delight on a college youngster's face on cracking a competitive exam or the delight on an office goer's face on receiving a bonus or a job promotion!

He noted this incident as his *best* observation and returned to the hotel.

'So class, I hope all of you have come up with something interesting. Would anybody like to begin?' Begum asked on the resumption of the session.

Surprisingly no one in the class wanted to be first, to read out their *best* observation.

'Class, this session will be interesting only if it's interactive. I sense a degree of inhibition among you all. Remember there's nothing like a right or a wrong observation during this workshop. Just express your observation.'

'Ok, I'll go first,' Raghu said in a rare display of taking the initiative.

'Sure Raghu. Go for it.'

'I have titled my observation as- *The mannequin spank.*'

'Interesting. Tell us more.'

He read out his observation.

Just as he finished, the entire class burst out laughing. He noticed even Roma laugh with total delight on her face!

He felt really conscious and felt like a complete idiot.

'Class! Please stop laughing. What did I just tell you all? Let's make a pact in which no one makes fun or criticizes anyone's work.'

Everyone stopped laughing. The odd chuckle still remained.

'Raghu, I found your observation interesting. There are however a couple of points which I want to discuss.'

'Sure Begum.'

'In your observation-the man changing the mannequin's dress and spanking her backside are the actual observations. The part in which you've described his state of mind as being happy isn't an observation but is your creative interpretation.'

'Oh, yes. I'm sorry. You are correct.'

'Also my experience as a writer has taught me that the quality of observations made by an individual, reflects his or her own inner feelings, beliefs and desires.'

Raghu reflected on this point with interest.

Begum's explanation was pretty much spot on. His observation clearly was a reflection that he himself was horny and his thoughts were raunchy! Even parts of *The Paperback Badshah* that he had drafted till now seemed to suggest the same. Even his short story *Romancing Roma in a Corporate Coma* was loaded with a fair bit of raunchy content! Was it even realistically possible for a cubicle dweller in a coma to have a hot nurse in a string bikini for company? It certainly wouldn't ever happen in the real world. But clearly anything seemed possible in his own creative world!

As Begum asked others to read out their observations, he noticed a hotel attendant enter the room with a pile of forty to fifty hardcover books and then place it on a table which was right next to Begum. On closer observation he noticed that it was Begum's own book, *The Stressed Indian Woman*. A few minutes later, as it was time to break for lunch, Begum made an announcement.

'Class, as you can all see and as most of you might be aware, this is my book,' she said, pointing at the pile of books.

'I request each one of you to purchase a copy right now, as in the post lunch session, I will be explaining various technical aspects of storytelling using my book as a reference point. You can make the payment of 450 rupees to him, right now,' she said, pointing to the hotel attendant.

Everyone slowly stood up to assemble in a queue to purchase the book.

Raghu stood in line behind David.

'Fuck. This book is expensive. Who willingly pays 450 bucks for a book especially given that it wasn't even a bestseller?' David asked him.

'I know,' he replied.

'At least if we had been informed before the workshop, we could have purchased the book online at a discount. What a waste of our hard earned money.'

'I agree with you.'

He really wished that when *The Paperback Badshah* was published, it would be at an affordable, 'within the budget' price point of two hundred rupees or lesser for a mass market reader.

A few minutes later, his turn came to buy the book.

'Raghu, enjoy the read,' Begum told him, as she signed a copy for him.

He honestly did not know if he would enjoy the read given the cost of book, but he nevertheless smiled politely!

'Sure, thanks Begum,' he replied, as he made the payment to the attendant.

With the book in hand, he walked out of the room to have his lunch.

✳

'Class, remember that a good story is one which has the right mix of emotion, humour, drama and conflict to get the attention of a reader,' Begum began explaining, in the post lunch session. 'A good story is written, when you feel passionately about it, in here.'

She pointed at her heart.

Everyone nodded attentively.

'Your heart is like a deep well which contains all your hidden emotions. It should never ever dry out. Always keep it open for new experiences…whether good or bad. As writers you should be ready to explore the various emotions be it happiness, anger, angst, jealousy, sadness, despair, irritation, excitement or any other. You need to tap into these emotions when you write. Writing *The Stressed Indian Woman* was a very liberating and fulfilling journey for me which came straight from my heart. It made me feel complete as a woman.'

She tapped her heart again.

The entire class clapped.

Raghu also clapped but wondered why he never found his own life to be complete. Maybe it was because none of his goals or dreams had ever been realized. He had just meandered along for the past twenty five odd years of his ordinary life. Maybe seeing *The Paperback Badshah* to completion would change all of that.

'Class, I shall now focus on a few technical aspects involved in storytelling,' Begum continued as she walked towards a soft board, which had been erected near her table during the lunch break. She wrote down terms such as-'Character development', 'Dialogue construction', 'Central idea', 'Main plot points', 'Conflict', 'Deepening of conflict', 'Resolution' and 'Climax', all of which definitely sounded like important terms for an aspiring author to know of.

She then asked the class to open their individual copies of *The Stressed Indian Woman* for further reference.

As she began speaking about the various technical aspects, Raghu's mind started to wander.

He thought about his own book.

He felt that *The Paperback Badshah* was a decent story which had a central idea, a decent plot line and an unusual climax (which he had thought of but was yet to write) which would definitely interest a reader.

An hour and a bit later, he looked at his watch.

Begum was nearing the end of her talk.

'....So class, storytelling has no definite structure. What I explained, was just a broad guideline and not a set of specific rules to be adhered to,' she concluded.

'Begum, in addition to your book, can you please suggest other novels which we should read to enhance our understanding of how to construct a good plot?' David asked, a few minutes later.

'Sure David. There are many literary classics which should definitely be read.'

Begum rattled off a list of twenty 'must read' literary classics.

Hearing the list, Raghu shuddered at his own literary inadequacy.

He had not even read one of them! And he considered himself to be an aspiring author! Hilarious!

'What about any of TB's books?' David continued.

'I don't know about you but I would hardly consider any of his books to be high quality literary fiction.'

'But he's so commercially successful.'

'David, commercial success driven by excessive marketing and promotion shouldn't be equated with the literary ability and talent of an author to tell a good story. All these 100-150 rupee type authors…aren't even authors! Their books can hardly be classified as literature.'

'But they are read by so many people in India.'

'That's because these books are low on intellectual content and very high on carnal content which perfectly matches the requirements of a non serious Indian reader.'

David made a note of her response in his notebook.

'Class, good writing should stimulate the mind and every word in the book should impact the reader. Can you say the same for 100-150 rupee type novels? You people, tell me.'

Begum had handled the situation deftly.

Raghu thought to himself.

He was a TB fan. But telling people that he was a TB fan wasn't ever going to get him admission into the closely knit literary circles or invites for the various literary festivals!

'Begum, what's your view on the state of Indian chick lit writing?' Roma asked, a few minutes later.

Raghu's interest levels suddenly perked up.

Roma had asked a really interesting question.

Chick lit writing always had a woman as the principal protagonist and story lines which generally dealt with matters of the heart, career blues in a light, non serious sort of way. The stories would typically have a smart, independent, sensible woman falling for the wrong man (or men) till she finally sorted out her life and fell in love with the man of her choice or decided that she didn't need a stupid man to complete her already rocking life. The cover of such books was usually in shades of pink or red to get the attention of a reader.

'To be honest with you, Roma, I find the genre very stifling and frankly very insulting for a woman of today. In most cases, the protagonist in such books is portrayed as a dainty little lamb lost in the woods who needs a knight in a shining armour for protection or a prince charming for a final union! Please! As women, we have outgrown such nonsense!'

'But Begum, what then accounts for the success of this genre?'

'I guess women especially in their twenties are suckers for romance and like a little mush, a little frothy fluff to keep themselves entertained. This in turn, keeps the publishers interested. But then again, this isn't the kind of serious writing which you, as an aspiring author should focus on.'

Roma nodded in understanding.

Just as the session was about to draw to a close, a girl in the row in front of Roma's, stood up all of sudden. She was big built like a military tank.

'Begum, my name is Sweety. I completely agree with your earlier point.'

'Which point?' Begum asked.

'All these chick lit books reinforce the bullshit stereotype that a woman needs a guy to feel secure and complete. What nonsense! As a woman, I don't need a stupid man to complete or compliment me. I don't need them to support or judge me. I'm a fighter. I'm not a quitter! I will fight out all my problems by myself. All men are anyways uncultured street dogs. I however had a real small dog….a Labrador puppy named Jimmy. I loved him a lot.'

Raghu wondered whether he was in a writing workshop or in a relationship rehab clinic!

Just then, a few seats to his left, he overheard a turbaned man mutter to himself, '*Oye Sweety, mera naam hai Guppi. Hame bhi de do ek do puppy.*' The turbaned man had a look of excitement on his face and was licking his lips. Clearly the man wasn't referring to a '*puppy*' of the canine kind!

Begum however had a concerned look on her face following Sweety's sudden emotional outburst.

'Sweety darling, clearly you seem to be under a bit of stress. Care to explain the context?' she asked.

'Sure Begum. One day, I was on a walk in my colony with my little doggie Jimmy. I had gone to collect my clothes which I had given to my dhobi wali to be washed. As we walked, a car came out of nowhere and hit little Jimmy. He yelped in pain. I rushed him to a nearby veterinary clinic. Thankfully the injury wasn't too serious. In a few days time, he was back in good health and became a great confidant for all my problems. Then one fine day, without any notice, intimation or announcement…he just left.'

'I'm so sorry,' Begum said sympathetically. 'My heartfelt sympathies are with you. I'm sure little Jimmy has left for a better place. A place called heaven.'

'No. He's not dead!' Sweety shouted.

'Oh!'

'He left for another colony. My bloody boyfriend who dumped me, took him away from my home to his!'

'But why did he take Jimmy?' Begum asked. She sounded surprised.

'That's because my boyfriend had gifted me little Jimmy on our three month "together-together" short term anniversary. But just after our break up, he took back all the gifts he had given and also returned all the gifts I had given him!'

'Oh. Did he have a key to your home?'

'Yes, he did. That's how he entered and took Jimmy away. Right from the beginning I knew my boyfriend was a total idiot. I don't care or miss him. But I miss little Jimmy. I still feel he connects with me. I can hear his doggie yelps and barks in my sleep. I also sense that he has taken to the bottle and is drinking whiskey to drown his "being separated from me" sorrows.'

'What! Who's drinking...your boyfriend or Jimmy?'

'I'm talking about Jimmy. I know you might find it hard to believe but that's the truth.'

Begum shook her head and reflected on the incident. Maybe it was an incident she could put in a future book of hers!

Raghu looked at his watch. It was 4 p.m.

It was time for tea.

As he sipped his tea, he reflected on Sweety's narration which he felt had the elements to form an entertaining story: Dog lover...to dhobi wali...to dog clinic...to dog heaven... to dog relocation...to dog drinking desi daaru and becoming totally talli!

*

'Class, my experience as a writer has taught me that generating fresh ideas is a combination of hard work coupled with moments of sudden inspiration,' Begum remarked as the final session began after the tea break. 'A sudden halt to your writing because of a lack of ideas can be really very frustrating. Tackling the dreaded writer's block is the chief discussion point of this session.'

Raghu opened his notebook to jot down a few points about the writer's block.

Begum explained that a writer's block, at a basic level was a situation in which a writer was stuck for ideas and couldn't make progress in his writing. The time frame of the block could vary from a few days to a few weeks to maybe even longer. He was thankful that he hadn't yet encountered a phase of this dreaded writer's block while writing *The Paperback Badshah*.

'Class, to cope with the block, I would suggest that it's important to break away from your normal writing routine once in a while and do other things to keep the creative juices flowing.'

'What other things?' David asked.

'Do things which you enjoy which aren't related to your writing. For instance, I'm passionate about travelling. On weekends, I love heading out of Hyderabad. The change of setting really helps in clearing up my mind. On weekdays if I'm stuck for new ideas, I just go sit in coffee shops and observe life go by. Before I know it, the creative juices start flowing again.'

David nodded interestedly.

'Class, I'm now giving you all a simple five minute activity. On a blank sheet of paper in your notebook, write down ten words which immediately come to your mind. You don't even have to think out of the box. Just write what you feel. Go for it!'

The moment Begum said the words 'out of the box', Raghu thought about the plastic lunch box he used to carry to school.

On a blank page in his notebook, he jotted down his first two words- *Lunch...Box*

His mind then wandered and he thought about how the electricity kept going off at his home and the constant need for a match box.

He jotted down his third and fourth word- *Match...Box*

His mind wandered further and he thought about cricket and the famous commentator Harsha Bhogle sitting in the commentary box.

He jotted down his fifth and sixth word- *Commentary... Box*

His mind then wandered to his time at work at SFPAL and to Mohan, the slimy fox.

He jotted down his seventh and eight word- *Slimy...Fox*

He then thought about Roma and how cool and attractive she was.

He jotted down his last two words- *Roma...Rocks*

He stared at the page.

Lunch...Box...Match...Box...Commentary...Box...Slimy... Fox...Roma...Rocks

He was happy. He had finished the activity in three minutes.

'Class, as you all must have realized by now, the idea of this exercise was to free up your mind and to allow you to get in touch with your thoughts,' Begum explained a few minutes later.

Everyone nodded.

'Raghu, would you like to read out your ten words?' she asked.

He nodded. He had no issues in reading out his words except for the last two words which were- *Roma...Rocks*! He had to think fast to make a change!

'Also if you wish, you can tell us what made you think of only these words.'

He nodded again.

He quickly replaced *Roma...Rocks* with *Rock...Frock*. The reason was that when he was a kid he used to play with small stones and rocks and till he was about two years old, his parents used to occasionally dress him up in a frock!

So his ten words finally read as-

*Lunch...Box...Match...Box...Commentary...Box...Slimy...
Fox...Rock...Frock*

He read out his ten words and explained how he arrived at them.

'Good work, Raghu. Interesting thought process. I'm sure you must have been quite cute as a frock wearing, cross dressing toddler!' Begum remarked.

He grinned.

When his turn came, David read out his ten words which were-

*Facebook...Posts...No...One...Likes...Why...No...Idea...
Get...Idea*

David gave an explanation that the blank notebook page reminded him of his Facebook wall on which none of his friends liked or commented on any of his wall posts. He combined that thought with the advertisement tag line of a cellular company.

A few others also read out the words which they had written.

'Sweety, would you like to read out what you've written?' Begum asked her, a few minutes later to keep her involved in the session.

Sweety read out her ten words which were-

*Boyfriend...Useless...Not...Loving...Not...Caring...
Jimmy...Loving...And...Caring*

Begum didn't even ask her for an explanation. The words were pretty self explanatory!

'Begum, I have something else to share with the class. May I?' Sweety asked.

'Sure, please go ahead.'

'The tough phase of my life made me question my existence just as a phase of the dreaded writer's block makes a writer doubt his own abilities and makes him question his very existence.'

David looked at Raghu and smiled.

Sweety seemed fully ready to unload further emotions out of her big, military tank like body for the benefit of the class!

Given an opportunity to express her views, Sweety unloaded not just emotions but also complicated gyaan!

She spoke about life in general and gave it a philosophical straight-out-of-a-religious-text spin by explaining that life was nothing more than mere 'maya', an illusion which distanced a person from his true inner self. Trappings like power and prestige were all just transient in nature. It was only the soul which remained forever! She then linked the same philosophy to the life of a writer and explained that a writer could ill afford to be caught in the maze of illusion. A writer had to remain brutally honest in his observations and be courageous enough to face varied reactions.

Raghu noticed that while Begum was nodding appreciatively while listening to Sweety's gyaan, there where many others (including him and David) who desperately wanted Sweety to say a final sayonara to the complex maya-maya talk!

He was relieved when she finally finished about ten minutes later. He had accumulated enough spiritual knowledge to last a decade if not a lifetime!

'Begum, I have a question.'

It was Roma this time, who wanted to ask a question!

'Roma, please go ahead,' Begum told her.

'No disrespect to Sweety or her thoughts, but is it wrong if an individual just adopts a fun, non serious outlook towards life despite the various complications? What's the need to get philosophical all the time?'

'I completely agree with you, Roma.' These six words came unexpectedly out of Raghu's mouth!

'Thanks Raghu,' she replied, turning around and glancing at him.

He felt excited. She remembered his name! Wow!

'Roma, your approach to life is a superficial one. Life is much...much...much more complex. Dwell deeper and tap into your hidden emotions as I had explained during the afternoon session. You will find your answers,' Begum explained.

'I agree with you, Begum that life is complicated but I'm still not too convinced....'

Others in the class (mainly Sweety's supporters) also added their two bits in response to Roma's question by stating that it was only by executing duties and responsibilities and by facing struggles and challenges, that an individual's journey in life was made complete and worthwhile.

'So class, we have almost reached the end of the workshop. A quick recap of the day's events,' Begum said about twenty minutes later. 'We began with the power of observation followed by certain technical aspects of storytelling and finally at a basic level we focused on how to tackle the writer's block. Before we conclude, let's break into a quick jig to relax the body, mind and soul.'

The entire class stood up.

A hotel attendant arrived with a laptop and played some kind of meditative trance music.

Raghu noticed Roma move in a delightful, engaging manner as if she was in total comfort with her body and soul. Her pen shaped earrings gently swayed in the air. She shook her thin, very much in 'work out mode' hips like a seasoned hoopla dancer with her low waist jeans offering yet another peek of her lower back, the tattoo and the book titles. He wanted the day to come when even '*The Paperback Badshah*' title would find a mention down there. He noticed Sweety standing all alone, a few feet away from him and singing the song '*Jimmy Jimmy Jimmy Aaja Aaja Aaja*' from the movie *Disco Dancer* followed by the heart wrenching song '*Why did you break my heart…why did we fall in love…why did you go away…away…away*' from the 90s superhit movie *Akele Hum Akele Tum* all to herself.

'Finally class, thank you all for coming. Hope you all benefited from this workshop. Go chase your writing dream which I'm sure is lying hidden somewhere within you. Don't ever give up on it,' Begum concluded.

The class gave her a warm round of applause.

The writing workshop had ended.

Raghu picked up his notebook from his seat. He exchanged best-of-luck-with-your-writing-plans wishes with David.

He then started to walk towards the exit of the conference room.

Just then he heard someone call out his name.

He turned around.

It was Sweety. What did she want?

'Raghu, can I speak to you for a minute?' she said.

'Sure Sweety. What?'

'Oh. You remember my name?'

'Yes, I do.' *How could anyone forget her name after the amount of talking she had done?*

'Can you please give me your phone number and email id?'

'For what?'

'I'm taking down everyone's contacts to stay in touch.'

She extended her notebook for him to write down his email id and mobile number.

'Are you on Facebook?'

'Yes. Why?'

'I'll send you a friend request.'

'Sure.'

'Ok, thanks Raghu. All the best with your writing plans.'

'You too.'

He noticed Sweety walking off in a hurry. Maybe she had another workshop to attend, in which she could download more of her complex thoughts and emotions!

Just as he was about to exit the conference room, he heard someone call out his name again.

He turned around.

It was Roma! Wow! What did she want now?

'Raghu, thanks for your support when I expressed my views,' she said.

'What support?' he asked.

'The part when I asked Begum why can't we as individuals, just have a fun outlook towards life.'

'Oh…that part! I actually do believe we should just go on with our lives without getting too serious or philosophical.'

'Yes, indeed. I was wondering…'

He noticed her biting her lower lip.

He never understood these kinds of complicated body signals. He however had decent knowledge about traffic signals!

He decided to end the 'lip biting' suspense.

'What?' he asked.

'Do you want to catch up for coffee or dinner sometime?'

'Let's meet for dinner.'

She smiled at him.

He looked back at her in disbelief.

He had actually wanted to say 'Sure, why not.' but the words 'Let's meet for dinner' came out of his mouth! This was the second time in the day, when words had just rolled out of his mouth!

'Raghu, dinner works for me. Here's my number.'

His heart started to beat faster. She gave her number just like that! Awesome!

He punched it into his mobile. He gave her a missed call for her to register his number.

'So Raghu, we'll catch up soon. I'll give you a call. Bye.'

She walked away.

He was in a trance. The hotel attendant should have played that meditative trance music right now!

He was unemployed, was writing a book and was now getting a dinner date with an attractive woman with a slim waist. What more could he ask for?

He left the hotel.

EMOTION

A week had passed after the writing workshop.
Raghu was at home. He was staring at his mobile phone. He was wondering how come Roma hadn't yet given him a call.

Was she playing hard to get?

He had no idea. He tried to reassure himself.

Maybe she had lost his number.

Maybe she was very busy with whatever she was busy with, and just didn't get time to give him a call.

Staring at his phone, he wondered whether he should take the initiative and give her a call. Or would it come across as being too desperate?

After thinking for about four minutes, he finally decided to give her a call.

He dialled her number.

He heard someone pick up the phone.

'Hello, who's this?' he heard her ask immediately.

He felt bad hearing her cold response. Had she forgotten him so quickly?

'Hi Roma, it's me, Raghu. We were together at the writing workshop,' he replied.

'Oh. Hey Raghu! I'm so sorry. I was just a little distracted. I didn't see your name flash on the display.'

He clenched his fist in triumph. So she did remember him!

'So Raghu, what have you been up to?'

'Nothing much. I've just been working on my book.'

'Book?'

'Yes. If you remember in the workshop, I had mentioned about it during my introduction to Begum.'

'Oh is it? Nice. What's your book about?'

'My novel, *The Paperback Badshah* is a love story.'

'That's awesome. By the way, where do you work?'

'I'm currently not working. I quit my day job as a financial advisor to write this book.'

'Wow Raghu, I'm seriously impressed. I never knew people like you existed… the kinds who quit a job to chase a dream. The kinds…who don't care for security or for money but who are passionate about their dreams. More power to you!'

For a second, he wondered whether she was making fun of him by highlighting his 'unemployed' status.

'Are you serious or making fun of me?'

'Why would I make fun? I'm dead serious. I think it is seriously cool to find someone who has sheer passion to chase a dream in this day and age of mounting EMIs, global economic shocks, uncertain job market times etc…'

'Thanks a lot, Roma. By the way, are you on Facebook? I searched for your profile to send you a friend request, but I couldn't find it.'

'I'm not on Facebook. I'm not really a fan of social networks. I believe in real networks and real friends. I don't need a virtual life to complete or complement my real life.'

He was impressed by such talk and logic.

'What about you, Raghu? Are you on Facebook a lot?'

'Not really. I login in whenever I take a break from my *gruelling* writing schedule.'

He lied. As if his writing schedule was that hectic! Plus, he didn't want to tell her the insane amount of time he spent online on FB and on other sites!

'So Roma, I was wondering….,' he continued.

'What?'

'….shall we lock in our dinner plans for Friday evening?'

'Works for me. Eight in the evening? Sahib Sindh Sultan, Forum Mall, Koramangala?'

'Oh cool. Yes. Pretty close to my home in Jayanagar.'

'I'll meet you there.'

'Why? I'll pick you up from your place.'

He suddenly realized that he didn't even know where she stayed!

'Look Raghu, thanks for the offer, but you needn't bother. I have some shopping to do in Koramangala. Once I finish that I'll meet you for dinner at the mall.'

'Are you sure?'

'Of course. I don't want to inconvenience you. I stay a bit out of the city.'

He was full of admiration for her thoughtfulness and sensitivity. She mentioned the name of a gated community where she stayed. He was dazzled by the name itself. It had a very aristocratic feel to it!

'So Roma, I guess, I'll see you on Friday.'

'Of course. Catch you then. Bye.'

She hung up. A few minutes later, he immediately called up the restaurant and made a reservation for a 'table for two.'

Before he knew it, Friday had arrived.

He decided to be a little proactive for a change.

Two hours before the date, he went to a bookshop near his home and decided to buy Roma a book (as she was a book lover) as a friendly 'first date' gift.

After browsing through a few titles, he picked up the global bestseller *The Girl with the Dragon Tattoo* by Swedish writer, Stieg Larsson. He smiled to himself as he held the book in his hand. He was gifting *The Girl with the Dragon Tattoo* to an attractive woman with a lower back book tattoo!

After getting the book gift wrapped, he returned home.

He rushed to his room, had a quick bath and got dressed in a white linen shirt and faded blue jeans. He also wore a casual jacket. He looked at himself in the mirror. He thought that he looked pretty cool!

Just as he was about to leave his home, his father arrived earlier than expected from office. His father stared at him and asked, 'Going somewhere, Raghu?'

He nodded. His father stared at him again. His father was possibly wondering as to how he could be so cheerful and for a change also fairly well dressed? Didn't the dark clouds of uncertainty hanging dangerously over his future cause him any tension?

He looked back at his father.

He was in no mood for a discussion or a gyaan session as he was feeling nothing but super excitement from within!

He walked out his home with an overall glow radiating from his fat face which suggested that his unemployed life was incredibly beautiful at the moment!

As he was en route to the Forum Mall on his bike, he spotted a roadside florist.

He didn't know what came over him. He suddenly braked and decided to buy a red rose for Roma!

He was surprised at his own display of 'first date' mush quotient. He had never done things like this ever before in his life!

He put the rose in the packet (which had the book) and continued to the restaurant.

At around 7.45 in the evening, he reached the restaurant.

He seated himself at the table reserved for him.

He realized that good things took time in arriving.

Roma was certainly one of them.

She had sent him a text stating that she was caught up in traffic and would be at least twenty minutes late.

As he waited, he saw an aged couple sitting at a table to his left.

The old man was merrily engaged in a bit of PDA by giving his missus a full on smooch much to the surprise of the waiters and the other onlookers! As a couple they seemed to have an attitude which suggested that even in the glorious sunset years of their life, if they had to confirm to bullshit societal diktats on love and romance and be made to feel conscious of their affection for each other in public...then well frankly, it wasn't a society worth living in!

His further observations of the romantic old couple were cut short as Roma finally arrived.

She was in a little black dress which displayed her toned legs.

She looked hot!

'I'm so sorry, I'm late,' she said, as she gave him a quick friendly hug.

'No problem at all....,' he said as he wrapped his arms around her.

He felt like he was in heaven…. in the presence of some celestial *apsara*!

She smelt so fragrant. He didn't know the perfume brand. It was probably an expensive high end one.

'Err…Raghu, do you mind?'

He realized that he was still hugging her! He let go. He felt embarrassed.

'I'm sorry. I was thinking about my book,' he lied. He noticed her smile as she took her seat.

Seeing her face to face, in such close proximity suddenly made him feel a bit conscious.

Talking on the phone was one thing. But face to face on a dinner date was another matter altogether!

He noticed droplets of sweat lining his forehead and neck.

'Raghu, are you stressed about something?'

Her question made him feel even more awkward and conscious!

'No…no…nothing at all,' he lied again.

He decided that the best way to avoid the attention was to make her the centre of attention.

'Roma, you're looking hot…I mean attractive….I mean very beautiful…I mean very nice…really nice.'

She smiled.

'Relax Raghu. I think you are looking kind of cute too.'

He couldn't believe it.

Apart from his mother, no one had ever called him cute!

'You know Roma, I'm not just cute. If you want I can also play the flute.'

He made a flute like musical instrument using his fingers.

She smiled at his lame PJ.

He relaxed.

The initial barrier of awkwardness seemed to have been breached.

'Roma, I've got you a gift.'

'Really?'

He noticed that she had a 'genuine' beauty-contest-winner look of surprise on her face.

'Here's the gift.'

'Wow, thanks.'

She opened the wrapping excitedly and held the book in her hand.

'Wow! I'm a huge fan of the Swedish literary sensation. Thanks a lot.'

'No problem. I remember in your introduction at the workshop, you had mentioned that you were a book lover.'

'You are right. I am. I'm also a big fan of Indian chick lit writing as well as of TB's writing. In fact, I have a couple of his titles inked on my body.'

'Oh is it?'

He deliberately made a 'fake' beauty-contest-winner look of surprise on his face. Little did she know that he had already observed the book tattoo and the titles inked on her lower back during the workshop itself!

A few minutes later, he gave her, the second gift- the red rose (which he had removed from the packet and placed separately once he had reached the restaurant).

'Roma, this rose is for you. *It's a rose for Roma in a restaurant which is known for its high quality aroma.*'

He noticed her smile.

'Raghu, does your novel also have such cheesy one-liners?'

'Well some of the lines in *The Paperback Badshah* may be cheesy, but certainly not sleazy.'

'Oh God! Please stop!'

She smiled again.

She then playfully hit his hand which was placed on the table.

As they placed an order for some starters, Roma told him that she wanted to know more about his book and his writing process.

He was more than happy to share details about his book.

He began telling her about the plot points (which he hadn't even shared with his close friends, Suresh and Nandu) which he had prepared in the Word document.

'As I was telling you on the phone, my book is essentially a love story. I'm trying to create a world for my readers in which they can enjoy the crackling chemistry, the emotions and the moments of raw sexual passion felt by the lead characters, Alok and Alka.'

He saw her listening attentively.

Seeing her seemingly genuine interest in his writing, he got carried away.

'Roma, I've also written a short story called *Romancing Roma in a Corporate Coma.*'

'What? A story about me?'

She sounded surprised.

'Actually, it's not about you. I had written it over a year ago.'

'Oh. What's it about?'

'Eh...eh....'

He suddenly felt a bit embarrassed. How could he tell Roma, that his short story had her namesake who was a hot nurse in a string bikini, who nursed a cubicle dweller in a coma?

'Raghu, you can tell me. We are both mature adults.'

He wasn't too sure…if he was a fully mature adult, but he decided to be honest and told her the entire short story.

A few minutes passed.

He was now curious to know her reaction.

Would she stop talking to him right away because of his horny imagination?

Would she think that he was just a pre programmed, mechanical horny robot with no feelings?

Would she think any lesser of him?

Would she be angry with him?

Surprisingly he saw her smile.

This was unexpected.

'Raghu, this is the most absurd, nonsensical story I've ever heard in my life! But overall it's very entertaining!'

'Wow. Thanks a lot.'

'You know something?'

'What?'

'Given your imagination, your dedication and your clear passion and interest for writing, I'm really confident that you will reach not just your current writing goal but also many future literary milestones. However always stay grounded and keep your head on your shoulders.'

'Wow, thanks a lot for this praise.'

'Raghu, I think you deserve another hug.'

He suddenly felt some chemistry brewing between them. He saw her getting up from her seat and walking a couple of steps towards him!

She bent down a bit and gave him a hug.

A cascade of her black, non streaked hair was on full view for him.

He couldn't believe it!

She had so much of dandruff!

He noticed little white flakes standing attentively all over her head. The little flakes were staring at him like they were outcasts who wanted inclusion back in civil society! While he needed to keep his head on his shoulders, she definitely needed to use the *Head & Shoulders* shampoo to eliminate the insane amount of dandruff!

Suddenly, he felt queasy.

He wondered whether he should tell her about her dandruff as a casual observation just as she had asked him earlier whether he was stressed about something.

But he then decided against it.

He got the feeling that if he said something about the amount of dandruff... he would be slaughtered. Finished! Khallas!

It would be game over even before the first date was over!

There would be no *'picture abhi baaki hai mera dost'* dialogues to share with her.

As she went back and sat down, he wondered whether he was overreacting and creating an issue out of a non issue.

She had been nothing but super nice to him.

And in return, he was acting as if he was perfect or as if he was some sort of angst ridden, flawed genius.

The truth of the matter was that he wasn't even a sweaty genius.

So what if she had dandruff? Why did it have to come in the way of the chemistry which was brewing between them? They could easily have daily shampoo showers together to eliminate the problem! Simple!

As they restarted their conversation, he gave her more details as to why he decided to write full time.

He then told her a bit about his family and also gave her some unnecessary bullshit details about-what all he ate, the time of the day he ate, when he took his afternoon nap and about the tasty masala dosas, idlis, rasam rice, sambar rice, upma etc. which his mother prepared for him!

He noticed that she was listening fairly attentively and patiently with a smile on her face.

He then casually glanced at his watch.

He realized that he had hogged all the 'first date' limelight! He had rambled on like a slow moving bullock cart on a highway for more than fifteen minutes!

He felt like a total fool!

It was only right if she did the talking from now on.

After all, it was the only way by which he could get to know the real Roma...hidden behind the little black dress superstructure which housed her attractive body, mind and soul.

'....Roma, enough about me and my boring life. I want to know more about you,' he said to her.

'What do you want to know?'

'Anything. I'm sure that it must be way cooler than my life.'

'Not really. On the personal front, I'm basically from Mumbai. My parents live there. But I have a place here in Bangalore as well. On the professional front, I used to be an airhostess. Working in the aviation industry has suddenly become a nightmarish experience as the "good times" have unexpectedly turned into "tough, turbulent times". I'm presently out of work and in the middle of a job hunt.'

'I'm sorry to hear that.'

'No need to be sorry. In fact it's because of the free time I've had that I could attend Begum's workshop and rediscover my interest in reading and writing.'

He wanted to tell her that even he was thankful for Begum's workshop as it had led to this awesome evening! But he didn't. He kept quiet. He had done enough talking!

'Raghu, I have seven principles cum areas of interest which serve as guide posts in my life,' she told him, a few minutes after they had ordered the main course.

'What are they?'

He was curious to know.

'They are as follows- *One:* I'm a book lover. *Two:* I believe in the free spirited triumph of woman power. *Three:* I wholeheartedly support gay and lesbian lovers. *Four:* I take pride in India being a nuclear power. *Five:* I dream that one day India will become a global superpower. *Six:* I am a diehard cricket lover. *Seven:* I hate it when women "cricket anchors and presenters" who lack intellectual cricketing firepower, dazzle stupid repressed Indian men with their "in your face" display of bosom power.'

She began explaining her various principles.

Principles one to six were pretty self explanatory.

He loved the fact that like him she was a cricket lover!

She rattled off cricket scores and statistics from various test matches, county cricket matches, Ranji trophy matches, Bangladesh versus Zimbabwe matches which really impressed him!

'Raghu, coming to my seventh principle. You know what irks me the most about cricket nowadays?'

'What? The number of useless T-20 and ODI matches being played?'

'No. Not that. It is when buxom, "noodle strap wearing" women anchors who don't understand the game one bit, mess up the pre and post match analysis of the game with their cricketing errors. An example for you-"*Dear cricket viewer…I forgot the cricket match statistics. Can I instead tell you about my vital statistics to boost the show's TRPs?*"'

He laughed at her imitation of a leading woman cricket anchor.

But in all honesty, he enjoyed watching the pre match and post match cricket shows presented by these anchors. But if he admitted to this, Roma certainly wouldn't be impressed!

'Raghu, in addition to my various principles, I also have pretty firm views on life,' she told him a few minutes later.

'What views?'

'You know, just as a writer is often misunderstood by the big, bad, insensitive commercial world, I also get the feeling that my views on life often come across as complex and complicated for people to understand.'

'Why do you think so?'

'I think it is because they question existing conventions and traditions.'

He grunted and also nodded his head even though he had no idea what she was talking about!

'I'm basically a complex individual with a complex personality and with a complicated life.'

He nodded again but wondered how she herself could know that she was a complex individual? Was it that she was actually just a simple, 'easy to decode' individual but wanted to come across as complex to give her personality that differentiating, mysterious edge to separate herself from the rest?

He didn't have a clue.

As she continued explaining about her complex personality and her complicated life, he felt a mild heaviness in his head. *In the next few seconds, his mind tuned out from what she was explaining and merrily wandered to an empty cricket stadium in which he was being seduced by her 'non complicated' bosom powers, right in the middle of the cricket pitch with her legs wrapped around him. He however kept nodding intermittently as she just went on and on……*

A while later, he heard someone ask him, 'So Raghu, are you ok with it?'

He suddenly realized that Roma was asking him something!

'What?' he asked feebly.

'I said, are you ok with it? Did you find my views too radical or difficult to digest? Will you really be fine with my existing situation?'

He had no idea about what she was even asking!

He just nodded his head.

'Raghu, I applaud your maturity and your sensitivity shown, in understanding more about me, my personality and my complicated situation.'

'Sure.'

He was happy that she was praising him but he still had no idea why she seemed so appreciative of him.

Then it struck him!

She had been speaking something about her complex personality and her complicated life when his mind had tuned out and wandered to an empty cricket stadium!

What if she now asked him questions from what she had been explaining?

He wouldn't be able to answer anything as he hadn't paid any attention!

Thankfully there were no complications as a few minutes later, she pointed in the direction of the old aged couple who were now busy hugging each other.

She made a noise out of her mouth which sounded like 'Awww....'

'Raghu, this old couple in my view is truly blessed by God as they seem connected at a spiritual level like true soulmates.'

'I guess.'

She then shared her views with him on the importance of 'finding that special someone' followed by her views on 'forging a special connect with that special someone' followed by her views on 'being in true love with that special someone'!

All these views got his complete attention!

He was surprised that she was giving him an insight into her inner world of romantic, mushy thoughts on what was just their first date!

Just then, she extended her hand and placed it gently on his hand which was on the table.

'Raghu, I think I feel that *"special connect"* with you. I think your presence will ensure that I never ever feel lonely or alone in a crowd...ever again.'

He was silent.

He tried to read between the lines.

She already felt a 'special connect' with him....so soon?

What loneliness? What crowd was she talking about?

Was she hinting at something more?

Whatever the reason, he started to feel very excited.

'Raghu, do you want to know why I feel that "special connect" with you and why I wanted to meet up with you in the first place?'

He was now all ears. He really wanted to know.

'Yes Roma. I want to know.'

'It is because of your smile.'

'My smile?'

'Yes. I noticed it for the first time during the workshop. Your smile reminds me of the early morning sunshine which stretches across the universe. If it's night time, it reminds me of the radiating stars which light up the night sky. It conveys to me, that you are someone who has no angst, no negativity and only pure undiluted happiness. I had always held the view that writers had a lot of emotional baggage, pent up angst, sadness, inner turmoil and were unhappy. But you are different. You seem happy, which I think is all thanks to your smile.'

He was amazed listening to the multiple interpretations about his idiotic smile which stretched across his fat face!

Was it her complex thoughts which made her arrive at these interpretations?

He had no idea.

He wanted to clear the misconception that he was cheerful and happy all the time.

But he then stopped himself.

If she was praising him so much, why stop her in full flow?

He might as well lap up the praise!

A few minutes later, as they were midway through their main course, Roma shifted the conversation topic from the emotional 'special connect' talk to what seemed like raunchy bedroom talk. The raunchy talk instantly stiffened an organ of his body into a hard rock and made his eyes pop out like he had got a 220 volt electric shock.

'Raghu, what are you views on a woman's G-spot?' she asked him.

'I'm sorry. What?'

'What are your views on the G-spot?'

'To be honest, I don't have too much of an idea,' he replied sheepishly. 'But I do know about Gold spot which I used to drink merrily during my school days.'

She smiled.

'Raghu, you're pretty funny and immature.'

'I think I am. But in my defence, I have decent knowledge about Gold spot, sun spots, blood clots, fairness cream related "dark spots", various religious holy spots and the "hot spot" cricket technology but really have no idea about the G-spot.'

'Ok fine. What are your views on the labia?'

'What kind of question is this? I really have no idea about the labia. But I do know that there is this guy in my colony who recently purchased an awesome new Skoda Fabia.'

'Raghu, you are funny.'

'I'm not trying to be funny. I'm being serious. I have no answers to your tough questions which by the way… don't even have options! I'm an aspiring author…not an encyclopaedia of knowledge.'

'Ok chill, Raghu. Do you want to know why I asked you these questions?'

'Why?'

'It is because of your description of *The Paperback Badshah's* plot. You had only told me, a bit earlier that in your novel, Alok and Alka share a fair bit of raw sexual passion.'

'Yes, they do.'

'It is surprising to know that while the creator is trying to ignite sexual chemistry in his plot, he himself hardly knows anything about such matters in real life!'

He was stumped for an answer.

He saw her laugh out loud.

'Err…err…I guess you are right,' he responded finally.

'Raghu, I can help. If you wish, I can share some inputs. Interested?'

'Can you please email me the details?'

He noticed her glare at him.

'Raghu, are you really stupid or just pretending to be stupid?'

'Truth be told…I'm a little stupid and hugely inexperienced especially in such *private* matters.'

'But you are honest. I like that.'

'I am. Thanks.'

'As you know, there is this T-20 match starting at 8 p.m. tomorrow.'

'I know.'

'I am free and if you want, you know…you can come over to my place. We can watch the match, discuss about the match and then maybe you know…you know…'

She left the last bit incomplete.

She then bit her lower lip.

This time…he understood the body signal!

He nodded in approval.

He also started to perspire a little.

She clearly wanted to see more of him at her place! Wow!

Her mind had clearly started to plan activities beyond just a simple dinner date. Activities which pointed in the direction of a dimly lit bedroom at her home involving a bit of night time shyness, friskiness and kinky naughtiness…..to teach him a thing or two about life which certainly couldn't be learnt over email!

A few minutes later, the bill arrived.

He offered to pay.

'Look Raghu, I don't believe in any of this forceful "male chivalry" nonsense. Let's split the bill.'

'Ok.'

He acted like he was sad, but secretly he was happy. The dinner had been pretty expensive!

Once they left the restaurant, he walked with her to the car park.

As she entered her car, she gave him a hug and a quick peck on the cheek. A peck which suggested that, she was equally excited about their next meeting.

'So Raghu, I'll see you tomorrow at my place.'

'Sure.'

She drove off.

Half an hour later, he reached home.

He changed, brushed his teeth and then turned on his laptop.

He logged on to Facebook.

Sweety had sent him a friend request. He accepted it. He skimmed through her profile. She was a student counsellor of sorts at an examination coaching institute. Her wall was full of sad, depressing posts on life, the journey of life, the importance of being spiritual and other blah blah blah. He wondered why Roma wasn't on Facebook. It would have been so much of fun! They could chat the entire morning, afternoon, evening and night away!

He came back to his profile page.

He stared at his empty wall.

It was very unlike him to post status updates to reflect his current state of mind. But this time he was genuinely excited.

He posted on his wall: *Life unexpectedly throws up opportunities. Good things happen to people who wait. Victory comes to those who wait the longest.*

Within a few minutes, he got a few likes and comments.

As he logged out off Facebook, a few questions suddenly came to his mind.

Were things moving too fast with Roma?

What had made romantic and reflective Roma suddenly transform into raunchy Roma?

Was he really that cool that made her want to meet him again?

Or was it a case that now...after twenty five odd years of his life, he had finally found a woman who found his wit impressive, his maturity levels irresistible and as a result couldn't get enough of him?

What would the following day lead to?

Would it just be a steamy one night stand or would it be the initiation of a full blown romance?

He felt excited just thinking about the possibilities.

PASSION

The next day.

It was around 4.45 in the evening.

Raghu had just woken up from his now customary afternoon nap.

He was feeling a little groggy. He had not slept too well during the night due to the nervous excitement building up within him.

As he stretched a little, he heard his mobile vibrate.

He had got a text message.

It was from Roma. It read:

I'm sitting here...thinking about you. Only all 58 kgs of me and nothing else. I wouldn't mind being gently spanked, like the mannequin you had described during the writing workshop. ☺

He stared at the message in disbelief.

Till now he had only heard of sexting or sex talk or flirtatious lewd talk while sending mobile text messages. But this was happening in real time! He liked it!

He replied:

I'm also sitting here…thinking about you. Only all 88 kgs of my sweaty self and nothing else.

He got an immediate response:

88 kgs?

He replied:

Yes. A combination of bone weight & over weight.

She replied back:

Funny. Be on time. I'm waiting. ☺

He was now fully energized.

He finally left his house at around 6.30 p.m.

Earlier in the day, he lied to his parents and had told them that he would be spending the night at a party at Nandu's place. He had to be fairly evasive and secretive as he didn't share a very open 'Hindi movie' type 'son-parent' relationship in which he could tell them that he would be going out on a casual (second) date and for them to encourage him by saying something like-'*Jaa Raghu beta, life is short. Zindagi poori tarah seh jee lay.*'

At around 7.40 p.m., after having navigated through the chaotic Saturday evening traffic, he finally reached the imposing main gate of the gated community where Roma stayed. At the main security gate, he was made to wait for a few minutes as the security confirmed with Roma about the arrival of her visitor.

He finally got the clearance.

As he rode inside the gigantic community to the phase in which she stayed, he noticed that everything seemed very peaceful, quiet and organized. There was no disturbance at these villa homes from the sudden arrival of roadside hawkers, painters, carpet sellers or suitcase sari sellers. In his colony, the bleats of goats, barking of dogs, loud noise from the cement mixers used in construction work, all played their part in making him partially deaf while enriching his daily mundane existence partially!

He also noticed many residents taking their dogs for a late evening walk. The dogs seemed to walk in a dignified, well coordinated 'march past style' manner by the side of well manicured lawns unlike the street dogs and the pet dogs in his colony, which roamed around with total disregard for any law and order!

A sudden commercial thought struck him as he observed life around here.

He never knew Roma was this rich!

A big villa all to herself! Wow!

It would be awesome if he could take his relationship with her to the medium to long term. He could meet her regularly at her place and make passionate love from dawn to dusk! He could also get to enjoy the comforts of her large villa and maybe even have a really big soundproof room for himself to write his book in silence!

He finally reached her villa.

He had reached just in time for the 8 p.m. start of the cricket match. *And hopefully also for the time of his life......*

He rang the doorbell.

Roma opened the door.

She gave him a friendly hug and said, 'Good to see you, Raghu.'

'Same here, Roma,' he replied.

He noticed that she was dressed in a tight T-shirt and black track pants.

He had secretly hoped that on seeing him, she would have jumped on him like it was shown in the movies and then within a few seconds, their clothes would be flung to a corner of the room! But clearly that had to wait!

He entered her living room.

The room was dimly lit. It had a romantic feel to it. He noticed scented candles placed in the corner of the room.

He sat down on a gigantic sofa which seemed to be made out of some imported Italian leather.

The T-20 cricket match had just started.

He heard the familiar voice of the cricket commentators.

One of the commentators was known for his clichéd style of commentary to describe match situations. The other commentator delighted some viewers (and irritated most others) with his over the top, *balle balle* style which focused less on cricket and more on non cricketing anecdotes, poetry, one-liners and nursery rhymes. Together, however, they made for a deadly combination.

He heard the voice of the clichéd commentator-

'...*The stadium is absolutely packed today. Not a vantage point is free...*'

He began to get involved in the match.

'Raghu, just like you surprised me with the book gift yesterday, I've also got a surprise lined up for you,' Roma told him, a few minutes later.

'What?' he asked excitedly.

'I've cooked something for you.'

'Seriously? For me?'

'Yes. In my view, a way to a smiling man's heart is first through his stomach and then via a region below his stomach.'

He grinned. He liked the way in which hunger for food and for the body was interestingly yet vulgarly stated.

'Give me two minutes. I'll be back.'

A couple of minutes later, she returned with a plate which had something on it, with a bit of ketchup by the side. She gave the plate to him.

'Here Raghu, taste it.'

'Sure.'

He stared at the plate.

What the hell had she made?

Did it contain some mysterious aphrodisiacs to power their night away?

He didn't know.

'By the way, what is it?' he asked.

'It's a masala dosa.'

At first, he thought that she was joking.

Then he realized that she was really serious about what she had prepared!

He looked at the plate again.

From no angle did it look like a dosa! It looked more like a burger with some aloo in between! Even the regular companions for a dosa-the chutney and sambar were missing!

Just then, he heard the clichéd commentator-

'...*the pitch is as flat as a pancake. There are no demons in them. The batsman should have no problems feasting on the bowling attack...*'

But clearly he was going to have a problem feasting on this weird food item!

He took a quick bite.

It certainly didn't taste like a masala dosa! It tasted more like a 'tasteless dosa-burger' which fell in the category of disgusting 'food items' which participants in adventure and survival based reality shows were forced to eat, to avoid elimination!

'Raghu, was it tasty?'

He knew this was a tricky situation. But he decided to speak honestly.

'Roma, the preparation is nice *but not* great. This "dosa-burger" has no oil, is fairly bland and seems to have been prepared for a calorie conscious eater and not for someone like me! My mother can make a good masala dosa blindfold!'

He immediately realized his error of having been fully honest! What was meant to serve as some sort of motivation came out of his mouth sounding all wrong.... like it was a comparison!

Too late! Too late!

He could sense that her mood was spoiled.

She moved away silently and sat on a chair which was a few feet away from the gigantic sofa on which he was seated.

With silence engulfing the huge living room, he started to think of ways in which he could apologize to her, to make her feel better.

Just then he heard the clichéd commentator-

'*...the match is interestingly poised at the moment. Either of the teams should look to seize the initiative. At this point however...we can safely say that cricket is the real winner...*'

He thought to himself.

Was the commentator stupid? How could cricket be the real winner? The match had just begun!

He then realized that while the commentator had no brains, he however had limited brains which he needed to use more sensibly and with discretion in the immediate future.

A few minutes later, he tried to break the silence with an attempt at humour.

He imitated the clichéd commentator to entertain her.

However, it didn't elicit a response from her.

He again heard the clichéd commentator-

'*...the teams need to get a move on. They surely don't want to waste the time of the fans and be docked a part of their match fee for slow over-rate...*'

He decided that it was indeed time to move on.

He tried to lighten up the situation by pretending to be an in flight male steward.

'Ladies and gentleman, on behalf of captain Roma, this is flight attendant Raghu speaking. Please settle down. Please fasten your seatbelts. We are currently experiencing some turbulence which should soon clear and make way for some erotic thunder.'

There was still no reaction. He was tired.

He decided to remain quiet.

A few minutes later, there was a change of commentators.

The camera focus also shifted to a 'noodle strap wearing' buxom woman anchor, who was the on field reporter for this match. Her role was to give television viewers a groundside report of the game to keep them more involved.

Facing the camera, the reporter told viewers that they could write in with their cricket questions.

A telephone number flashed on the TV screen.

The reporter then walked to a corner of the ground where the cheerleaders were dancing.

She interviewed them.

A new telephone number flashed on the screen.

The reporter told viewers that they could speak exclusively and in private with the cheerleaders for only one rupee per minute by dialling this number.

Raghu felt excited hearing this.

He silently took the mobile phone out of his pocket to save the number.

Just then, Roma glanced in his direction!

She had an angry expression.

'Raghu, what the hell are you doing?' she asked him.

'What did I do now?'

'Don't you realize that what you just did…is a gross violation of my seventh principle? You allowed yourself to be seduced by this stupid busty reporter's bosom power!'

He was at a loss for words to come up with a meaningful explanation.

Roma got up angrily and switched the TV off.

He tried to think of new ways to diffuse this volatile situation.

Thankfully a few minutes later, she walked up to him and gave him a hug.

'Raghu, I think I overreacted.'

'I'm also sorry, for not respecting your principles.'

The fight was resolved. Finally!

Romance definitely seemed like it was back in the air.

He wanted to know when would they kiss and undress each other, to begin the proceedings which would hopefully burst open the floodgates for some deadly sexual thunder.

Via some sort of mental telepathy, she seemed to actually interpret his thoughts!

'Raghu, I know why you are here. I can sense your excitement. Let me go change into something different. I'll be back.'

She walked in the direction of her bedroom.

He was excited.

In the match, a strategic time out was about to begin.

As he waited for her to return and for the match to resume, he got up and walked around the sprawling living room.

The villa seemed like a carbon copy of a suburban US home.

What furniture! What artefacts! What floor rugs! What exquisite wooden flooring in one section! What exquisite marble flooring in an adjacent section! He could see his own reflection! As he looked around, he spotted his gift (the book) lying on an expensive looking table.

He also noticed a fireplace. Unreal!

Was a fireplace in the living room, the new status symbol for the rich residents of Bangalore? Was there also a wine cellar and a swimming pool tucked away somewhere? Just then, on the wall, next to the fireplace, he spotted a few photos. In one photo, he saw Roma hugging an old man.

Maybe it was her father who was based in Mumbai.

He suddenly remembered how he had tried to hug his father after Mr. Prasad's motivational session and how his father was completely surprised by the sudden display of affection! Hilarious!

He looked at the photo again and muttered, 'Hello Uncle. I'm Raghu. How are you? Can I please do advance marriage booking for your daughter? Thank you.'

He chuckled to himself.

He walked back to the sofa.

The match had resumed after the time out. The clichéd commentator was also back live on air.

He then noticed Roma return.

She was in a black satin robe with little underneath.

He heard the clichéd commentator-

'*...the match is not yet over...but one can safely say that a viewer has got his money's worth...*'

For a change, the commentator was spot on!

He reduced the TV volume.

Things were finally happening!

He started to feel the full impact of her bosom power seduction. There was hardly anything left for deduction. He felt a hardening erection.

He removed his shirt and tossed it in the air.

As his shirt went up in the air, he also looked skywards to thank God.

God was indeed great but only for a few seconds as he casually asked Roma a question which resulted in an unexpected revelation......

'Roma, do you miss your dad a lot?' he asked, pointing at the photo.

'Raghu, are you an idiot?'

'I'm sorry. I know it's an inappropriate time to ask such a question.'

'You idiot, that's not my father. *That's my husband.* He's out of town.'

'WHAT?'

Raghu was shocked. *Roma was married! What the hell was going on?*

The sexual excitement in him fizzled out.

He heard the clichéd commentator have his say as well-

'...*It's all happening here at the cricket ground! All of a sudden... the batsman has no clue as to what's happening. This is a crucial phase of play which can determine the outcome of the match...*'

It certainly was a crucial moment of the evening!

He stared at the photo again.

Roma was around his age. The old man looked so...old! *A sixty plus something man married to a twenty something attractive woman?*

It just didn't stack up.

Unreal! Unbelievable!

Was God deliberately playing with his emotions because he had smirked insensitively while listening to Sweety's various observations during the writing workshop?

He had no answer.

But what he did know was that he wanted answers right now!

How come such a significant material disclosure was conveniently forgotten by Roma?

How come during their dinner she had not mentioned even once that she was married but instead had spent a lot of time telling him about her stupid principles?

He looked at her.

'Roma, I want an explanation.'

'For what?' she asked.

'You are married! You never told me this.'

'Raghu, are you joking? I told you last night while having dinner that I'm a married woman.'

'Really?'

He didn't remember her mentioning it even once!

'I clearly told you everything when I was telling you about my complex personality and my complicated life. And if you remember, like a mature adult, you had been nodding intermittently in understanding of my situation!'

'Oh.'

He felt a sudden sinking feeling in his gut with this second revelation.

Did she really tell him all of this? How come he hadn't even reacted?

A few seconds later, it struck him as to what possibly might have happened-

During the dinner, when she had probably mentioned that she was married, he wasn't even listening to her as his mind had already tuned out and was busy in another world...a world in which her legs were wrapped around him in an empty cricket stadium!

As he gasped silently thinking of this likely possibility, he noticed that she was staring at him with a questioning look on her face.

'Raghu, now I'm having doubts of my own. Did you pay attention to anything at all, that I said last night?'

'Yes. I paid full attention to everything you told me. But this part...possibly must have slipped my mind. If you don't mind, can you please give me a quick one time recap of the entire situation?'

She made a 'not-too-pleased' face and then began her narration-

It was little over a year ago, when she was an airhostess that she had first met her husband, a Bangalore based businessman in the business class section of a Delhi-Bangalore flight. By the end of the flight they had exchanged phone numbers. A few weeks later, phone numbers made way for hotel room numbers. Hotel rooms became the launch pad for their physical intimacy. The businessman followed up the acts of physical intimacy by showering her with expensive material gifts which made her very happy. A few months later, they decided to get married. The businessman's parents were already in heaven and her parents opposed the union on account of the thirty five year plus age gap. They passed cheap remarks which really hurt her. Remarks such as: 'Awara buddah jo hai tharki... uss se Turkey mein karogi shaadi?', 'Buddah se pyaar...kahan gaye tumhare sanskaar?', 'Will the buddah have energy in his haddi to play with you night time sexual kabbadi?', 'We are warning you right now...buddah se shaadi will lead to barbaadi.'

She however decided to follow her heart and stood firm in her decision to get married.

Her parents snapped all ties with her.

She moved in with her businessman husband to this spacious house in the gated community.

But looking back now, her parents seemed to be right all along.

The problems began a few days into the marriage.

Her husband started having an affair with a female business associate of his in Delhi.

The knowledge of the affair jolted her.

She felt broken from within.

She realized that there was no love between them.

And to top it all, instead of focusing on her emotional and sexual requirements, her husband began irritating her even further by discussing the performance of his monthly mutual fund investments.

Roma paused and reflected on her situation.

Raghu was silenced listening to this narration!

It certainly was an interesting yet complicated situation to be in.

He never ever had a girlfriend who had shown interest in him but now a married woman who was battling deepening cracks in her marital life was showing interest in him and was clearly knowledgable and experienced enough to teach him a thing or two about a woman's various body spots (A, B, C, D, E, F, G etc.), body parts, techniques and positions.

'Raghu, this sadness about my situation is all a thing of the past,' she continued. 'I've adopted a new outlook towards life. Do you remember the opinion I had expressed at the workshop that life is all about being lived to the fullest, despite the various complications?'

'I remember clearly,' he replied smiling gently.

It was an opinion of hers which he had supported.

'Raghu, do you know, this smile of yours is what first attracted me to you.'

'I clearly remember everything you told me about my "sunshine" smile!'

He deliberately broke out into an extended 'sunshine' smile.

'Your smile reminds me of Akash. He too had a "sunshine" smile,' she stated casually.

'Who's Akash?'

Who was this new additional fucker in the already complex love plot who had a 'sunshine' smile like his?

'Errr....err...no one.'

'Roma, who's Akash?' he asked again. 'Did you tell me about him as well during our dinner date?'

'No, I didn't. It's a closed chapter in my past. It's a chapter which can freak anyone out. Let it not spoil our evening together.'

He wanted to tell her that nothing could freak him out more...than she being married to such an old, sixty plus buddah to begin with!

Pointing a finger in her direction and speaking in a deep baritone like a famous TV quiz host, he asked her for a quick narration.

Rather grudgingly, she began telling him-

She had met Akash for the first time, a few months after the cracks in her marriage had surfaced. He had just joined her airlines as a commercial pilot which was before the job cuts had set in. In their first meeting itself, he smiled like the sunshine which reduced her pain and thoughts of her unhappy marriage.

During their time off from work, they got to know each other better.

He was in his late twenties. He was born and brought up in Netherlands and had come to India to work. His dream from first standard itself was to be a pilot and rule the skies. Though he was a commercial pilot, he had the energy and the competitive fighting spirit of an air force pilot. He loved living life on the edge. 'Top Gun' was his favourite English movie. 'Border','Refugee','LOC Kargil' and 'Lakshya' were his favourite Hindi movies.

One thing led to another and eventually they ended up having an affair.

More than the physical intimacy, it was the small gestures of love which mattered to her, which made her feel important, special, loved and cared for. Things were going on fine until one day, when her husband confronted her regarding her affair with Akash. She admitted to the same.

Hearing this, her husband's old age ego was hurt. He started to behave like a possessive lover. He threatened her with dire consequences.

She realized that while his string of affairs on the side had to be pardoned or conveniently ignored, her contentment didn't make him happy.

She immediately called up Akash and informed him about the situation. He told her confidently that he wouldn't be intimidated by any sort of pressure tactics and would instead explain matters face to face to her husband.

She felt reassured.

But before she knew it, a few days later, Akash just disappeared from her life. He had unexpectedly severed all ties. She tried contacting him but to no avail. The HR at the airlines also confirmed that he had just left the job without any sort of intimation!

She knew that deep down something was terribly wrong.

How could Akash just disappear into thin air?

She suspected her possessive husband's hand in it.

But she was too scared to ask or confront him.

It was yet another jolt in her quest for everlasting love and happiness.

But somehow she had managed to pick up the pieces and move on.

It was an incident from her past which had taught her about true love.

As Raghu finished hearing Roma's full story, he was totally freaked out!

And also very scared!

He realized that this evening with her could turn out to be very dangerous.

Would he become the new object of attention for her buddah husband? Would he become the latest victim of a passion related crime?

He could imagine a scary scenario play out in his mind.

He would be sitting at home, all alone, working on his novel. Goons sent by the husband, dressed as gas inspectors would suddenly appear. They would first beat him with a hockey stick. Then they would break his laptop into pieces. Then just before leaving, they would reconfigure his head with a few bullets. *The Paperback Badshah* under creation would suddenly become orphaned and his dreams of becoming a published author would remain unfulfilled.....

His thoughts were interrupted by the ring of the landline phone.

Seeing the number flash on the display, Roma told him to remain silent.

'It's my husband on the line,' she told him.

He froze. *Her husband on the line! Oh fuck!*

She spoke for a few minutes while trying to sound somewhat cheerful.

She finished the call and then told him that her husband had finished his business work earlier than usual, and was landing in Bangalore in a few hours time!

Just then he heard the clichéd commentator in the background-

'*...the game of cricket is a great leveller. One moment you are up in the air basking in cricketing glory and the very next moment you are back, with your feet firmly planted on the ground! One moment a six hit by you, is busy kissing an airhostess in the skies and the very next delivery, you are bowled and out of here...*'

He arrived at a decision.

He wanted to leave.

'Roma, let me honest with you. I'm actually getting very scared. I think it's best if I leave,' he told her.

'Why? What happened?' she asked.

'I thought all along, that you were single and ready to mingle. But now, given the unexpected revelations, I'm pretty scared of the consequences. As your well-wisher, I think it will be best, if you first visit a divorce lawyer to disengage from the current situation you are in.'

He waited for her reaction to his assessment of the situation.

She first ruffled her hair. Flakes of dandruff floated in the air and parts of it fell on her black robe and started to shine like little attention seeking diamonds. And then, before he knew it, she screamed on top of her voice.

'WHO THE HELL ARE YOU TO GIVE ME ADVISE? ROMA COMMANDS YOU TO STAND UP AND REMAIN SILENT LIKE A STATUE!'

He stood up silently.

Not even in his wildest dreams did he imagine that she was capable of such anger!

Plus he had no idea as to why she had spoken suddenly in third person!

Was it a part of her complex personality which she had told him about during their dinner date?

It seemed possible.

'Raghu, I'm frankly hurt, surprised, angered and insulted by your decision. You clearly came here with the intention of having your fair share of "fucking fun" but the moment it got a little complicated, you got scared and want to run?'

'I guess,' he muttered feebly.

'You know what you are?'

'What?'

'You are a L-O-S-E-R!'

She made the 'loser sign' by using her forefinger and thumb, and placed it in line with her forehead.

'You know something else?'

'What?'

'*The Paperback Badshah* has the most bullshit plot ever! I had said nice things about it earlier to only make you feel good about it. It is nothing but complete nonsense!'

He felt really bad hearing this sudden, unexpected criticism of his work-in-progress novel.

He noticed her walk towards the book which he had gifted her.

'Look at me, Raghu! *The Girl with the Dragon Tattoo* is a superb book which has been read and loved by readers the world over. *The Paperback Badshah*, if ever published, will be a total washout! It will be given the thumbs down by readers and will not sell more than five copies all over the world!'

As he stood silently and listened to her outburst, he really hoped that her book sales prediction wouldn't come true!

Just then, she suddenly threw *The Girl with the Dragon Tattoo,* in his direction. He was supposed to be a statue but he instinctively put his hand out to his right like a fielder at backward point and caught the book!

He was proud of his catch.

He heard the clichéd commentator in the background-

'...*What a catch! Catches do win matches! Fielding is really crucial in the shorter format of the game. Overall the catch has resulted in an extraordinary moment of real estate success....sorry, I actually meant banking success...sorry, I actually meant mobile phone success...*'

He started smiling as the commentator was confused as to which sponsor's tag line to use, to describe the catch!

From the corner of his eye, he noticed that Roma was glaring at him.

'Raghu, wipe that "stupid" smile off your idiotic face. It sickens me!' she shouted.

He was surprised. This was too much!

Till just a while ago, he had been the recipient of various 'sunshine smile of the year' compliments and now suddenly, she wanted him to wipe the smile off his face?

Maybe it was all her pent up frustration coming out on him.

A few minutes passed but she wasn't yet done with her outburst.

'You know what?' she asked him.

'What?' he asked.

'I want a *real man. A real man...*who wouldn't mind taking a few blows, a few broken bones, a broken ribcage, a broken nose, a broken knee in the face of hostile opposition, to win me over. *A real man...* who understands what volatile, edgy, passionate love is all about. *A real man....*who will sacrifice everything for love including his own life, if required and be worshipped by the romantic couples the world over. I'm in search of that kind of *real man*…who will truly, madly, deeply love me for days, weeks, months and years to come!'

'But….'

'Don't interrupt me, Raghu! I've realized one thing. You can never be that *real man* for me. You are someone for whom I've lost all respect. You are nothing but an idiot…an overgrown 88 kg *man-child* who can only sit on your ass, eat properly, have cups of coffee, take afternoon naps, sit in front of your laptop, check your Facebook updates and work on your stupid novel! Someday you will have to grow up and you will realize that life and especially matters of the heart are not always laid out perfectly in clear black and white! It is messy and complicated!'

Listening to all these '*real man*' versus '*man-child*' back to back dhamakedar dialogues, he wanted to ask her just one question- *How could fight for her to reduce her pain, if thanks to her buddah husband, he himself was left with no brain?*

Before he could even ask her that logical question, she told him to get lost. She pointed at the front door.

He picked up his crumpled shirt and buttoned it on as he walked towards the front door.

'Raghu, one final thing.'

'What?'

'I'm confident that even the cricket cheerleaders will never ever pick up your call! Not even in your dreams! Now just get lost!'

He walked out of the villa.

Roma slammed the door on his face.

Unlike the cricket match which was still in progress, their 'love match' was sadly all over.

Forty minutes later, he reached his home.

He saw his father watching TV.

'Raghu, how come you are home so early? You said you are going to be at Nandu's party, right?' his father asked.

'Yeah, the party got over early,' he lied.

His father looked at him curiously.

'Were you thrown out of the party?'

'What do you mean?'

'I have a feeling that you were thrown out of the house. I'm pretty sure the party must have been only for employed people who work hard on weekdays and party harder on weekends!'

His father burst out laughing at his own comment!

He wanted to tell his father that he had actually been 'thrown out of a house' but for altogether different reasons!

*

A week had passed since the Roma episode.

Raghu was making substantial progress in his writing.

Having attended Begum's workshop, he had understood that as a writer, he had to occasionally draw inspiration from the 'well' of emotions which was locked inside of him, to add that extra 'something' to his writing. The time he had spent with Roma had certainly added to his bank of experiences and some of the moments had made their way into his draft!

Just as he was about to begin work on a new chapter, he heard his mobile ring. It was Nandu.

'Raghu, what's up? Nandu asked.

'Dude! Nothing much. Just working on my novel.'

'Oh cool. I'm passing through Jayanagar. Do you want to catch up for a quick coffee?'

'Sure. Coffee day?'

'Done.'

Twenty minutes later, they met at the Café Coffee Day in Jayanagar 4th block.

'Raghu, growing your hair huh? Trying to look like Lasith Malinga?' Nandu asked him as he made a slinging, round arm bowling action like the Sri Lankan speedster.

'Not really, dude. It's just that I've not gone for a haircut. How come you are in such a chilled out mood?'

'Kavita has taken Gopu to her parents place for a few days for some family function. I'm just chilling at home, all alone!'

'How come you didn't go?'

'It's a long boring story. What's up with you?'

'Nothing much apart from the writing….no wait…there is something!'

'What?'

'There was this chick who was hitting on me, big time.'

'And what happened?'

'Things didn't work out.'

'Why?'

'Well…forget it.'

'Why are you acting so shy? We have discussed everything from a chick's vital stats to cricket stats right from our school days. So just spill the beans…oops….I mean the coffee beans…ha ha….'

'Ok, here goes…..'

Raghu spent the next fifteen odd minutes detailing his time with Roma. He described the various interesting moments and finished his narration by describing the series of unexpected back to back revelations.

He waited for Nandu's reaction.

'Ha…ha…ha….Raghu! You are such a loser!' Nandu burst out laughing. 'You had the chance to get some high quality action but you felt a lot tension and so you ran away! You got scared of a sixty something buddah husband? Hilarious!'

'Dude, you seem to be in a really funny mood. Did you not hear my narration clearly? Roma is married. It was so complicated. I was scared of crossing a seriously dangerous matrimonial line.'

'But why did you get scared? She liked you. She made the first move. You had an open invitation. You thought she will come on a show like *Sach Ka Samna* or what in which the host will ask her, "So Roma, is it true that you have had an extramarital affair with an aspiring author?" to which she would moan and take your name, following which, her husband sitting in the audience would track you down, remove his revolver and shout, "Oye South Indian, main hoon North Indian! Chal haat upar karle. Goli chalne wali hai. Koi aakhri khwaish? Idli, dosa, sambar vada, upma?" And before you can even apologize and say something like, "Sir, maaf kardo. Galti ho gayi…," the oldie would shoot you-dishoom…dishoom…dishkaww…dishkaww? Shit! I'm so creative. I think even I should quit my job and write a book…ha ha!'

'Dude, you think it's funny? I was really scared.'

'Raghu, if I was not married…I would take Roma's number from you right now and I would give her a call.'

'Ok, before doing that, look…Kavita's behind you.'

'What! Where?'

Nandu turned around! There was no one! Raghu had pulled a fast one!

'You idiot! You had me stumped for a second.'

'Sorry dude! Now you see what I'm saying? Even my reaction to leave was instant! It was an automatic flight to safety approach.'

'Ok, I think I get your point. But take my advice right now.'

'What advice?'

'An opportunity to write a book and all will come and go but an opportunity with a chick will definitely not come and go! With Roma you have lost your chance for good. But going forward with chicks, please act like a mature, grown-up man and don't position yourself as a man-child. You may still get lucky. But how to get that luck to get lucky is a separate issue altogether.'

'Hmm.'

'I have a question to ask.'

'What?'

'When Roma threw *The Girl with the Dragon Tattoo* right back at you…where exactly were you fielding?'

'I think I was at backward point. I caught it one handed!'

Both of them laughed.

'Raghu, we should seriously catch up more often. I've not laughed this much.'

'We should, dude. Everything may seem funny now, but it certainly wasn't when I was at her place!'

IRRITATION

A month later.
It was yet another Saturday.

It was mid morning.

Raghu was at his writing desk.

His enthusiasm levels were lower than usual.

It was because he was suffering from a bad case of the dreaded writer's block. For over two weeks, he had not been able to come up with even a single new idea to further his plot. It was so frustrating especially given the encouraging progress he had made in his writing until now.

During this time, he even tried the exercise taught by Begum at the workshop to cope with the block, but it didn't seem to help.

He however decided, that it was now high time he stopped thinking and rather started fighting it.

Deep down he was still optimistic as he knew that he needed just that one new idea, thought or observation to reignite his imagination which would get his writing back on track.

He switched on his laptop.

He opened a new Word document in the hope of writing a sentence or two.

The sheer *whiteness* of the blank document however intimidated him!

It reminded him of the imposing cricket grounds in Australia. The *whiteness* which stretched horizontally across his laptop screen reminded him of the never ending, square boundaries at the Melbourne Cricket Ground. The *whiteness* which stretched vertically across his laptop screen reminded him of the incredibly long, straight boundaries at the Adelaide Oval.

He felt like pulling the hair out of his head.

He also felt a bit of sudden tension as certain questions came to his mind.

How much longer would this block last?

Would a change to his existing writing routine help break the block?

Would his free flowing style of writing be curbed because of the block?

What if he never got any new ideas to further his plot? Would it cause his months of hard work, to come to naught?

As he stared at the blank Word document again, his mother suddenly barged into his room.

She gave him a sheet on which she had written a list of items that she wanted him to purchase from a nearby discount shopping store. He knew that if he went now….the rest of the morning which he had earmarked for his writing would be gone! Poof! This was because he knew that it would take him about thirty minutes to locate the various items in the store and another forty odd minutes would then go by, waiting in a long serpentine Saturday morning queue to get the items billed!

Thinking of this loss of time, he asked his mother if he could get the items a couple of hours later, as he was busy with his writing.

'Raghu, go get the items right now,' his mother told him firmly. 'If you were in office, you would have been actually busy. Now you aren't even busy. You are simply wasting time at home. Don't get confused and bring items which aren't on the list. Or else I'll send you back to exchange them.'

His mother walked out of the room.

He felt irritated.

How many times did he need to explain that he was a creative entrepreneur in pursuit of a dream and had a daily routine which needed to be followed?

Why was his sitting at home and writing a book perceived to be a waste of time?

When would this perception change?

Didn't writing require time, thought and effort?

Or was it a case that he was now simply overreacting and feeling irritated because of the lack of progress in his writing?

He wore his sandals rather uninterestedly and left for the store.

Twenty minutes later, he felt he had reached a crowded railway station.

Of course it was the shopping store, but seeing people aggressively push past each other with their shopping carts in front of them, in search of a bag of 'ten kg' atta or a packet of tur dal or a red plastic bucket with a blue mug free, made the store seem more like a busy, crowded railway station!

As he grabbed hold of a shopping cart, he suddenly realised that witnessing the hustle and bustle of this Saturday mid morning crowd, wasn't a bad way at all of picking up some observations which could be useful for his writing.

As if on cue, he noticed something.

A small kid who couldn't perhaps take all the commotion, vomited in a corner!

A store attendant ran towards the spot and started shouting further vomit inducing words which added to the overall commotion. In an interesting combination of a Hindi version followed by a Kannada version, the attendant repeatedly screamed the following for the benefit of the general public-

'ULTI! CHOTA BACCHA KO ULTI HO GAYA…*CHIKKA HUDAGA GAY ULTI BAN DI DEY…*!'

About forty minutes later after the vomit entertainment, he had finally finished locating the various items in his list.

He pushed his shopping cart towards the billing counter.

He stood in the queue.

The queue progressed slowly.

In front of him in the queue, a woman was standing with her husband and young son. The son was repeatedly thanking his mother as she had allowed him to purchase a small toy car.

'Thank you, Mummy for this gaadi,' the son thanked his mother once again, with obvious childlike glee radiating from his face.

'Beta, I haven't yet billed it,' she replied.

'Bill it fast, Mummy. I promise I will play a lot with this gaadi. I also promise I will never trouble you and Papa. Pakka promise.'

The mother smiled and hugged her son.

A few thoughts came to Raghu's mind as he witnessed this display of mother-son 'gaadi' love.

Years later, the small son would probably arrive at a store to do some shopping in a real car. Would the son still retain his childlike excitement and enjoy the Saturday morning crowded shopping experience?

Seemed highly unlikely!

Twenty odd minutes later, his turn finally came at the billing counter.

He started unloading the various items from his shopping cart onto the counter. The cashier glared at him seeing the amount of shopping he had done. He wanted to tell the cashier that he was only shopping as per his mother's instructions!

Half an hour later, he was back home.

He placed the shopping bags on the dining table.

'Raghu, Gopi is coming home tonight for dinner. He had called while you were shopping,' his mother told him. She then began checking the various items he had purchased.

He nodded and then went to have his lunch.

While having his lunch, he thought about Gopi.

Gopi was a distant relative, but with each passing year he tried to make himself less distant with his regular visits to Bangalore! He was a businessman based in Erode but of late, his business interests often got him down to Bangalore to meet new distributors and his other business partners. Before the end of each visit, he tried to make it a point to merrily hop over to the Balakrishnan household to keep the 'family ties' alive!

What irked him the most about Gopi, was the number of bullshit questions he usually asked during each of his visits which could test the patience of any normal human being. Questions such as-'Raghu, what are you doing?', 'Why are you doing?', 'Why are you doing this, not that?', 'Where are you going?', 'How are you going?' among various other kinds of questions. This time, he got the feeling that the topic of discussion with Gopi, during the evening would centre around why he had quit his job to write a book.

He tried to anticipate the various possible questions and the suitable responses he would have to come up with.

In the early part of the evening, just after he had woken up from his afternoon nap, he heard the doorbell ring. His mother told him to open the door as she was busy in the kitchen with the dinner preparations.

He opened the door thinking that it was his father.

It turned out to be Gopi!

Oh fuck.

Gopi had come earlier than expected. He was supposed to come for dinner but had already come by 5 p.m.!

'Hello Raghu! How have you been?' Gopi asked, in his trademark loud booming voice, so that even the neighbours could tune in, if interested.

'Good Uncle.'

'It's so good to be back in the Balakrishnan household after so many months.'

'I'm sure it is.'

He put on a fake 'sunshine' smile to act as if he was really happy to see his relative after so many months!

Just then, his mother also arrived from the kitchen to exchange some quick pleasantries with Gopi. A few minutes later, she rushed back to the kitchen to resume her dinner preparations.

He walked with Gopi to the living room for some general chit-chat till his father came home from work.

A few minutes later he heard his mother calling him from the kitchen.

He ran to the kitchen and returned with a tray which contained a cup of piping hot filter coffee and a plate of biscuits. He placed it gently on a small side table by the couch.

'Raghu, I heard something about you. Is it true?' Gopi asked him, while sipping on the coffee.

'What?' he asked.

'That you quit your job to write a book?'

'Yes, it's true.'

The next few minutes were spent in answering the questions which he had anticipated such as- 'When did you quit your job?', 'Why did you quit?', 'What's your book about?', 'What's the title?', 'What's the progress?', 'When's it getting published?'

All in all, he answered with clarity and gave a rough overview of his novel.

He could, however, sense that Gopi wasn't fully satisfied with his answers and was keen on taking the questioning to an altogether different level.

And that's exactly what happened!

'Raghu, it's good to see youngsters like you doing something different. But writing and all can be done even when you are old and retired. Right now what's more important is for you to have a regular, full time job. When are you going to get one?'

'I will look for one, once I finish my book.'

'Ok. But please be aware of the realities of life. Please realize that the cost of living is very high nowadays. You will feel the impact of the rising price of food items like atta and dal only when you once start living on your own in a different city. I'm telling you all this, because as a member of the family I'm concerned about your future.'

'Sure Uncle. Thanks for your concern and insight.'

He was proud of himself.

He had easily absorbed Gopi's questions, opinions and free advice without getting even a little irritated. Gopi was trying to impress upon him the importance of stability and regularity of income. But little did Gopi know…that he had already discussed all these points with his parents, before he had resigned from his job!

The next few minutes passed by in an awkward silence.

Gopi looked at the wall clock. He also looked at the wall clock and thought of making some small talk by asking Gopi about his business, clients, sales, orders etc.

But thankfully, just then the doorbell rang.

He opened the door.

It was his father.

He was relieved as he could now go back to his room while his father could take over and talk to Gopi.

A couple of hours later, the irresistible aroma of his mother's cooking drew him from his room to the dining table for dinner.

He pulled up a chair at the table. His parents and Gopi had already started eating. He noticed that Gopi who earlier had given him deadly gyaan on the rising prices of food items like atta and dal, was merrily devouring with full gusto the various tasty food items which his mother had prepared! They included his all time favourites-onion sambar, pulav and vegetable kurma.

'I'm of the view that while today's generation is very clear about its goals, it is all about themselves and their interests,' Gopi remarked suddenly.

Raghu noticed his parents glancing in his direction!

He looked back in their direction and then loaded his plate with a generous helping of vegetable kurma and pulav.

'By the way, I spoke to Raghu earlier about the importance of having a full time job. I'm sure he will do something about it,' Gopi continued.

'Oh. You did?' his father asked interestedly.

'Yes, I did. Hope he takes my advice seriously. There's another point which I want to talk about.'

'What?'

'One of my business associates in the US sent me an article recently, which highlights a rising trend among adults who prefer to stay in their parents' home with no intention of ever moving out. The main reason for the trend is not recession or job loss. It's because these "adult kids" find life much more comfortable in their parental homes.'

'Gopi, I fully agree with you on this point. One should move out of the house by the time he or she is 21. Staying with parents and enjoying home comforts only curbs their independence and ability to exercise independent decisions in the long run,' Raghu's father commented while glancing at him again.

He wanted to stand up, clap and give his father '*the dhamakedar dialogue of the year award*'. He also wanted to tell his father and Gopi that this was India and not the US! Here it was all about loving your family and parents. They had never seen Bollywood movies or what?

'You are very right. But will Raghu ever move out of this house?' Gopi asked his father.

His father was silent.

'As a parent you've given him good education and good nutrition but maybe you've failed to give him adequate career direction.'

He wanted Gopi to keep quiet!

This was just too much! The fucker was crossing all acceptable limits! Why was the fucker on a demolition mission to highlight the realities of his life to his parents? Why was the fucker hell bent on creating some unnecessary tension?

Before he knew it, his mother also added her two bits to the discussion.

'Gopi, maybe Raghu being directionless is in our karma…… rama rama…,' she started off.

He glared at his mother.

He started feeling irritated and lost interest in the tasty kurma on his plate because of this sudden stupid talk about fate, destiny and karma. Just before dinner had started, he had thought that he had answered Gopi's inquisitive questions. But clearly Gopi had outsmarted him by leaving the best for the last by giving extra bullshit gyaan and showing fake concern in front of his parents!

He noticed that his father was still silent and seemed to be in deep thought.

This irritated him even more.

He regarded his father as someone who took pride in forming an own independent view on a subject matter. But now even his father seemed to be under the influence of Gopi's views and opinions!

Half an hour later, Raghu was relieved as Gopi had finally left his home to catch a bus back to Erode.

As he walked to his room, he overheard his parents talking to each other.

They sounded worried.

'Why is Raghu like this?' he heard his mother ask his father.

'He's a useless fellow. Why are you acting so surprised?' he heard his father reply.

'Why don't you talk to him again? Where will writing a book take him? It will take him nowhere! He should have a job. That's more important.'

'I agree. Let's speak to him.'

'Raghu! Where are you? We need to talk to you,' his mother shouted.

'Why are you shouting? I'm right here!' he shouted back, standing just a few feet away. His mother was shouting out his name as if their modest home was a big villa!

'Raghu, what's your plan?' his father asked him bluntly. His mother stood behind his father like the second in command...like the vice captain of a cricket team.

'We have discussed all of this when I resigned. I gave you all my explanations. I will finish my book and then get back to a job.'

'No. This time I want a specific deadline. I want to know your exact time frame of execution. Tell me.'

'Ok. I've written about 70% of the first draft.'

'Ok. So how many more days, weeks, months or years will you need to finish it?'

'Creativity doesn't work that way. On somedays I write a lot, on some a little and on others nothing at all. So I would say I need at least one more month to come up with a complete draft.'

'And after that?'

'I will start sending my manuscript to various publishers.'

'And after that?'

'I will wait for their response.'

'So are you basically telling me that you are going to be spending the next three-four months doing this?'

'Umm…yes.'

'But I remember that when you resigned, you told me that your entire writing wouldn't take more than a few months. But now you are again telling me that you need another few months! So when are you going to look for a job?'

'Relax. I know what I'm doing. I'm really in control.'

'I don't think you are in control. You are drifting. You've wasted enough time. Just get your life on track.'

'I'm not drifting. I'm in control.'

'Raghu, don't talk like you are in control. If you were… you would already have plans in place to finish your book quickly and to then start reapplying for work.'

'Maybe it's my personality type which gives me the confidence that I'm in control.'

'What's this new rubbish you are talking about now?'

'I think maybe I'm an Omega male.'

'What do you mean?'

'I recently read an article which explained that an Omega male unlike a hypercompetitive Alpha male is someone who's laidback yet focused and happy in doing his own thing. The competitive rat race doesn't really worry him. He's an individual who has his own goals and works towards them.'

'Raghu, please keep all these Omega and Alpha male theories to yourself. Whether you are an Omega idiot or an Alpha idiot is to be seen in future. But right now, just get a job and get your life back on track.'

His father walked off in the direction of his bedroom.

'Raghu, why are you doing this to us? Life isn't meant to be easy. You have to take on responsibility. You can't escape the challenges of life by just sitting at home all day in front of your laptop. You've wasted enough time. Please get a job and get your life back on track,' his mother also added.

As she walked off, he noticed tears streaming down her cheek. Not copious amounts of filmy tears but a steady trickle which fell onto her cheek like a series of tossed up deliveries bowled by an off spinner which initially looped up in the air and then eventually landed on the pitch.

He suddenly felt very emotional.

Why couldn't his parents just understand and be supportive of his goals and aspirations?

Why couldn't he do his own thing without any interference?

Why did they always get brainwashed after getting gyaan from external sources like relatives for instance?

Was chasing a dream and being self absorbed in the process necessarily a bad thing? Was it a selfish thing to do?

How could he explain to someone…the sheer joy and happiness which a combination of solitude, cups of coffee, a laptop and ideas in his head could conjure up?

Why was he expected to clam up and react apologetically or defensively each time he was asked what he was doing with his life just because he didn't have a job or a monthly salary to show for his efforts?

Why couldn't they appreciate the hard work, time and effort that he was putting into his writing?

Was it because it wasn't in an office-like setting?

He knew for a fact that he was writing *The Paperback Badshah* because he was really excited about telling a story.

There was no ambiguity on that front. It wasn't some sudden spurt of teenage angst or 'wanting to be different and cool' which had spilt into adulthood.

He shuddered even to think about how it was for entrepreneurs who invested their time, effort and capital to try something different.

How did their families react? What would they be going through?

How did the entrepreneurs react to their relatives' taunts, negativity and pesky questions which tried to find 'logic' in every dream of theirs before it even took flight?

In his case, he knew that the curiosity, interest in what he was doing would last till his book was published. Till then he probably had to just stomach the pesky questions from all and sundry.

He switched on the TV to take his mind away from these heavy, energy sapping thoughts.

He flipped channels. Nothing interesting was being telecast.

The day couldn't get any worse.

He switched off the TV.

His mind suddenly wandered back to his past, to a time when he had one other significant dream to speak of, which he hadn't even bothered to pursue.

The dream which he had was of wanting to become a proud Indian cricketer.

After his tenth standard exams, he wanted to become a left arm spinner for India like Venkatapathy Raju. All of a sudden in the eleventh standard, from a spinner, he wanted to become a left arm fast bowler like Wasim Akram.

The first step to achieve this dream presented itself in the form of a 'state level' cricket trials selection process which was soon to be held in Bangalore. However before deciding to go for it, he wanted to have a discussion with his father. Since those days, his father thought that he was actually a directionless teenager who needed guidance, his father decided to listen to his explanations attentively.

Sitting face to face, he spelt out his cricketing dreams to his father.

He waited for his father's reaction.

His father finally shared his thoughts on the same.

'So Raghu, do you want to be a fast bowler who will get 0/142 in the 1st innings and 2/123 in the 2nd innings on flat, unresponsive Indian batting tracks? Yes or No?' his father asked him.

'No.'

'Why not?'

'I want to get 7/32 in the 1st innings and 5/46 in the 2nd innings and win matches for India. I want to demolish the opposition with my left arm in swingers, out swingers, bouncers and yorkers.'

'Raghu, do you think you are playing in England or Australia? It isn't about whether you know how to swing the ball, bowl a bouncer or bowl a yorker. It's about your own self belief that you can be a fast bowler on Indian pitches. Do you think you really have the stamina to sprint in daily…ball after ball in the hot sun?'

'Maybe not. I feel tired even if I run for two minutes nonstop.'

'Good. That answers your question. Forget this dream. You aren't a child prodigy like Sachin Tendulkar. You are Raghu Balakrishnan. Continue to watch cricket on TV. Play book cricket. Play cricket on the computer. Read books on cricket. Discuss cricket with your friends. And become a fast bowler only during your exams to knock down all the subjects with confidence!'

His father patted him reassuringly on his shoulder and walked away.

Looking back now, he realized that he had left that dream incomplete.

He had conveniently allowed it to fall by the wayside without even giving it a try.

The fact that he hadn't even felt bad about missing out, just showed his lack of passion for the dream to begin with!

Later that night.

Raghu was in deep sleep.

He was in the middle of a dream.

A test match was in progress.

The ball was turning square off the pitch.

It was his test match debut. He was the last man who had just arrived at the crease to bat. At the non-striker's end was superstar VVS Laxman who was still going strong.

'Raghu, concentration is the key. Focus on each delivery being bowled. Play each ball on its merit. Take it as a challenge,' he heard VVS encourage him, as their objective was to bat out time and save the match for India.

He nodded in understanding.

He felt inspired listening to these words.

He also drew inspiration from his own bowling performance for India during the match. In the 1st innings he had bowled as a left arm fast bowler and had taken 2/114. In the 2nd innings he had bowled as a left arm orthodox spinner and took 3/78. Overall it was a pretty decent effort as a bowler.

It was now time for him to show his grit as a batsman.

He took strike.

The silly point fielder standing in his eye line was making a lot of unnecessary comments to try and break his concentration. He noticed that the fielder was none other than his irritating relative Gopi! The wicketkeeper and the first slip fielder also started muttering something. He turned around. The wicketkeeper was his father and the first slip fielder was his mother!

Unbelievable!

He decided not to react.

Instead, he decided to focus on each delivery and play it on its merit.

He survived a few deliveries.

At the end of the over, there was a drinks break.

VVS started walking towards the boundary edge as a substitute had come running in, with a set of bats and a pair of new gloves.

He was now all alone in the middle. He had a look around.

He noticed a small dog waving at him from one of the stands.

Before he could wave back, the dog crossed the boundary line and ran towards him!

It then handed over its visiting card. He was really impressed seeing such a 'visiting card' handing over real dog!

He read the card. The dog was none other than Sweety's little doggie, Jimmy!

He was amazed as Jimmy began to talk to him!

'Hey Raghu, I'm sorry for running onto the field. But there is something important I wanted to tell you.'

'What?'

'Dude, when we read cool dialogues, quotes, motivational lines on how to chase dreams, live life to the fullest and all that jazz…we feel really positive, inspired and optimistic about everything. But when we actually do try to chase dreams…the ground realities aren't that easy. The optimism fades away and leads to pessimism and cynicism.'

'I know.'

'No disrespect to your parents, but what do they know about chasing a dream? They know nothing! But I do believe that they have the full right to taunt, advise, question and irritate you because deep down they love you and have your best interests in mind. But can the same be said about relatives who don't even give a fuck about you? Their constant prying, advising, questioning, probing all under the giant umbrella called "the great Indian reality check of life" can get too much to handle, right?'

He was super impressed listening to Jimmy, who was speaking with such clarity!

'I think you are right,' he told Jimmy.

'I know I'm right. But what about you, dude? A bit of needling from others and you feel upset? Buckle up man! Life is tough. You can't let external pressures bog you down. A little pressure is good but not a lot. I still think you are doing the right thing. You should chase your dream, execute it sincerely and then think about the various other aspects of life. Who knows whether ten to fifteen years later, you would even be able to write a line, let alone a full-fledged novel!'

As he reflected on what Jimmy had just said, he saw three cops with lathis in hand suddenly run towards Jimmy.

'Jimmy, watch out!' he screamed.

'Dude, do you think these unfit idiots can catch me? Watch me now…'

He stared in disbelief as Jimmy ran across the ground with the cops in hot pursuit. The crowd also joined in the fun as they were getting to watch some Olympic type running, hurdle crossing contests on the cricket field itself!

The unfit cops gave up the chase. They were out of breath.

Jimmy then ran out of the field and climbed to the top of one of the floodlight towers!

On top of the tower, Jimmy held a placard for him which read- *'Dude, these fools couldn't even catch me! Similarly don't let anyone stop or demotivate you from chasing your dream. Right now go save the test match with VVS sir while I enjoy myself a bit.'*

He thanked Jimmy for the message.

He then noticed that Jimmy was enjoying himself more than just a bit!

Jimmy had started dancing with a model who was slowly removing her clothes. Unlike some of her other high profile peers in the 'nude streaking and stripping down' business segment, who stripped only if India won important tournaments like the World Cup, this model however enjoyed stripping towards the end of every domestic cricket match irrespective of the final result!

He looked away.

The drinks break was over.

He had to refocus on the task at hand along with VVS and save the match for team India…..

Raghu woke up the following morning.

His head hurt.

That was some dream!

After having his breakfast he logged on to Facebook. He had not checked his account for a while.

Nandu had sent him a FB message which read:

Hi Raghu, I'm Rita. Would you like to sip a margarita with me? I'm married but I'm available. I'm lonely. I could do with some company. Can you please come? Actually…you know what? Please don't come. You will get scared and start running! Ha ha…

Days had passed since the Roma episode but Nandu was still at it!

He replied:

Stop this, you fucker. I'm not in a good mood. I already have enough on my plate.

He was surprised when a couple of minutes later, he got a reply from Nandu!

His message read:

Raghu…what happened to your sense of humour? Why so sensitive? Chill out! Last joke on this matter: What do you have on your plate? A dosa-burger? Ha ha…ha ha….

He decided not to respond to this follow up message and went back to his wall.

He noticed that Sweety had not just liked but also had recently commented on his last FB post which was over a month old: *Life unexpectedly throws up opportunities. Good things happen to people who wait. Victory comes to those who wait the longest.*

She had commented: *I knew it, Raghu. You are a good guy. You deserve the best that life has to offer.*

What the fuck? What did she even know about him to write something like this?

He casually checked her wall.

Her latest status update read: *Irritation, frustration, rejection and depression makes a person's life worthwhile and complete.*

He didn't want to read any more spiritual or depressing wall posts.

Instead, he just wanted to focus on his book.

He thought to himself.

Regardless of what anyone said, he was clear that he wasn't going to leave his book dream incomplete. As the creator, he was going to refocus, work around the creative block, knock down all the obstacles in his path and see *The Paperback Badshah* to completion.

DETERMINATION

A week later.
Raghu was in his room.

He was sitting in front of his laptop and had resumed work on his novel.

He finally had some new ideas to work with!

He was in a really determined frame of mind.

The immediate environment around him also egged him on with live examples of focus, determination and dedication. Above the window in front of him, he saw an ant make a slow trek along the length of the wall, which included a climb over the tube light as well, as a part of its obstacle course training for the day. Just outside his window, he saw a squirrel make a quick guest appearance after a long time. The squirrel was skillfully carrying some twigs to build a little nest of sorts.

A couple of hours later, he took a break from his writing.

He saw his room was in quite a mess.

As he put things back in order, he came across an old calendar stacked under a pile of papers in the corner of the room. It had a motivational quote printed for each day of the year.

He flipped through the calendar.

The quotes were inspiring. Similar variants of such quotes also kept popping up on Facebook in the form of updates posted by people. Some of the quotes were-

'Attitude is everything', 'Failure is not an option', 'You are a Champion…yesterday, today, tomorrow and even day after tomorrow', 'Winners don't give excuses. They don't blame circumstances. They control the circumstances.'

The last quote got him thinking.

Incidents from his past suddenly came to his mind.

He remembered how he had blamed everyone and everything around him (except himself and his lack of preparation) as reasons for not clearing most of the management exams which he had appeared for, before his MBA. During one management exam, he had come up with the excuse that the girl sitting next to him was constantly muttering which really disturbed his concentration. In another exam, he came up with an excuse that the guy sitting next to him was flipping through the exam booklet like it was a game of book cricket which really disturbed him and made him lose focus on his own exam booklet!

The bottom line was that being a self starter and taking initiative to control a situation (instead of blaming circumstances) was something which had been missing in his arsenal for tackling challenges in life. But now however, while writing the book he had rediscovered these positive traits. He was determined to chip away and see his dream to its logical completion without the need to make any further excuses or exhibit any unnecessary volatile reactions in case random people passed pesky comments.

Later that evening when he went to have his dinner, he saw his parents watching TV in the living room.

He loaded his plate with food and came to the living room. His healthy appetite suprisingly didn't seem to reduce even in this current 'cold war' climate!

They saw him.

But they kept quiet.

He pulled up a chair and sat a few metres away from them.

From the corner of his eye, he knew his mother was looking at him.

The uncomfortable, uneasy sound of silence best described the home environment at the moment. Given the amount of weight he had put on, over the past few months while writing the book, he was quite literally the sweaty little elephant in the room, whose presence his parents were aware of but didn't really want to acknowledge or address at the moment!

The same authoritative news anchor (who had earlier conducted a panel discussion about the Pak foreign minister's visit to India) was on TV.

This time on the anchor's show, it was special report on whether or not it was right for 'pushy' parents to aggressively monetize the talent of their precocious children. The focus of the report was primarily on 10 year old Shashikant Sharma aka Chota Jadagur (CJ) who was the latest singing sensation on the block. CJ had catapulted to national stardom after winning a recent singing reality TV show. He sang in both Hindi and English.

Both CJ and his father were present in the studio with the news anchor.

The anchor was busy grilling CJ's father on how he dealt with the celebrity status of his son and the perils of CJ growing up too soon. The anchor asked questions such as-

'Did CJ have a normal upbringing?', 'Were there sacrifices to make?', 'Has he lost out on his childhood because of this fame?', 'Is he going to study further?'

CJ's father began answering the various questions.

He told the anchor that as a parent he believed in living in the present without thinking too much about the future. He believed in letting CJ do his own thing and was not a 'fame crazy' or 'money hungry' pushy parent as was widely reported in the press.

The anchor did not seem too convinced by CJ's father's responses.

A few seconds later, an audio-visual clip of CJ was played out-

'I'm CJ,

I'm a dreamer,

I'm an achiever,

I've got a good sense of humour,

All in all....I'm a low cost Indian version of western singing star Justin Bieber,

I've faced disappointments and loneliness but I've worked very hard to not remain penniless,

If you want me to endorse your products,

All you have to do is to contact my manager, who by the way is none other than my super supportive, super awesome father!'

As the audio-visual clip finished, the camera zoomed in on CJ's father, who was beaming with pride.

'Unlike our son, CJ works very hard for a living and more importantly listens to the advice given by his father,' Raghu heard his father comment to his mother, all of a sudden.

He wanted to react but did not.

He just smiled to himself and continued eating.

He was suddenly reminded of an entertaining incident from his school days, when he could talk to his parents openly about things without it being linked to his academic future or his future in general. In that particular incident, he wasn't just thankful for his father's support but was also super impressed with the final solution which his father had come up with!

The incident had taken place during a history class.

An impromptu quiz was being held by the history teacher. It was his turn.

He was made to stand next to the blackboard, in front of the whole class.

He felt very nervous. History was a subject which always intimidated him as he had to mug up a lot of dates and the names of various places, which in combination invariably left him totally confused.

Standing right next to him, the teacher fired away like a machine gun. She asked him-

'When was the first battle of Panipat? When was the second battle of Panipat? When was the third battle of Panipat?'

He scratched his head. He had absolutely no idea!

He then thought, that the three battles must have happened in the same year like three back to back cricket matches of an ODI (one day international) series.

So he answered, '1947.'

He realized that his answer was wrong when he heard his classmates roar in laughter.

'Raghu! Don't play the fool or else I will send you back to nursery school! "1947" was the year of India's independence!' the teacher screeched.

To teach him a lesson, she slid her thumb and forefinger into his right shirt sleeve and pinched him on his bicep. As she pinched him, he noticed a sweat patch under the right armpit of her tight blouse. Clearly teaching history was as much a struggle as the real freedom struggle, which India had undergone to gain her independence!

'Be serious, now. Locate Patiala on the India map,' she commanded him, a few minutes later.

As she stood breathing down his neck (quite literally!), he took a pencil and pointed at a place on the map, which was hung in front of the blackboard.

'Madam, this is where I think Patiala is,' he told her confidently.

'Raghu! You idiot! You haven't been studying at all. You are pointing at a place near Karachi in Pakistan!'

The entire class burst out laughing.

The teacher gave him 0/10 in the quiz and sent him back to his seat.

To entertain his friends, he deliberately walked back slowly to his seat with his head hung in shame and his hands behind his back as if he was a traitor who had betrayed the nation! 'Raghu is a gaddar. A desh drohi. Let's spit on his face! He needs to be sent right back to a military camp and not a cricket camp across the border!' he heard one of his friends comment cheekily.

Later that day, he told his father how the history quiz had gone.

He then told his father that since he didn't have a brain like a supercomputer to process a lot of information, it caused him a lot of confusion. He explained that he always got confused with names of places like Porbandar, Panipat, Pathankot, Patiala and Peshawar as they were all places of some historical significance and found a mention in his history textbook.

'Well, let me be honest with you, Raghu. I totally agree with you. It's difficult to learn all of this. This is mental torture at its worst. Continue with your strategy of thinking of the various dates and places like they are all cricket events and just keep mugging. The Indian education system rewards you for mugging and not for understanding. So, don't worry. Today you got 0/10. Next time mug properly and try to get at least 5/10,' his father told him sympathetically.

He was relieved that his father had taken his side.

The pep talk had helped him.

Post the pep talk, the floodgates of entertainment opened.

He told his father how his teacher had pinched him.

His father had a good laugh first and then gave him a killer idea.

He told him that the next time the teacher tried to pinch…. he needed to raise him arm and move it swiftly in such a manner, that it would trap her long forefinger under his armpit *like a thermometer*! That would automatically teach her a lesson!

Raghu suddenly looked at the TV.

CJ was sharing a hearty laugh with his father about something, which made even the news anchor smile.

If his memory served him right, his father had repeated the 'thermometer history' incident on at least fifty occasions to close family and friends in the form of a well timed, three minute entertainment capsule!

COMPLETION

A month later.
It was sometime before noon.

Raghu was in his room.

He pumped his fist in the air.

The moment was worth celebrating.

He had taken a significant first step in the direction towards becoming a published author.

His first draft of *The Paperback Badshah* was complete!

73,500 odd words in the Word document was evidence of the hard work which he had put in (and brief struggles which he had encountered) over the past few months.

He emerged from his room to inform his parents about this development.

'I did it!' he shouted proudly to no one in particular.

'What did you do?' his father asked from the living room. His father had taken a day off from work.

'I finished writing my book.'

'Oh. Congrats. I thought you got a job interview or something.'

He was disappointed by the lukewarm reaction.

He thought that on hearing the announcement, his father would run towards him with a box of sweets and stuff his mouth with a Mysore pak or a ladoo to celebrate. But clearly there wasn't any of that infectious, over the top celebrations.

Instead there were questions.

'So Raghu, what's your book about? What's the title?' his father asked.

'My book, *The Paperback Badshah* is a love story. Do you want to read it and give me some feedback?'

'Sure. Why not?'

'Ok. So I'll go take a printout and give you a spiral bound copy to read.'

In the evening, Raghu was at a stationery shop near his home to get his book printed and then spiral bound. A while later, as he walked back home with the spiral bound copy in hand, he spotted a new fast food joint on the main road.

Images of calorie rich, trans-fat loaded burgers stared at him. These burgers looked really tasty unlike the 'dosa-burger' which Roma had prepared for him not too long ago!

His mouth salivated seeing these images.

He decided to treat himself. After all, one phase of his mission had been accomplished.

He ordered two vegetable burgers as a takeaway.

Fifteen minutes later, he had reached home.

'So this is *The Paperback Badshah*. Please read it and give me your feedback,' he told his father proudly as he handed over the spiral bound copy.

'Ok, I will. But what's in that packet?' his father asked, pointing at a thin plastic packet in his hand.

'Oh, it's just two burgers which I got for myself from this new fast food joint which has opened on the main road.'

He walked with the packet to the dining table.

He opened the paper wrapping gently and began eating the first of the two burgers.

It was junk delight at its best.

'Give me a bite,' he heard a voice ask suddenly from behind his back.

He turned.

It was his father!

Before he could respond, his father grabbed the burger and took a really big bite!

And before he knew it, his father had finished the entire burger and had started opening the wrapping of the second one!

'What are you doing?' he asked his father.

'Raghu, what's the big deal? You go for another walk and get yourself another burger. More exercise will do you good. Health is wealth, remember?'

'That's bullshit. Given your age, you shouldn't be eating this burger!'

'I heard something about a burger. Who's eating a burger?' his mother asked, as she walked in from the kitchen.

'I had got two burgers for myself. But he nicely grabbed the first one and ate it. Now he's started eating the second one as well,' he replied, pointing at his father.

His mother stared at his father.

She was waiting for an explanation as to why non-nutritious, non home cooked food was being eaten. There was no explanation from his father, as a large chunk of the second burger was in his mouth!

She exploded.

'People want nutritious food but you are eating this junk food? You still think you are young or what? In a few years…

both of us are going to be senior citizens. The food which I've been preparing in the kitchen is going to go waste!'

His father stood silently.

He was enjoying seeing his father being caught in this awkward spot!

Before he knew it, his mother suddenly turned the spotlight on him.

'Raghu! You are no less. Your body had started to age. Eat right. As it is, you are giving us enough tension by being unemployed and on top of that, you are also making yourself a ready candidate for a heart attack!'

'By the way, Raghu gave me his book to read,' his father said, changing the topic of discussion.

'I know. I heard him shout something about *The Paperback Zamindar* in the morning,' she replied.

'The title is *The Paperback Badshah* not *The Paperback Zamindar*,' Raghu said, correcting his mother.

'Raghu, who cares whether your book title is *The Paperback Zamindar*, *The Paperback Thanedar*, *The Paperback Havaldar*, *The Paperback Patrkaar*, *The Paperback Atyaachaar* or *The Paperback Samachar*? I don't think readers will read your book more than once. They will read it once and then forget about it. They however always remember a literary classic as it is of high quality, just like my nutritious, home cooked food!' his mother said rudely.

'I totally agree. The flavour of a burger remains only for the moment. The aroma and flavour of ghar ka khana lingers on for generations,' his father conveniently chipped in with some fake praise.

'By the way, Raghu, I just thought of another title for your book,' his father told him, a few minutes later.

'What?' he asked.

'Instead of *The Paperback Badshah* why don't you change the title to *The Paperback Berozgar* as you are anyway unemployed?'

'Yes, I agree. That really sounds like a better title,' his mother added sarcastically.

He was stumped. He never knew a small food fight could result in such hostility towards his book!

But overall he was happy.

The food fight had resulted in his first proper interaction with his parents since Gopi had left!

After sometime, as he walked back to his room, he thought about the title of his novel.

The reason for having a 'Hinglish' title like *The Paperback Badshah* (as opposed to a simple but more staid English title like say, *The Paperback King* or say *The Paperback Writer*) for a novel written in English was because his novel had a smattering of Hinglish in parts and especially in conversations among the various characters. Also he felt that a Hinglish title could create some sort of buzz among his intended target audience, who were essentially college youngsters and working professionals in their twenties, who themselves spoke in Hinglish in their daily lives.

An earlier title which he had in mind was *The Horny Desi Lovers.*

He however realized that having a title like that, would catapult him straight to the erotic or porn novel category and not to a mass market reader category which was his intended audience!

But the bottom line he had realized, was that getting a reader's attention was more than just having a 'catchy or fancy' title. The story had to get their attention!

*

Over the next few days, Raghu did a bit of research to get a sense of how to go about getting published.

His research helped him understand the two ways in which one could get published-

An author could either send the book manuscript directly to a publisher as per the submission guidelines mentioned on their website or an author could seek the assistance of a literary agent. Just as a job consultant tried to find the right job for a candidate similarly a literary agent as an intermediary tried to find the right publisher for an author's work.

He noted that irrespective of the route adopted, an author needed to begin by first sending across something known as a 'book proposal'. A book proposal basically had to contain a synopsis (a brief 2-3 page document which captured the entire story) and 3-4 sample chapters from the manuscript. If the book proposal interested the publisher or the literary agent, they would ask for the complete manuscript for further evaluation to take the matter forward.

He emailed a few literary agents that he had identified via his research process.

He got a response from only one.

In the email to him, the agent mentioned that they (the agency) would like to evaluate his entire manuscript to gauge the quality of his writing and to suggest changes. But for doing so, they would charge an evaluation fee of fifty paise per word! The evaluation fee also in no way guaranteed that they would be able to find a publisher for his work! However if after the evaluation, they did feel that the work was worth pitching to publishers, the representation fee charged by them (to secure a book deal) would be separate and would reflect as a percentage share in the author's royalty payment.

It was now decision time for him.

On one hand, a literary agent could guide him through the complexities of the publishing world and try locking in a good book deal for him as their fee would be linked to his royalty payment. But on the other hand, they could also decide not to pitch his work to publishers, but still extract money out of him by charging him for their preliminary manuscript evaluation services!

He finally took a decision.

He decided not to go via any agent. Instead he decided that he would directly submit a book proposal to various publishers as per their submission guidelines and wait for their response.

He also decided to take a break from all the 'process of getting published' research.

He walked out of his room and went to the living room to watch some TV.

A few minutes later, his father walked up to him.

'Raghu, I started reading your manuscript a few days ago. You've written so much. I don't think I'll have the energy to read the entire thing,' his father told him.

'Ok,' he replied, sounding a bit dejected.

'But I can tell you one thing.'

'What?'

'It's an impressive effort. Remember like fine wine....your writing will only get better with time.'

'Really?'

He couldn't believe that his father was praising him! Some respect and importance from his family....finally!

And for a change, the conversation wasn't even linked to his employment!

'Let's hope that *The Paperback Badshah* gets longlisted for a prestigious literary award like the Booker,' he told his father, fishing for some more praise.

'Raghu, don't get so ahead of yourself. Go, get a job first.'

And once again the conversation was linked back to his employment!

Just then, he heard his mother scream from the kitchen.

He and his father ran to the kitchen.

'The pressure cooker! There's a problem. It's not working,' his mother explained.

'Again?' his father asked.

'Yes…again.'

Raghu smiled to himself as he suddenly remembered the earlier occasion when the cooker had stopped working. It had stopped working just as he was about to tell his father that he wanted to quit his job to write a book.

'Raghu!' he heard his mother command him suddenly.

'What?' he asked.

'Tomorrow I want you to go buy a new pressure cooker.'

He made an irritated face.

Again…domestic work was dumped on his creative shoulders. He had to make another visit to that crowded discount shopping store.

His father looked at him and grinned.

'What?' he asked his father.

'Raghu, I'm sure of one thing. You may or may not ever bring home the Booker, but tomorrow you will certainly be bringing home a new pressure cooker!'

He smiled as he heard this mild PJ.

A thought came to his mind.

While the cooker had clearly outlived its time and practical purpose in their household, his book however was gaining importance and was soon going to enter the business end of things!

SUBMISSION

Four days later.
Raghu was exhausted.

He had just finished writing yet another version of the synopsis of *The Paperback Badshah*. He realized that writing a book was one thing but writing a succinct, well worded synopsis to grab the attention of a publisher was another matter altogether!

It was certainly very challenging.

He decided to re-read the latest lengthy version of the synopsis which he had prepared which covered all the major plot points of his story. It read as follows-

THE PAPERBACK BADSHAH

Part 1- College Love

The Paperback Badshah is a story of two lovers, Alok and Alka, final year students of a college set in some part of India in the late 1990s. Only a few days are left for their college life to get over. They go on a college trip to Shimla. On the final night of the trip, they jump onto a pile of hay in a barn for a quick hill station romp. While having an intimate conversation the following morning, she asks him what he wants to do with his life. He tells her that he has no idea, but would like to write a book someday. She tells him that her father, a widower is pressurizing her to settle down and plans on getting her married in the next few months. He wants to console her. He pats her head lovingly as flakes of dandruff fall merrily on his hand! He promises her that he will one day become a real responsible, successful man and ask her father for his beautiful daughter's hand. She hugs him and applauds the spark of cheesy creativity in him but wonders whether it will be too late by the time he acted.

A few weeks after the trip, she gives him a call.

She tells him that she's pregnant. He is supportive of the situation and is excited about being a father to a baby even though he has no job or money.

Part 2- Confrontation

Alka breaks the news to her father, a senior vice president in a big MNC. He first gives her a quick lecture on morals, scruples, society, tradition and family reputation. He then tells her to go for an abortion. She tells him that the only thing which deserves an abortion is his old world ideas. She tells him that she has decided to keep the baby and is planning on getting married to Alok. He is stunned. He tries a different approach to make her understand. He tells her how

Alok is worthless and useless. She tells him that her heart however still beats only for Alok. Hearing this, he storms out of the house and heads to work.

The family caretaker of many years, working in the house, who sees this father-daughter confrontation, gets emotional and tries to offer his two bits of advice to Alka. She has however made up her mind. She wants to be with Alok and start a new life together with him. She gives Alok a call and informs him about the developments at her home. She tells him that she will move out of her home and come stay at his home. Before leaving finally, she goes to her bedroom and packs five gigantic suitcases with all her clothes, makeup kits, shoes, belts, boots, high heels among many other items.

A couple of hours later, she reaches Alok's home.

She sees him sitting on the doorstep. He looks dejected. He tells her that his father has thrown him out of the house. They arrive at a decision. They decide to elope and begin a new life in the jungle which is just outside their city. They also decide not to take any help from their friends or relatives.

When Alka's father comes home from work, the caretaker informs him about the sudden turn of events. Alka's father rushes to Alok's home, expecting to find his daughter. Instead he meets Alok's father. Alok's father tells him that he told Alok to get lost with Alka. Alka's father is surprised hearing this. Both the fathers then exchange wry smiles. They are confident that their directionless kids will come back soon. After all, for how many days, weeks or months can a couple survive only on love without money?

As the days roll by, Alka's father gets tense. He fears the worst. Using his connections in the police force, he organizes a nationwide hunt for the missing couple. He also decides that once he gets hold of his daughter, he will marry her off to a man of his choice.

Part 3- The Jungle Experience

Life in the jungle meanwhile, is rather enjoyable for Alok and Alka.

They go on with life without a care in the world. They sing, they dance and occasionally also make wild jungle love. During the day, Alok cuts logs of wood with the tribal men while Alka weaves baskets with some of the tribal women. In the evenings, they all sit together and eat tasteless 'dosa-burgers' for dinner. A couple of months later, Alok and Alka get married as per the jungle customs. A few months after that, a heavily pregnant Alka gives birth to a little baby boy. She names him Chintu which means the 'little tiny one'.

As time passes, the police still haven't been able to locate them. Meanwhile in the jungle, Chintu starts making a lot of friends. A little white tiger spots him and decides to become his guardian angel for life. Though physically Chintu is still a toddler, he has the maturity of a small boy in third standard! Chintu treats the white tiger like a small horse and roams around in the jungle while singing songs like '*Chal mere ghode... tik...tik...tik*' to entertain himself.

As Chintu now has a routine of his own, Alka gets more time for herself.

She becomes extremely fitness conscious and sheds her post pregnancy flab. Alok is amazed by his wife's amazing transformation but really misses her curves. He now feels that he is married to a lean-mean, well toned army officer. As a part of her gruelling daily fitness routine, Alka does hundred stomach crunches on the spot, two hundred push ups-some of them one handed and occasionally also lifts Alok and gently tosses him in the air, like a chef tossing vegetables in the air to make a salad!

Part 4- The Urban Experience

Love without financial stability can lead to marital tension.

This thought strikes Alok one fine day. He decides it is high time for him to start looking for work. It is time to take on some responsibility. Till now, he and his family had been guests of the generous hospitality of the tribals. He walks out of the jungle. As he nears the city limits, he notices a massive construction site. He walks to the site. The construction is taking place for an international sporting event called the 'Athletic Games 2020.' A supervisor working at the site asks him whether he would be interested in the job of a brick layer. He can't believe his luck and jumps at the opportunity. He is happy as there is enough work to keep him employed for at least the next 5-10 years of his life!

Time passes by.

Months later, after having settled nicely into his job, Alok starts penning a love story during his free time in a notebook based on incidents from his own runaway love story. He finishes writing the entire story in record time, in just over five weeks! He titles his story '*A love saga in which I dance to the musical beats of my own raga.*'

One day at work, his supervisor happens to notice the notebook. He picks it up and begins to read parts of the love story. He is super impressed. He especially enjoys the sex scenes written as a part of the heartfelt story. He tells Alok to get the story published. Alok is surprised on hearing that his story actually has the potential to get published. He tells his supervisor that he doesn't have contacts in the publishing world. The supervisor decides to help him out. He takes photocopies of Alok's story and sends it across to various city based publishers.

In the days that follow, Alok continues to work really diligently at the construction site. One day, a senior official in the company notices the passion and dedication with which he is laying bricks. He is impressed. He promotes Alok from being just a 'brick layer' to a well respected 'assistant manager'. Alok can't believe it. Overnight his luck has turned! From being a micro man in a sweaty vest, he is now fast turning into a complete man in a business suit!

Further exciting changes take place in Alok's life.

His story is accepted for publication! It also begins to gather a fair bit of pre-publication buzz and is touted as being one of the most promising romantic stories to be ever published in India! Various sections of the media add to the frenzy by calling him the next big thing...*a paperback badshah*...a 'king' in the making, who is going to take Indian writing by storm. They predict that the story will be a runaway hit with the reader and that the paperback book sales will be unprecedented. Their reasoning is that a story of a lover's trials and tribulations, filled with complex human emotions and loaded with steamy moments of sexual passion, is indeed the perfect recipe for success with an emotional, teary eyed Indian reading audience!

As other publishers begin to express their interest to publish his future works, Alok's existing publisher gives him an unprecedented fifty book deal along with a cheque as an advance payment, which has so many zeroes in it...that his eyeballs for a few seconds pop out of their sockets when he first looks at it!

Witnessing this unbelievable turn of events, Chintu is tongue tied and wonders how on earth is it even possible for such a lame story written by his father be touted by the media as a bestseller even before its release? Unlike Chintu, Alka is however super excited witnessing this remarkable turn of events. She tells

Alok that it is the right time to go and meet her father and his parents to patch up and clear all ill feelings. He immediately agrees. After all, he now has a steady job at the site and well...*money isn't really a problem anymore*!

Along with Alka and Chintu, he bids goodbye to all the tribals in the jungle and thanks them for all their love, friendship and assistance. The white tiger promises to visit Chintu in the city sometime in the future, as long as he doesn't fall prey to a poacher and then get featured as a vital statistic in some 'save the white tiger' campaign! Thinking about this scary possibility, Chintu decides to take his friend along. He spray paints him in black, to conceal his identity. From a white tiger...his friend now resembles a black coloured dog like animal.

Part 5- Reunion

Alok and Alka finally re-enter the city, which they once called their own. The inept police force which has been looking for them for what seems like forever... finally spots them. Alok tells them that he is no longer in hiding and as a matter of fact, is actually en route to meet Alka's father. Hearing this, the police lets all of them go.

Seeing his daughter, a small boy, his daughter's five big suitcases, a small ferocious looking black dog and Alok for the first time in this particular descending order of preference after so many years, makes Alka's rich father very happy and also very curious. He realizes that for happiness, money is not everything. *The sudden source of money is everything*! He makes this observation after noticing Alok in a stylish, finely cut business suit. He is amazed by this sudden transformation! He wonders how the worthless loafer is now wearing such an expensive designer business suit. He decides to embrace Alok, not out of love or affection but to feel the texture of his suiting fabric! Thinking that it's a warm embrace of instant reconciliation, Alok returns the favour.

The caretaker who witnesses this emotional scene of reconciliation tells Alka's father that as per an article he recently read in a newspaper, Alok is a manager at the 'Athletic Games 2020' construction site and is also a famous paperback author in the making. He then quotes the advance cheque amount which Alok is rumoured to have received for his fifty book deal. Alka's father is stunned on hearing this sudden rags-to-riches story. He is surprised that he isn't aware of any of this and the fact that the caretaker knows all of this, but has not once bothered mentioning any of this to him until now!

A few minutes later, Alka's father tells Alok that he was wrong about him all along and that Alok is indeed the right man for his daughter. He then tells Alok that he will call his parents up right away to finalize plans for a week-long combined family celebration. Alok nods his head happily on hearing this. Alka's father then walks towards his grandson Chintu and hugs him. His stone heart melts just like the melting bowl of custard which is on the dining table. Seeing this genuine display of affection, Alka gets emotional and goes and hugs her father.

Half an hour later, as they are all seated at the dining table, Alka's father asks her details about her time spent in the jungle and her marriage in particular. She tells her father that she hasn't yet had a legal marriage but she did have a jungle marriage. Hearing this, her father loses his cool. 'So are you telling me that Chintu is a bastard?' he thunders. She nods sheepishly. Just at that very moment, Chintu asks for an extra helping of custard. His grandfather refuses and tells him rudely, 'No custard for a bastard!' Chintu starts crying as his grandfather has used a bad word. Seeing his master cry, the black dog (tiger) which was rather silent until now, roars loudly to protect Chintu. Hearing this sudden roar from the small dog like animal especially after all the earlier display of family love, makes the caretaker lose consciousness. He faints and falls to the ground. Alok rushes to him. He checks his pulse. Thankfully the caretaker is still alive.

The caretaker gets up slowly a few minutes later and mutters gibberish like-'Where am I?', 'Who am I?', 'What happened?', 'Is there any chance that the ugly small black dog bites?' He immediately gets an answer to his last question. The white tiger bites his arm off to show him the difference between a baby dog bite and a ferocious tiger bite! The caretaker's arm pops out of his shoulder socket! Chintu tells his tiger friend to behave and then walks to the caretaker and pushes his severed arm, right back into the shoulder socket! The caretaker then starts rotating his arm like a fast bowler during a warm up session to confirm that thankfully everything is back in order!

Witnessing all this unwanted, unexpected, unbelievable nonsense, Alka's father decides to put an end to it by formally accepting both Chintu and the white tiger also as part of the family. A few minutes later, they all hug and pose for 'picture perfect', 'happy family' portraits with the caretaker playing the role of the photographer. Looking at the white tiger in fear from the corner of his eye, the caretaker promises to give it special attention and a daily dose of tandoori chicken, chilli chicken and butter chicken! Everyone is happy. Love is back in the air. *After all...it is all about loving the family and the ferocious pet of the family!*

The story ends.

Raghu smiled to himself as he finished reading the detailed synopsis which he had prepared. He however needed to reduce the length of the synopsis substantially further to a single page or at the most to two-three pages before sending it to publishers.

As a writer, he noticed that in *The Paperback Badshah* he had drawn on inspiration from certain real life incidents. For instance- The dandruff which falls on Alok's hand *(in part 1 of the book)* was inspired from the dandruff incident from his dinner date with Roma. Alok being clueless about his career plans and life in general but having a dream of wanting to write a book someday *(again in part 1 of the book)* was inspired from his own life. Alok and Alka having dosa-burgers for dinner in the jungle *(in part 3 of the book)* was inspired from the dosa-burger incident from his second date with Roma. Chintu playing with the white tiger in the jungle *(in part 3 of the book)* and treating it like a horse was inspired from his observation of the woman at the discount store who had purchased a toy gaadi for her son. Alok's supervisor at the construction site who encourages him to get his story published *(in part 4 of the book)* was loosely inspired by his 'resignation related' conversations with Shekhar at SFPAL. The white tiger becoming a dog *(in part 4 and 5 of the book)* and featuring as an important character right at the end of the story was his way of giving importance to dogs and in particular to Jimmy, who had once come in his dream.

All in all, he felt that as a love story, *The Paperback Badshah* offered an interesting plot which was 'different' from the usual run of the mill love stories. Hopefully the publishers too would feel the same!

✳

A few days later.

Raghu finally decided on his strategy to get published.

He decided to send his book proposal to multiple publishers at the same time.

He shortlisted eight publishers to whom he was going to send his work.

He emailed them stating that he had written a novel and wanted to submit it for evaluation.

He got a response from all of them.

Some of them stated that they wanted only an email

submission of the proposal while the rest wanted a more strict 'double spaced and only one side of the page to be printed' hard copy submission of the proposal by registered courier.

✳

A week later.

Raghu had managed to trim down the detailed synopsis version to a more compact two page version. He had also prepared a single page version which was a requirement for some of the publishers. He also spent time re-reading his three sample chapters and rectified all the basic errors (typos, spelling errors etc.) to the best of his ability.

With the synopsis and the sample chapters now in place, he submitted his book proposal to all eight publishers.

The response time for the proposal as per their various evaluation guidelines was a minimum of four to six weeks.

All he had to do now was to wait for a response from them.

REJECTION

Three weeks later.

Raghu was in his room.

He had just finished checking his email.

He felt very dejected.

He had received his fifth straight rejection email from a publisher.

What compounded his misery was the fact that the publishers had not given any specific reason for rejecting his book proposal. Each of the five rejection emails more or less contained the same following cryptic response-'*We regret to inform you that we will not be able to publish your work as it does not fit our publishing profile. We wish you the very best and hope that your work finds a home with another publisher.*'

He really wanted to know why his proposal had been rejected.

Was the fault in the synopsis which he had sent across?

Or was it in the three sample chapters?

Or was the rejection because of the quality of his writing which was simply not good enough to get their attention?

Sadly, he would never get to know the actual reason(s) for the rejection.

With so many negative thoughts clouding his mind, he decided to take a break.

He got up from his desk and walked around his room. He spotted the calendar which had the motivational quotes printed on it, peeking out from under a pile of papers. He flipped through to a date which had a quote, which read-'*Try, try, try till you succeed. You will succeed one day.*'

What an awesome quote but it didn't offer any solace at the moment! Even if the remaining three publishers rejected him, he had to keep on trying and send his book proposal to a whole bunch of other new publishers in the market. It was not like he had any other choice!

He then came across another quote, which read-'*It is the journey and not the destination that matters.*'

Another awesome quote! He had already visualized the destination-

The destination would be a beach in Goa. It would be a beach party to celebrate the success of The Paperback Badshah. He would be parasailing in the morning breeze. He would then make a swift descent onto a specially constructed stage on the beach. The people gathered at the party would begin to clap excitedly and give him an awesome rock star like reception......

He stopped thinking.

For that dream scenario to happen, he first needed to get a positive response from at least one publisher, which at the moment clearly wasn't happening.

He again sat down at his writing desk.

He stared sadly at the tube light and wondered to himself.

Why was this happening to him?

Was it some sort of cruel joke being played at his expense?

How could a publisher just reject his work?

How could they be so insensitive?

Didn't they care about the amount of hard work he had put into his writing?

The fact of the matter was that…they didn't.

When he had received the first couple of rejections, he had felt that it was "the publisher's loss…not his". But now with five rejections (and maybe more to come), clearly it was only his loss, not theirs. *They didn't even care!*

Suddenly, he felt very lonely.

He didn't know with whom to share his dejection and rejection travails.

He had told his parents about the first couple of rejections. They had casually dismissed his rejection 'sadness' and told him to just move on with life. *They did not realize the gravity of the situation.* Now if he told them that he had received five rejections, maybe his father would even say something like-'5 rejections? *Ek do teen char paanch…*' and start dancing like Madhuri Dixit in the hit song from the movie *Tezaab*. His friends too, being incredibly busy with their own lives would perhaps not understand the extent of his rejection sadness. At best they could offer comforting words of sympathy. Something like-'Raghu, don't worry. Be positive. Be patient. Things will turn around.'

He suddenly remembered how Roma during the dinner date had told him, that his presence would ensure that she would never ever feel lonely in a crowd. Back then, he had trivialized her serious thoughts in the form of humour by wondering how his presence could make her feel less lonely.

Well the fact of the matter was that the joke was now actually on him.

He had to cope all alone.

There was no escaping this fact.

The real world rejection by the publishers of his 'creative baby' was a very bitter pill to swallow.

It was a horrible feeling.

Later in the day, he was on Facebook.

He was going through the various status updates posted by his school, college and other virtual friends. It seemed that except himself, everyone else had played their cards well and were enjoying their lives. Seeing their smiling faces in their profile pictures made him wonder where his life was headed. A few months back, he was all determined and resolute after his relative Gopi had given him gyaan on life. But now he was back to square one and had begun to wallow in self pity.

The self pity turned to mild envy as he read new status updates and saw photos of what people were doing with their lives. One girl from his schooldays had gone skydiving and jumped out of a plane in Spain while a guy his age from his college had proposed to his girlfriend on top of a crane in an unheard of love spot in Ukraine! Another guy from his college had purchased a holiday home and had flooded his timeline with around hundred photos! Another batchmate had backpacked across Europe and had posted about hundred and fifty photos!

And here he was....an unemployed idiot who was just sitting on his fucking ass after having quit a job to write a book, which clearly no one except himself gave a shit about! Maybe it just didn't make sense to be a dreamer anymore in such fast paced, super competitive, commercial times. Maybe all the reports that he had read in the newspapers, that the publishing industry was steadily growing in India was perhaps nothing more than just baseless media generated talk!

What if his parents were right all along?

Was he just a good for nothing unemployed lump? A slacker who would stay at their home all his life without contributing any money but adding to their worries and problems?

He felt like a social outcast.

And like a total loser.

Just as he was about to log out off Facebook, Sweety pinged him on FB chat.

Sweety: Hi Raghu, long time.

Raghu: Hi Sweety. Long time indeed. Tell me.

Sweety: How have you been?

Raghu: Ok. Why?

Sweety: No, I generally asked. What's up?

Raghu: Nothing much. All down actually.

Sweety: Why, what happened? Can I help?

Oh God…why did he have to say that things were down? Now she would jump in with her gyaan! Oh no!

Raghu: No, don't bother. Nothing important.

Sweety: Classic guy problem.

Raghu: What?

Sweety: It is the classic guy problem of not being able to open up and share your problem freely. Just let it out.

Raghu: No, seriously, I don't have any problem.

Sweety: You are facing some sort of problem. Just drop the façade of being able to tackle everything alone and let me offer you some insight. I've helped many students cope with peer pressure issues, low self esteem issues, broken relationship issues in my capacity as a student counsellor.

Raghu: But I don't have any of these problems. Mine is different.

Sweety: Ah….now you are talking. Tell me more.

Raghu: No.

Sweety: Are you not being able to open up and express yourself right now because it is over an impersonal chat?

Raghu: I don't know.

Sweety: Do you instead want to meet face to face?

Raghu: Where?

Sweety: Where do you live?

Raghu: Jayanagar. You?

Sweety: I live in Vivek Nagar. My office is in Koramanagala. We can catch up for a drink someplace there, tomorrow?

Raghu: Ok.

Sweety: Thanks Raghu. I can feel your pain. I'm telling you that I will definitely be able to help. We all need help at some point or the other in our lives. Life is short and it is very important to enjoy the precious gift called life.

What was wrong with her? He was not dying or some shit! He was just sad that his book had been rejected!

Raghu: Ok. Let's see. By the way what are your charges?

Sweety: Charges for what?

Raghu: Your counselling? What else?

Sweety: I'll do it free of cost for you…as you are not my student. ☺

Raghu: Oh cool. I'll give you a call tomorrow to confirm. I'm logging out now. Bye.

Sweety: Bye.

He logged out.

He thought to himself.

Why did Sweety...*the same Sweety who hated men and called all men dogs* suddenly want to help him? What was in it for her?

He had no idea.

Maybe she thought of herself as some sort of spiritual counsellor or 'full of life' motivational specialist like Kareena Kapoor in *Jab We Met* or Katrina Kaif in *Zindagi Na Milegi Dobara* who would help the guy forget all his sorrows, tensions and problems in two to three hours flat, and then enable him to start living life to the fullest by appreciating every nanosecond of life!

Later that night.

Raghu was in deep sleep.

His mind had transported him to another world.

A world which was far away from the madness called urban life.

He was lying all alone in a small hut in some part of rural India. He was single and unemployed. He had no money except for two thousand five hundred rupees which his parents had sent him for his various expenses, which he had stored carefully in a small pencil box in the corner of his hut. He had only four shirts, a kettle, an onion, three rotis, two-three pieces of cow dung, a small bleating goat and an unpublished spiral bound copy of *The Paperback Badshah* to give him company.

He spent most of his time drowning his 'being rejected by publishers' sorrow in low quality liquor which had chipped away to corrode his liver. On the rare occasions when he was not boozing, he was busy typing his login details into an imaginary computer in the air in a desperate attempt to log on to Facebook to check the latest updates of his virtual friends and to see whether they even cared about his stupid existence! But clearly no one cared!

Then all of a sudden, a baby faced leader of a political party entered his hut followed by his entourage of party workers and photographers. The leader sat next to him and told him that it was part of his vote bank building exercise. He promised his full political support to the leader and asked for ten bottles of scotch in return. The baby faced leader smiled and agreed. The leader then held the solitary onion lying in the hut as a sign of solidarity with the aam aadmi's concern over rising food prices. The photographers began clicking photos.

Seeing them clicking away, he suddenly got an idea!

He placed his right arm around the leader like they were really good friends! In his left hand he held the spiral bound copy of *The Paperback Badshah* and proudly posed with it for the photographers! He figured that this way, his book title along with the onion held by the leader would prominently feature in some of the photos which would get published in newspapers, which in turn would then somehow get the attention of a publisher!

Just then, one of the party workers walked up to him and asked him whether he had ever voted before. He replied sheepishly that he had never voted. The reason for this, he explained was that because the only time he had tried to vote during an election, instead of landing up at an electronic voting booth he had landed up at an STD telephone booth located near a toll booth!

Hearing this bullshit explanation and for having wasted everyone's time, the party worker pushed him violently to the floor. To teach him a lesson, the baby faced leader then took his onion, his pencil box containing money and his small bleating goat! The leader then sat on his goat and wore a garland made out of his 'pencil box' notes! The leader along with the rest of the party workers and the photographers then stormed out of his hut.

Writhing in pain on the floor, he shouted for help.

No one was there. He wanted to walk to the nearby police station to file a complaint. He however had no energy left. What pissed him off further was that while his goat, money and onion were taken forcefully, no one had bothered to even touch his book! Clearly no one gave a damn about his creativity!

He shouted out for help again....

Raghu woke up the following morning.

That was some crazy nightmare.

He sat on the edge of his hard bed and wondered to himself.

Why on earth had the leader taken his goat? Was it because he didn't know how to vote?

He had no answers to these questions just like he had no concrete answers as to why the publishers had rejected his book proposal.

In the afternoon, he was contemplating whether to go meet Sweety or not. He finally decided to give it a shot. He had nothing to lose. Maybe she could actually come up with a quick fix solution.

He gave her a call and they decided to meet up at a pub in Koramanagala.

He reached the pub at around 8.15 in the evening and was waiting for her to arrive.

A few minutes later, he saw a huge military tank walk towards him. It was Sweety.

'Hi Raghu. It's been a while,' she said.

'It has been,' he replied. They exchanged a handshake.

'I hope you didn't have to wait for long. I just finished my aerobics workout.'

He smiled to himself, thinking about Sweety bringing down the aerobics floor with her moves!

'So Raghu, let's begin,' Sweety said, diving straight into the purpose of the meeting.

'Let's begin what?'

'Tell me about your problem. Don't be conscious. Open up and let it all out.'

'Ok, I will. But before that I really want to know something.'

'What?'

'How come you are so keen to help me? I thought you hated guys? You had bitched about your ex-boyfriend in front of everyone in the workshop.'

'I know. Thinking about it now, I regret that outburst about Vikrant. Anyways all that is in the past. I attended a three day spirituality workshop which has deactivated me from my past and reactivated me positively for my present and future.'

'Hmm.'

He was not too convinced. The waiter interrupted their conversation and took an order for a pitcher of beer along with a few starters.

'Raghu, I think you have real trust issues. You don't seem to take things at face value, do you?' Sweety asked once the waiter left.

'I've no idea. Please don't ask me such complicated, confusing, mind twisting questions. As it is, I have enough problems to deal with.'

'Such as?'

'My book has been rejected by five publishers.'

'Ah. The cat is finally out of the bag. So this has been the cause of your worry.'

'Yes, it has been.'

'Why don't you tell me everything about this book journey of yours…right from the beginning?'

'Hmm.'

'I know you are hurting from within but you feel that by talking about it, will make it worse. Trust me…it won't. There is nothing unmanly about opening up and sharing your problems. In fact, I think it is cool. Let it all out. Take your time.'

Just then the waiter returned with their order, placed it on the table and walked away.

Raghu stared at the mug of beer in front of him.

In real life (unlike in the dream which he had had), he had never ever been a heavy drinker.

In fact, he hardly ever drank. In college and during his MBA, his friends used to make fun of him as he never had the capacity to drink even two mugs of beer! Many times, his friends would catch him gulping down two to three glasses of water for a few sips of beer to avoid getting drunk or talli! He would explain to them that it was his way of neutralizing the alcohol content in the beer! Observing this, his friends would burst out laughing and say things like-'Raghu can have only rasam and rava idli. The moment he has one mug of beer, he becomes totally talli….'

Looking at the mug again, he picked it up and gulped down almost half of its contents in one go!

Vitalized by the beer in his system, he started off like a moderately depressed book devdas and told Sweety about his journey right from the time he quit his job for writing *The Paperback Badshah* to getting the five rejections. '…I'm still not able to understand how come a good story like mine has been rejected. At least the publishers should have given me a proper reason for the rejection. Till recently, I used to visualize my book being in the front display of bookstores, but I guess I now need to forget this book dream,' he concluded.

He looked in Sweety's direction. While the beer had made him talk, she appeared deep in thought! He eagerly waited for her analysis and her solutions.

'Ok Raghu. I've understood your problem,' she said finally.

'And what do you suggest I do?' he asked curiously.

'I would suggest that you remain patient and keep faith in God. He has a plan for you. He is watching you from above and is analyzing your actions. I'm sure that before you even know it…things will turn around in your favour.'

'That's it? This is your advice?'

'Yes. What else did you want to hear?'

He scratched his head in frustration.

He had blabbered so much for this advice? Even the calendar with the motivational quotes in his room gave better advice! If he had spoken to Suresh or Nandu, even they would have given him this 'Stay positive. Things eventually will turn around gyaan!'

'Sweety, I was expecting some clear cut methods to cope with the book rejection. What you gave me is just general gyaan,' he told her.

'No it isn't. Think of the situation you are in, this way-'

'Which way?'

'-You are a lonely man who is chasing a dream away from the herd. These rejections are just temporary road blocks before you confidently walk straight into a glorious creative sunset.'

'Or maybe I will fall straight into a bottomless pit of depression,' he cut in listening to her additional 'sunset' gyaan.

'Stop being so negative and cynical! Let me tell you something.'

'What?'

'After the workshop, I wanted to write short stories using my experiences as a student counsellor. But I gave up after a couple of months because I couldn't motivate myself to write. It was then that I realized that it is so difficult to plug away systematically till completion. So, seeing someone like you reaching your goal...at least half way is really noteworthy and a victory in itself.'

'I guess so. Thanks.'

'Always remember that good things take time to happen. Remember you had put up a Facebook post about victory coming to those who wait the longest? Think of this phase as the struggle phase before you eventually emerge victorious!'

He nodded. *But that post of his was in the context of hoping to get lucky with Roma and nothing else!*

'I guess you are right, Sweety. I'll have to be patient and just struggle for the next hundred odd years,' he remarked sadly. 'After all, Roma was not built in a day.'

'Raghu, did you just say Roma *instead of* Rome?'

'Did I?'

'Yes, you did!'

'Oh. Maybe her name came out by mistake! Any idea what she's been up to?'

'I've no idea. I'm not in touch with that arrogant bitch.

Remember how she had disagreed with my views on life during the workshop?'

'I remember.'

'You were no less. You also supported her opinion.'

'I know. I got carried away.'

'Ok whatever. Have you been in touch with her?'

'Not really. I haven't met her after the workshop,' he lied.

'Oh ok. Getting back to your book rejection, I just wanted to tell you one thing.'

'What?'

'Matters or decisions taken by "following one's heart" are indeed tricky and complicated. It's something which cannot be explained and invariably causes the person concerned a lot of tension, uncertainty and pain.'

'You are right.'

He was impressed with this bit of gyaan given by Sweety. He could relate to it at some level. Incidents from his recent past came to his mind-

At SFPAL, he had followed his heart and not his brain and had laughed merrily at Shekhar's 'mental-dental' joke which had created a bad impression...

On the writing front, when he told his parents that he wanted to write a book, they called him an idiot...

Roma too had followed her heart and married her buddah husband which led to complications. She again followed her heart and fell in love with Akash...which led to further complications...

So clearly decisions taken from the heart were not necessarily rational in nature and couldn't be explained...just like the sizzling chemistry between Alok and Alka in his novel which couldn't be explained but hopefully would be felt and enjoyed by a reader...that is if his book was ever published!

The ring of his mobile interrupted his thoughts.

It was his mother calling.

'Raghu, where are you? Do you want dinner or not?' she asked.

'I'm in Koramangala. Keep some dinner for me. I'll come in sometime.'

'Who was that?' Sweety asked him once he had hung up.

'My mother.'

'Ok.'

'Do you also stay with your family?'

'No, my parents stay in Chandigarh. My uncle and aunt stay here. But I don't stay with them. I've taken up an apartment in Vivek Nagar.'

'Cool.'

'I stay separately because I love my independence and also because I don't want to inconvenience them. My work is pretty hectic. Initially I was in the Delhi office. Then I was in Pune. Now for the last year and a bit, I've been in Bangalore. In the coming months, I'm going to be travelling to the new branch offices in Hyderabad, Visakhapatnam, Chennai and Trivandrum.'

'Wow…pretty hectic schedule lined up for you. But don't you counsellors have to be in one branch or in one city all the time to counsel the students?'

'We have to be. But this time around, I'm one among a select few who have been chosen to train the new batch of counsellors in these branches.'

'Cool. Have you always wanted to be a counsellor? What are you future plans?'

'At this point in time, this line of work really interests me. But as part of my overall life plan, I want to travel the world, meet new people, soak in new experiences and absorb new cultures. I want to live in the great cities of the world like

London, Paris and New York. What are your plans, once your book gets published?'

'No plan in particular. I guess, I'll get back to a regular job.'

'How boring! We should travel the world together! It will be so much fun!'

'Let's see. Or maybe you travel the world and send me postcards.'

'Maybe I will. So shall we get going?'

'Ok.'

'How did you come?'

'I came by auto as my bike's punctured. Why?'

'It doesn't look like you can even stand straight! One mug of beer which you have managed to finish with great difficulty seems to have knocked you out completely!'

He saw her grinning. She was right. He did feel a little talli as he hadn't neutralized the beer with gulps of water, like he always did!

'Do you want me to drop you to an auto?' she asked him, once they were outside the pub. He nodded. He was surprised to note that there weren't any autos in their immediate perimeter eagerly waiting like greedy vultures to swoop down on exiting pub-goers.

He walked with Sweety towards her bike: a scooty.

The thought of riding pillion made him grin.

'What's so funny?' she asked him.

'Nothing. A funny thought came to my mind.'

'Let me guess. You were thinking that just because both of us are a little heavy…the scooty will not move. Am I right?'

'Unbelievable. You are right.'

'Don't worry. Nothing like that will happen. Riding on my cool scooty is probably the best way to beat the shit traffic in this city.'

'I guess so. But tell me, how did you know what I was thinking?'

'Raghu, I'm not trying to boast but I can read a person's mind if the person is present within a distance of five feet near me. I had purposely deactivated the mind reading for this evening as I wanted you to let out the excess baggage out of your mind at your own pace. But now I've reactivated the mind reading.'

'As if....'

'I'm serious. I can mind read.'

'Ok, if you say so.'

'Don't challenge me, Raghu. I know what you are thinking right now.'

'What am I thinking?'

'You are thinking: "*Sweety has such a big ass. How can she counsel me and others on matters when she can't counsel herself to lose weight?*" Am I right?'

'Yes, you are! How did you know?'

'I just told I can read the human mind.'

'Ok, what am I thinking of right now?'

'It is something very vulgar. You are thinking: "*Sweety's got such a big upper body and her boobs are like juicy melons which I really want to squeeze.*" Am I right?'

'Oh my God! This is really unbelievable. I'm really sorry for my thoughts.'

'It's ok. I have mind read worse shit which goes on in the human mind which I'm not comfortable talking about.'

'That's fine. But how did you develop this mind reading?'

'It's a skill I've acquired over a period of time.'

'Is it possible for you to predict the fate of my book?'

'I'm a mind reader, not an astrologer.'

'Oh. Do your friends also know about this mind reading ability of yours? Do they enjoy it or do they freak out?'

'A bit of both actually. That's why I don't use it often. But personally I consider it nothing more than just a harmless quirk. They however find it weird when I talk to Reema and Seema in public. I really don't know why that's such a big deal.'

'Who are Reema and Seema? Your friends from work?'

'No. They are my boobs...the melons which you were nicely thinking about earlier.'

'WHAT?'

He was shocked. Sweety spoke to her boobs? And she told him this so casually as if it was a mundane occurrence like a cow crossing the main road! He had to agree with her friends completely. This was freakishly weird!

'Sweety, I know I'm a bit high, but did I just hear right? Did you just tell me that you speak to your....'

'Yes, I did. Don't act so surprised Raghu!' she interrupted him. 'Don't tell me that you have never had a frank conversation with your body parts or with the voices in your head? It's a perfectly natural thing to do.'

He felt his head spin! Did he ever speak to his dick, his other body parts or to the voices in his head? NEVER!

'Sweety! *How can you talk to a body part?* Which world are you living in?'

'For your information, I'm living in a normal healthy world in which the body is spiritually, physically and mentally connected to the mind.'

'Ok whatever. But what do you talk about?'

'I talk to Reema and Seema whenever I need reassurance or a second opinion or a boost to my self confidence. They comfort me with their words of wisdom. They have been my trusted confidantes ever since Vikrant left.'

'Whenever I need to boost my confidence, I come and meet counsellors like you…ha ha.'

'Not funny.'

'Ok, I'm sorry. By the way, are they talking to you right now? I'm just curious.'

'Yes. Seema just said something.'

'What?'

He looked on in rapt amazement as Sweety pressed her left boob like it was doorbell!

'A bit of girl talk. Seema, by the way wishes you a very good evening. Say hello, Raghu. Don't feel shy.'

'I'm not feeling shy. Good evening, Seema,' he replied, waving in the direction of Sweety's left boob. Unbelievable!

'Sweety, I think I might faint. Can you please deactivate the mind reading and boob talking and just drop me to an auto?'

'Ok, I will.'

'Sweety is such a crazy, fat freak,' he muttered to himself.

'I heard that, Raghu!'

'I'm so sorry!'

He rode pillion as Sweety rode the scooty in full speed like it was a Ferrari towards an auto stand.

'Sweety, I know this is cheesy but I think you are really sweet. You are a good person except for your "quirks". Thanks for listening to my problem,' he told her as he was about to get into an auto.

'Raghu, there's no need to thank me. I'm just happy spreading cheer over mugs of beer.'

A sudden thought came to his mind.

He had seen in many movies that the terminally ill patients often had an infectious enthusiasm for life as they were living on limited time, before going to the other world to meet their creator. Was Sweety also living on limited time?

'Sweety, I know this is very awkward to ask, but are you suffering from something?' he asked, sounding genuinely concerned.

'Suffering from what?'

'I mean…are you like dying or something?'

'Raghu, as you can clearly see, I'm in good health.'

He smiled.

'Ok cool. Will you be able to ride home safely?'

'I'll manage. Not everyone is like you…one mug of beer and knocked out.'

He smiled again.

'Raghu, we'll stay in touch on Facebook, right?'

'Of course.'

'Do keep me updated with the progress on the book front.'

'I will. Maybe whenever we meet next, you can hypnotize me and use me as a bakra for a black magic experiment or a past life regression experiment. I can use those experiences for a future book.'

'Maybe I will. But let me consult Seema and Reema to see if it makes sense.'

'Do that,' he remarked sarcastically. 'Ok bye, Sweety, Seema and Reema. Sleep well. Take care.'

En route home in the auto, he couldn't say that he felt better about his current 'book rejection' situation but he definitely felt a tad relieved. Sweety actually was a lot of fun to hang out with! Quite an amazing transformation from the sniffing and all-the-problems-in-the-world-rests-on-my-huge-shoulders Sweety from the writing workshop!

INTERROGATION

A few days later.
Frustrated with the current situation, Raghu decided that it was time for him to reapply for work.

But just then, negative thoughts came to his mind.

He thought about how he had quit SFPAL confidently thinking that he would write his book, get published and then re-enter the work force by easily justifying his work break.

But right now the situation was totally different.

Would recruiters look favourably at his job break? He had quit his job to write a book which wasn't even published. They might appreciate his effort and decision to have followed his passion. But where was the tangible final result which he could show them at his end?

It was certainly going to be a challenge to find a new job.

He decided to reapply for roles as a financial advisor in wealth management, similar to the one he held at SFPAL.

He began his job hunt by first updating his resume.

He had an old single page resume saved in a document folder on his laptop.

He used buzz words like 'hard worker', 'target oriented', 'good team player' etc., to juice up his modest work achievements at SFPAL! Right at the bottom of the page, he created a new section titled 'Hobbies and Additional Information' in which he mentioned a couple of points about *The Paperback Badshah*.

His resume now finally looked complete and fairly balanced.

It had an interesting combination of professional work achievements and incomplete book achievements!

A few hours later, he uploaded his final polished resume on various job sites. He immediately got an acknowledgement email from a job site, followed up by another email in which they (the site) offered to redesign his resume in a better manner for him to secure a 'handsome package'! All he had to do was to pay a one time fee of ten thousand rupees with no hidden charges!

He smiled as he read the email. He had no money and these fuckers wanted to make money at his expense!

Just then his mobile rang.

He picked it up.

'Hello? Am I talking to Raghu?' the voice asked.

'Yes,' he replied.

'Sir, I was wondering if I can tell you about this assured income plan. I'm calling from....'

'Not interested.'

'Sir, the reason I'm calling is because your name came up in my database of preferred customers. My records tell me that you are a salaried working professional at Star Financial Planners & Advisors Limited.'

'What you have is old data. I no longer work there.'

'Oh, thank you for the update. Where are you working now?'

'I'm *self employed*. But I'm still not interested in your assured income plan.'

'Please sir, your name came up in my database of preferred customers....'

'Arrey what please? I have no money. I'm not interested.'

'Ok sir. When can I call again?'

'Call me next year. Thanks.'

He disconnected the call.

Irritating as these call centre agents were, he had to applaud them for their enthusiasm and persistence. Maybe even he should adopt a similar dogged approach to deal with his book rejections. He had to take the rejections in his stride as part of the learning process.

Deep down, he still had a lot of confidence in his book.

He had to be patient and wait for a response from the three remaining publishers before taking any further book related decisions.

＊

A month later.

Raghu was in his room.

His mobile rang.

'Hi, am I speaking to Raghu?' a professional sounding voice asked.

'Yes,' he replied.

'Hi Raghu, I'm Rachel Karen Green from Right Fit Job Consultants.'

He smiled to himself. She had the same name as Jennifer Aniston's character in the serial *Friends*!

'Hi Rachel,' he said finally.

'Raghu, I came across your resume on a job site. I'm aware that you are currently on a work break and you wish to reapply?'

'That's correct.'

'There's a job opening with XYZICZIM Securities. The position is for that of a financial advisor.'

'Ok. That sounds interesting.'

'I'm sending you the job description by email right away. It contains all the details. I would really appreciate it, if you can go for this interview.'

'Sure. Let me check my email and get back to you.'

He hung up the call. He was surprised.

A job interview had come sooner than he had expected! No publisher had responded positively but a job consultant certainly had!

He checked his email.

The job description attachment in the email explained the role on offer. It was similar to the role he had at SFPAL. He confirmed to the email and got an immediate reply from Rachel stating that she would confirm the date of the interview.

'I got an interview call!' he told his parents, a few minutes later.

'Finally!' they replied in unison. He gave them the details. They listened interestedly. They were sick of listening to his tales of book rejection which he had restarted telling to them over dinner everyday for the past several days!

A few days later, Rachel gave him a call and confirmed the date for his interview.

He realized that his life was slowly moving back from the comforts of his room, his home, his afternoon nap and his unemployment right back to the grind called work life!

He decided to do some sort of preparation for the interview.

He read through some financial concepts and stock market happenings which were related to his work. He realized that he was really rusty on that front. He also realized that his office shoes were really dusty! Also his office pants didn't fit as he had gained a lot of weight! He needed to overhaul his wardrobe before going for the interview.

An interesting thought came to his mind.

In *The Paperback Badshah*, Alok had started off as a directionless man and had ended up as a successful man. Would he also be able to make that sort of transition now... from being an unemployed man to a focused 'job ready' man?

The day of Raghu's interview arrived.

It was a Friday.

He was feeling pretty nervous.

Just before leaving his home for the interview (which was scheduled during an afternoon slot), he quickly scanned through the business pages of the mass market newspaper just in case the interviewer(s) decided to check his business awareness.

He came across a news item which made him laugh.

The news item was about how an official in an important statistical organization had messed up big time while preparing a report on the state of the Indian economy. In the report, the official had incorrectly mentioned that the economy was growing at 3.7% per annum instead of the actual rate of 7.3% per annum!

Hopefully he wouldn't mess up his interview this badly!

Forty minutes later, he had reached XYZICZIM Securities's office in Vasanth Nagar for his interview.

The sun was beating down.

He was in a business suit. His suit stuck to his sweaty body.

Thankfully the draught of a/c air inside the reception area in the office cooled him down. A security guard directed him to an empty interview room on the second floor. On the second floor, as he walked towards the interview room, he walked past a cabin in which a middle aged guy was sitting. The door was open. The guy was speaking to someone on the phone and at the same time staring at a PowerPoint presentation with such interest, as if it was a porn star commanding his full attention with her arresting, irresistible presence.

Just then the guy screamed at someone on the phone.

'Stupid fool! How are you even a financial advisor? Don't you know basic arithmetic? 8550 divided by 50 is 171 not 85! How can you just cancel 50 from the Numerator and Denominator of the fraction? Are you stupid? You don't need a calculator or Excel for such a simple calculation! Go redo the entire calculation and update it correctly in the presentation. I want the presentation in the next ten minutes!'

Raghu smiled to himself.

His basic maths was certainly better than that!

He walked past the cabin and entered the interview room. He waited for his appointment with the HR manager.

A few minutes later, the HR manager walked in.

She had a copy of his resume in her hand. He noticed that she had circled the 'Hobbies and Additional Information' section in red. Without introducing herself and without even engaging in a bit of the usual mundane pleasantries, she began by asking him questions.

'Why do you want to work, Raghu?' she asked him.

He was surprised by the question. He actually had no idea why he wanted to work!

'To pay the monthly bills,' he replied uncertainly.

'But that's not a good reason why one must work.'

'But isn't that why, the majority of us work?'

She smiled and left his question unanswered.

He also smiled and felt at ease. He also noticed that she was making a note of his various answers.

'Will you be comfortable working full time?'

'Yes, of course.'

'Do you know how to use a laptop? A desktop?'

He nodded. A few months out of the job market and the HR manager thought that he had gone back to the stone ages!

'Ok Raghu, I'm done with my preliminary questions. As a part of the recruitment process, you'll now have to take a computer based finance test. The test has 75 questions. Each question has four options and there's no negative marking for a wrong answer. So answer all the questions. The test times out automatically at the end of 45 minutes. After the test, there will be a personal one on one interview with your manager.'

He nodded digesting all this information.

'Follow me.'

He followed her to a desktop system.

She punched in some access code and magically a test appeared on the computer screen!

'Good luck,' she told him and walked away.

His test began.

He noticed that the good thing about the test was that he could scroll down to any of the questions and revisit it later, if he didn't know the answer at first. The test covered a range of finance concepts such as alpha, beta, duration, convexity, interest rates, inflation, stock markets, global economy, mutual fund basics, regulatory aspects etc.

About ten minutes later, he felt a little tense.

While the questions were fairly simple, the wording in each of the answer options made the selection of the correct option, a challenging one.

His attention wandered a little.

A few metres beyond his desktop screen, he spotted a water cooler.

By the water cooler, he noticed two women standing. They seemed cordial but were not really exchanging friendly vibes with each other. They also seemed to be in some serious cleavage competition. Each one had a deeper neckline than the other. Maybe that explained the tension between them on what was a chilled out, casual 'Friday dressing to work' afternoon.

He scolded himself for getting distracted by this cleavage competition right in his eye line. He didn't want to give it as a reason for messing up his exam. He refocused all his energy back on the finance test.

As he scrolled down to a question on 'whether interest rates should be cut......', he first thought about the cricket strokes 'square cut' and 'late cut' and then about the women with their respective 'low cut' dresses!

He then thought about Sweety and how she spoke to her confidantes, Reema and Seema! It distracted him further!

His mind then wandered back to the women.

He thought about a boxing contest between them in which he would be the referee to decide the winner. But those thoughts were too graphic in nature and were automatically blocked out by the self imposed censor board in his brain. At best, they could be passed for late night 'thinking' after obtaining an adult 'A' certificate instead of a more accommodating 'U/A' certificate from the censor board!

All of a sudden, he realized that only fifteen minutes were left for the test to time out!

He felt a mild buzz in the pressure points in his head.

He had answered only 37 questions! He had to answer the remaining 38 questions in the next fifteen minutes!

He didn't know what to do.

Then an idea came to his mind.

He resorted to a tactic which had never paid any dividends to him but was the best under the current circumstances. He decided to randomly guess the answers to the remaining questions!

Fifteen minutes later, the test window automatically shut down.

The test was over.

He knew he had screwed it up but he now had a personal interview to attend. He walked back to the interview room.

About twenty minutes later, the HR manager walked into the interview room with a middle aged guy. It was the same guy who had been screaming on the phone at someone about the arithmetic error!

'Raghu, this is Digvijay. The position you are being interviewed for, is in his team. He'll now interview you,' the HR manager said.

He nodded.

'Meanwhile I'll go get your test results and be back.'

She left the interview room.

It was now a one-on-one between him and his potential manager.

Just then, an office assistant entered the room with a plate of Marie biscuits balanced on his left palm and a cup of piping hot tea (or maybe coffee) balanced on his *bare* right palm! The assistant placed both the items on the table in front of Digvijay and then left.

Raghu was impressed witnessing this balancing act of the office assistant!

Maybe the office culture of this company was all about putting in one's 100% on the job every single day! Maybe it was about putting one's body (and palm!) on the line and performing every task at hand (and on the palm!) with selfless dedication!

The assistant returned a few minutes later with a glass of water for him.

The interview finally began.

'Raghu, let's get cracking. Why do you want to work with us? What value can you bring for us? Can you bring in new clients? What's the business plan you have in mind to achieve your targets? Where do you see yourself in the next 5-7 years? Will you put in your 100% for this job? What assurance can you give me that you will stay with us if selected? Why don't you write full time? What's more important for you-money or success? Tell me! Tell me fast!' Digvijay began, by asking him a series of back to back questions.

He couldn't believe it!

Fuck! This interrogation seemed like an interview straight out of the popular novel *Corporate Atyaachaar: the comical journey of an office doormat* in which the protagonist in the story is also asked similar questions by his boss, a character called the Human Ball Scratcher (HBS)! People often thought that fiction writing is loosely based on real life incidents but in this case, incidents were unfolding in front of him in real time, straight out of a work of fiction!

'C'mon, Raghu! Where are you lost? Are you dreaming? I want answers to my questions. I don't have all afternoon,' Digvijay said.

'One minute....,' he replied.

He took a deep breath. He then gulped down the entire glass of water which was in front of him.

'You seem to drink a lot of water, Raghu. Good for you. You will have fewer kidney problems later on in life. But in case you are selected, I might however need to include "water" as a cost in your overall CTC salary calculation!' Digvijay commented and burst out laughing.

He tried to smile in return but couldn't. He felt a mild tremor running through the side of his head at the very thought of working for this manager!

Just then, the HR manager entered the room with a sheet in her hand.

It was his score on the finance test.

She passed the sheet to Digvijay. Digvijay had a quick look and burst out laughing! Again! Even the HR manager was grinning.

'Raghu, it's unfortunate but I regret to inform you that your score is in the bottom three of the "all time" lowest scores for this role, since the time I've been interviewing candidates in this company,' she told him.

'What? Really?' he asked, sounding surprised.

'Yes.'

'How much did I get?'

'You net score is 4 on 75!'

He was shocked. The score was embarrassingly low! He thought he had answered at least 30 questions correctly!

'I got only 4 questions correct?'

'Yes Raghu. You answered 18 questions correctly and 56 were answered incorrectly. You also missed out a question.'

'Oh. But then how did I get a score of just 4?'

'There was negative marking in place. One point was awarded for a correct answer and 0.25 was deducted for an incorrect answer.'

'What? But I thought you told me that there was no negative marking?'

'I lied. As a recruiter, I wanted to see if a candidate actually reads and then answers the various questions, or whether the candidate just resorts to random guessing.'

He was totally stumped. *This was pure evil.*

The HR manager laughed. Digvijay joined in. It seemed like they were having total Friday afternoon, recruitment entertainment at his expense!

'So Raghu, that's it for the moment. We're done. I'll keep you informed about the second round of interviews,' the HR manager told him.

'Sure,' he replied with a weak smile even though he knew that there wouldn't be a second round of interviews. They had already made up their mind after seeing his low test score!

En route home, he tried to reassure himself that the interview was anyway just like a warm up match to get back into the work mode. Plus the work environment was more like that of a hostile jail. It certainly didn't seem like a place where a sane person would willingly want to join and work!

He reached home.

'Raghu, how did the interview go? Will you get the job?' his father asked expectantly.

He did not get into any specifics. Instead he just looked down at the floor.

His father got the answer.

'Do you know how to shout properly?' his father asked him, a few minutes later.

'Yes. Why?'

'Why don't you join them? You might do well.'

His father pointed at the TV screen.

A clipping from the popular reality show *Bigg Boss* was being aired on a news channel, in which a few small time celebrities were howling at each other like attention seeking barbarians within the confines of a big house.

He thought to himself.

Given his book rejections and now a more than likely job rejection, it wouldn't be a bad idea for him to try his luck on a reality TV show if given an opportunity. He could shout out loud to boost the show's TRPs!

He wanted to smile at the thought of seeing himself on TV but his present situation was really no laughing matter. Nothing was going as per plan.

Things were heading from bad to worse!

PART 3

CREATIVE OUTBURST

ACCEPTANCE

A week and a bit later.
It was mid morning.

Raghu was in his room. He was sitting at his writing desk and mulling over his future. Just then, through the window beyond his desk, he noticed a filthy cow standing outside his house. It had a bell around its neck. It seemed like a holy cow on a religious yatra of sorts. It was pressing itself against the gate.

He couldn't help but smile to himself.

In the past, he had seen street dogs loiter on the road outside his house but he had never ever seen a cow trying to enter his house!

Would such a thing ever happen in Roma's gated community?

Not a chance.

He decided to investigate. He opened the front door and walked towards the gate to witness live action.

The mystery unravelled itself.

On the other side of the gate, the cow had a companion who was hidden behind its large backside! The companion was a baba, a guru of sorts who had a tin can in one hand and a twig in the other hand. The baba was busy drumming some musical beats on the tin can while howling some indecipherable religious chants to exhort people to put money in the can.

Suddenly, the baba looked in his direction.

He wanted to turn around and run back into his house. But he then wondered whether he would be cursed if he ran away without putting in, any money into the can. What if the baba suddenly pulled out a coiled rattle snake out of the can to teach him a lesson?

He didn't ever want to land up in such a dangerous situation.

He searched for some loose change in his shorts pocket. He found three rupees! He dropped it into the can. The baba in return began howling some religious chants while pointing the twig in his direction to bless him! A few minutes later, the baba stopped howling and walked away with his bovine companion in the direction of the other homes in the colony.

Later that evening.

Raghu had just finished reading three emails.

He couldn't believe it. He had often heard people use the saying *'when it rains, it pours'*.

He now knew why.

He had received positive responses (that too on the same day!) from each of the three remaining publishers to whom he had sent his book proposal!

All of them were all interested in publishing *The Paperback Badshah*!!!!!!

The good times were rolling in…finally!

He read through each of the emails again.

The email from the first publisher stated-'....We read your proposal with interest and we would directly like to go ahead with the publication of your manuscript. However in our publishing model, we would require you (the author), to share in the costs of publishing the book. In return, you get to share in the profit from the sale of the book which will be significantly higher and more lucrative than a fixed royalty percentage which most other traditional publishers in the market offer....'

Reading this email didn't make him feel too happy.

He wasn't comfortable with this concept of self publishing in which he had to share in the various costs of publishing (for editing, proofreading, printing, marketing, promotion and distribution) in the hope of extraordinary book sales in return. In his view, in this case, the publisher was conveniently trying to deflect the entire responsibility of publishing the book based solely on its merit and was instead more keen on treating it as a business venture with the author! If this was the case, wasn't it then better for an author to just go to a printing press and get his book printed by spending his own money? Why even bother sending across a book proposal for evaluation in the first place?

The email from the second publisher stated-'....Our team screened your proposal. We request you to send across the full manuscript for evaluation. We will get back to you in twelve weeks time.....'

This email was certainly interesting.

But there was an issue. What if after further evaluation, the publisher decided to not extend a book contract to him and not publish his work? Then what would he do?

The email from the third publisher stated-'....Our team screened your proposal. We are keen on publishing your book. We will be sending across a book contract in the coming week. At your end, do send across the entire manuscript for evaluation....'

This email was certainly the best of the lot!

They were sending a book contract!

The email was from Indian Mass Market Fiction Publishers (IMMFP), a domestic publisher which specialized in publishing mass market fiction novels at an affordable price point of hundred rupees. Their target market was mainly college youngsters and working professionals in their early twenties. *The Paperback Badshah* certainly did fit in nicely with the target audience they had in mind!

Having read the three emails, a few thoughts came to his mind.

Were the three emails, a direct result of the baba's 'three rupee worth' magical chants? Or was it simply an input-output result for the hard work which he had put into his writing? Or was it simply a random, unexplained result of God's intervention...a God for whom his faith had been fickle and inconsistent over the last few months?

He had no answers but he was super relieved and excited.

He marched confidently out of his room to tell his parents about these exciting new developments.

'I HAVE SOME GREAT NEWS,' he announced loudly, to his parents who were watching TV.

'What?' his father asked.

'Guess?'

'Raghu, I'm not good in "twenty question" type games. Tell me quickly.'

'Ok. I'm getting a book contract for *The Paperback Badshah*.'

'What! Really?'

'Yes!'

'Superb. That's great news indeed.'

He quickly told his parents about the three publishers from whom he had received emails and about the book contract which IMMFP was sending across in the coming week.

'What are the various points which should be in a book contract?' his father asked him.

'No idea,' he replied.

'What will the royalty payment be like? Will there be overseas distribution? How are you going to promote the book? Will the publisher spend for the publicity and promotion?'

'I have to first get the contract to check all of this.'

'Will an e-book version also be available?'

'First, let a paperback version come out and then let's talk about an e-book version!'

'So Raghu, how are you feeling now as a publisher has finally shown interest in *The Paperback Zamindar*?' his mother asked him.

'For the last time I'm telling you that my book title is *The Paperback Badshah* and not *The Paperback Zamindar*!'

'I know. But let's ask the people of Bangalore for their opinion.'

'What?'

'People of Bangalore which do you think is the better title? Also people of Bangalore do you think that my son, Raghu is Bangalore's most desirable? Please tell me….please tell me.'

'What are you doing?'

'She's trying to sound like the host of the show,' his father chipped in, while pointing at the TV.

He smiled as he realized what was happening.

His parents were watching an episode of *Simi Selects-India's Most Desirable* hosted by the famous yesteryear actress Simi Garewal in which the 'desirable' guests on the show were asked various questions about their lives including questions about their love life, relationship status etc.!

He went back to his room.

He turned on his laptop and logged on to Facebook.

He posted on his wall: *Breakthrough! Finally…light at the end of the tunnel. There is a God. Thank you.*

Lots of friends including Suresh commented along the following lines- What happened, Raghu? All ok?

He sent Suresh a FB message: *Dude, my book is going to get published! I'm super excited!*

At around ten in night, he got a call from Nandu.

It was a little over three months since they had last spoken.

'Raghu, what's up? Ignoring me huh?' Nandu asked.

'No dude. Why?'

'Oh cool. I thought you were still pissed off because of those Rita-Margarita messages…ha ha.'

'No dude. Forget that. Listen to this-'

'What?'

'My book's going to get published. I'm getting a book contract.'

'Seriously? Wow!'

'Yes dude!'

He quickly updated Nandu about his book rejections, his meeting with Sweety, his unsuccessful job hunt and the fantastic news of getting a book contract from IMMFP.

'Raghu, I'm really happy to hear this! I'll share this awesome news with Kavita right away.'

Just as Nandu mentioned his wife's name, a couple of question suddenly came to Raghu's mind.

'Nandu, can I ask you a couple of questions?'

'What questions?'

'Don't take it the wrong way as we have been friends for really long. Does Kavita talk to her body parts?'

'What kind of vulgar question is this, you fucker?'

'No dude. Let me put the question in context. When I had met Sweety, she told me that she talks to her body…and in particular to her boobs. She calls them Seema and Reema affectionately. Can you believe that?'

'Unbelievable! This is just too much. How come such incidents happen only to you?'

Raghu didn't know whether Nandu was sad that such incidents never happened to him!

'What do you mean?' he asked.

'Raghu, with Roma it was her "bosom power" principle and with this Sweety woman, it is her boob talking and boob nicknames! I'm really getting the feeling that you are deliberating adding low quality Bollywood masala to spice up our conversation.'

'No dude. No extra masala. Just the truth, the way I heard and saw it.'

'As if! Anyways to answer your earlier question, I don't think Kavita has any nicknames for her body parts. Even if she did…I will not tell you! What's your other question?'

'Dude, do you talk to your junior?'

'Yes, I do. I talk and sing songs to Gopu all the time!'

'Not baby Gopu, dude! I'm talking about your junior down there in your body!'

'Raghu, this is too much! You have been up to too much of unemployment nonsense!'

'Dude, I'm not making this up! I swear! Sweety told me that guys also talk to their bodies. I didn't believe her one bit.'

'She really told you this?'

'Yes, she did.'

'I hardly get time for normal talk with my family...so I'm pretty sure I don't do this! If I do all this kind of talking, Kavita will throw me out of the house. The other day, I didn't hear my own name!'

'Are you serious?'

'I'm serious. Kavita was shouting, "Nandu! Nandu! Go pay the bill!" I was in the same room but I was busy working on my laptop. I heard it as "Bindu! Bindu! Go pay the bill!" So I didn't move. She got so wild! She thought I was deliberately avoiding household work. She then linked this behaviour of my mine to some fight which we had last year, which I had totally forgotten about but which she suddenly remembered.'

'Oh.'

'But thankfully after the full day had gone by in a fight, we made up rather sweetly in the night. I kept making this tiger noise "Grrrr…" which she liked a lot and it powered us for the night.'

'Dude, I don't want to know all these details from your personal life.'

'You are right. I think even you should forget all this

nonsense Sweety stories and just focus on your book and on your job hunt.'

'You are right. I will.'

'Your parents must be relieved that you at least restarted your job hunt, right?'

'Yes, they are. I think that they are also pretty excited by the positive developments on the book front. My plan right now is to focus exclusively on the book till its release.'

'Good stuff. Ok Raghu, I've got to hang up. I've got some pending work to complete. Congrats once again. And in case of more Sweety developments, do inform me!'

'Really? But I thought you said it's all nonsense?'

'It is. But I would like to know. I'm someone who is never too busy for masala gossip and stories…ha ha.'

∗

The following week.

Raghu had just finished having a late breakfast.

The doorbell rang.

He opened the front door. A courier guy was standing with a cover in hand.

The book contract sent by IMMFP had arrived!

He quickly signed the courier guy's delivery sheet, took the cover, shut the door and ran to his room.

He sat at his writing desk. He ripped open the courier to check the book contract. There were two copies of the contract. He liked the quality of the paper on which the contract was printed. He had to sign both copies and return one signed copy to the publisher, for their records.

The contract ran into ten pages!

He first expectantly flipped to the page which had the

clause regarding the payment of royalty.

He finally located the royalty clause and saw the royalty percentage.

There was nothing *royal* about the royalty percentage!

It was very modest indeed.

He did a quick mental calculation of the kind of money he could make.

The conclusion he arrived at, was that the money he would be making would be modest at best. If however there was an extraordinary scenario in which *The Paperback Badshah* became a gigantic bestseller on the first day of publication itself and was followed by sustained demand from readers right through the year, he would then definitely be laughing all the way to the bank!

After focusing his attention on the *not-so-royal* royalty clause, he focused his attention on the whole bunch of other clauses in the contract relating to-grant of rights, distribution rights, reproduction rights, electronic rights, production rights, promotional aspects, author proofs, author's copyright, accounting treatment, cancellation of contract, reversion of rights etc.

An hour later, he felt as if he had aged considerably given that he had read (and understood) each and every point mentioned in the various well worded clauses of the contract. There was however one aspect in the contract in which the wording was pretty ambiguous. It was regarding the publisher's specific role in the promotion of the book. No specific details were mentioned as to how they would promote the book.

Did the onus of promotion and publicity rest entirely on his own shoulders?

He needed to check with the publisher on that front.

In the afternoon, just after his nap, he was on Facebook and was doing some timepass checking of updates. Sweety had liked and commented on his previous week's status update: *Breakthrough! Finally…light at the end of the tunnel. There is a God. Thank you.*

She always seemed to react to his FB posts with a lag effect!

She commented: *If it is what I think it is…then congrats! My prayers for you have worked. This calls for a celebration* ☺ *See you in Bangalore in a few months time. I'm super busy with all the work happening in the new branches* ☹

'What prayers?' he wondered to himself. But he felt happy that someone had actually prayed for him.

Later in the evening when his father was back from work, he gave the contract to him to read through.

His father cracked three to four jokes about the modest royalty percentage. As per one of his calculations, the likely yearly royalty wasn't even going to be enough to cover the costs involved in creating a marriage profile on the various matrimonial websites!

He smiled. His father's 'seriously low' earning-from-the-royalty projections was funny!

In a reasonable scenario he could visualize buying at least a Nano with the royalty amount. He could take his parents for a spin around the colony in the Nano and then he could stop in the middle of the main road and dance to the energetic tunes of *Jai Ho* from *Slumdog Millionaire*!

As his father commented on the other aspects in the contract, a sudden matrimony related thought came to his mind.

Generally people on their marriage invitation cards listed their impressive qualifications (such as a B.Tech from an IIT or a PGDM from an IIM). While he had no great qualifications to list (just a modest B.Com and a tier-2 MBA), what he certainly would mention was the fact that he was a (soon to be) *published author*!

TRANSFORMATION

Two and a half months later.

Raghu was excited.

The final manuscript and the cover of *The Paperback Badshah* had gone for printing.

He recognized the amount of effort which had gone into his book to reach this stage. And the *story* behind how his book had reached this stage.

To begin with, after receiving the contract from IMMFP, he sent regret emails to the other two publishers, to stop further evaluation of his work.

Then on the book front, at the publisher's end, his manuscript was about to be edited.

He had always heard that the process of editing would be a fairly time consuming process as the editor would play an important role in removing the excess content, help iron out the grammatical flaws and suggest appropriate changes to be made to the manuscript.

His editor, a lady named Sangeeta, who had worked in publishing for around four years immediately put a set of deadlines in place. She informed him that while a few editorial changes would be made, the focus would be on retaining his original 'voice' and in staying true to his 'style' of storytelling.

He felt reassured hearing this.

This was because he had often heard that the author-editor association often got a little damaged by the end of the editing process on account of the collision of the creative egos. But thankfully none of that would happen in this case, as he was confident that his book was in good hands.

A couple of weeks later, there was an unexpected announcement in store.

He received an email from Sangeeta informing him that she was moving on from IMMFP as she had received a job offer from a competing publishing house! She wished him luck on the book front and signed off.

He felt taken aback by the dramatic turn of events.

First, he felt sad.

Then panic set in.

With his editor leaving, would his book be left in the limbo? Would the book editing be stalled for some time?

Someone from the editorial team at IMMFP immediately assuaged his fears by telling him that a new editor had been assigned to take over the task of editing his book.

He felt a sense of relief.

Jasjeet, the new editor (with a MA in English Literature but with just under a year's experience in the publishing field) though was sadly nothing like the mild mannered, meticulous, careful 'attention to detail' Sangeeta!

One telephonic exchange with his new editor made Raghu realize this!

Jasjeet's cocky, arrogant 'I-know-it-all' attitude gave him a feeling that this author-editor association was going to be eventful.

And it turned out to be just that!

He sent an email to Jasjeet asking for the revised editing deadlines.

He didn't get any response.

A week passed by.

He sent a new email which again went unanswered!

Before he knew it...another week had passed by!

There was still no communication!

He was now getting anxious. What the hell was happening on the book front?

Surely one email or a phone call to confirm that the editing was in progress and going on smoothly was not too much to ask for, was it?

A few days later, he finally got an email with an attachment.

In the email, Jasjeet informed him that the first round of editing was complete.

He was happy to know that the editing had been done in super quick time!

Replying to the email, he told Jasjeet that over the past couple of weeks he has sent a couple of emails which had gone unanswered. Jasjeet replied back stating that while he was aware of the emails, he had been too involved with a 'personal problem' to revert.

Raghu left it at that.

He focused his attention on the edited manuscript.

To begin with around 5000 odd words were hived off from the manuscript thereby reducing the overall word count from the initial 73,500 odd words to a more compact

68,500 odd words. Jasjeet had also suggested a list of minor changes and had inserted comments in various parts of the manuscript.

Over the next few days, Raghu responded in detail to each and every comment made in the manuscript. He also made a few additional corrections and changes of his own, before emailing the 'revised' edited manuscript back to Jasjeet.

In another round of speed editing, the manuscript was trimmed further to reach a final word count of 65,500 odd words which was re-sent back to him for another round of author corrections and changes.

He re-read this revised 'speed edited' manuscript in detail.

Prima facie most of the errors had been rectified and the various minor changes had been incorporated.

He finalized this manuscript of *The Paperback Badshah* as 'the manuscript' which would be sent across to the typesetter working at the publisher's end who would convert 'the manuscript' in its present form into its final 'book layout' form.

With the final manuscript locked in place and being worked on by the typesetter, the other important book production process to be carried out was the cover design of *The Paperback Badshah*.

A couple of days later, Jasjeet sent him an email informing him that he was also in charge of designing the book cover and asked him whether he had any cover ideas in mind.

Reading this bit of news, he burst out laughing.

While he perfectly understood that IMMFP was a small publishing house as compared to the industry bigwigs which had well defined editorial, art, design, marketing and distribution departments...this was however the first time that he heard of an editor also being in charge of designing the book cover!

He decided to keep the humour aside for the moment.

He had a fairly simple book cover idea in mind which he felt best captured the essence of *The Paperback Badshah* as a love story. He wanted images of a man, a woman, a tiger and a toddler in some form on the cover to represent- Alok, Alka, the white tiger and Chintu respectively as they were the main characters in the story. He sent this idea to Jasjeet who was now in his new avatar as the 'cover designer'.

A week later, Jasjeet came up with a cover design.

Placed in the centre of the cover was a heart shaped design. The heart was cracked along its perimeter to denote a broken heart. Inside the broken heart, images of a woman, a toddler and a *lion* were included. The image of a man (with a really glum expression on his face) was surprisingly excluded from the heart shaped design and was instead placed all alone, a few inches away, close to the edge of the cover!

Raghu had two main questions in his mind after viewing this cover.

The first was- What was this cover trying to convey?

The second was- Why was there a lion instead of a tiger?

He emailed Jasjeet asking for an explanation.

Jasjeet wrote back explaining that the 'neglected' man on the cover represented a man who had been neglected by his loved ones, especially by a woman!

Raghu was surprised reading this bullshit reason.

The Paperback Badshah was a happy love story! It wasn't a tragic love story. There was no heartbreak! Surely Jasjeet had to know this being the editor of the book! So where did the issue of the man being 'neglected' arise?

He sent across another email asking for an explanation.

There was no response.

He then gave Jasjeet a call asking for an explanation. It was then, that Jasjeet shared the 'thought process' behind the cover design. He told Raghu that he was suffering from a prolonged case of a broken heart! His girlfriend had dumped him. It was the 'personal problem' which he had alluded to earlier as well during the initial phase of editing!

While Raghu absorbed this surprising overdose of personal information, he tried linking it to his book cover. Was Jasjeet expressing his 'I'm dumped and neglected' state of mind on a debutant author's book cover by isolating the image of the man on the cover?

He seriously hoped not!

He told Jasjeet to take it easy and requested him to place the image of the man back in the heart design, remove the jagged edges of the broken heart and to replace the lion with a tiger. Jasjeet promised to make the changes.

A few days later, Jasjeet came up with a much improved cover.

Everything was in place...*except for the presence of a lion which had still not been changed to a tiger! What the fuck!*

He called up Jasjeet and asked him to make this one final change.

This seemingly innocuous requirement resulted in an unexpected flare up.

Jasjeet lost his cool. He howled- '....Raghu, how many changes do you want me to make? Do you think I'm a machine? Do you think I have only your book and book cover to work on or what? What do you *knew* about cover design anyway? Let me handle it.'

Hearing this, Raghu wanted to tell him that while he didn't know anything about cover design, what he certainly knew...was the grammatical difference between *knew* and *know*! And between them Jasjeet was supposedly the one with an MA in English Literature! Hilarious!

He quickly realized that he had to maintain his calm despite the flare up as the final objective of designing the best possible cover had not yet been met.

He apologized to Jasjeet for sounding a tad too pushy.

Jasjeet grunted hearing his feeble apology and also mumbled an apology of his own. '...Look Raghu. I'm also sorry. Please understand my situation. I don't think I've been mentally present here at work for the last couple of months. Earlier I used to feel like a *sikandar*... a total winner and conqueror as I was in love. But now I'm feeling low and worthless like a *bandar*...like a discarded monkey because my girlfriend left me!'

Hearing this, Raghu felt bad and also very worried.

He just prayed to God that Jasjeet's mind had been in place when his book had been edited!

A couple of days later, Jasjeet came up with the final cover sample.

He had done a really good job.

All the changes had been incorporated.

While his heart and mind may or may not have been in proper working order (on account of his personal problem), the heart shaped design flush in the centre of the cover was certainly in order! He had also exercised his creativity and given the image of the animal on the cover...the face of a tiger and the body and hind of a Doberman, which was in line with the white tiger's transformation into a dog in *The Paperback Badshah*!

As the final input at his end to the cover design, Raghu sent across the story blurb, a photo of his, a brief note about himself and his email contact for correspondence which were going appear on the back cover.

The following day, Jasjeet sent him a final 'complete in all respects' cover (comprising the front cover, the spine and the back cover). All in all, in a combination of red, light blue and a sprinkling of green, the front cover with the title *The Paperback Badshah* positioned right at the top looked very attractive to grab the attention of a reader!

Coinciding rather nicely with the completion of the cover design was an email from the typesetter containing his 'book' in its final form as an attachment for his final approval and for a last round of author corrections and changes (if any). A few days later, after reading through his book in this final form, he gave his approval that everything was in place. A week later, his publisher informed him that his 'book' along with the cover was being sent to the printing press and that 5000 copies were being printed as part of the 'first edition'.

He was excited.

The amount of effort which had gone into the book to reach this stage had been totally worth it!

PROMOTION

A week later.
Raghu's publisher informed him that with the printing and binding almost complete, *The Paperback Badshah* was going to be available for purchase at a price point of hundred rupees from the various online stores as well as from the regular bookstores in just a little under two weeks' time.

While Raghu was really excited that his book was going to be available soon in the public domain, he realized that he didn't have a specific book promotional plan in place.

He visualized an ideal scenario in which he was already an established, successful author with a well defined promotional plan in place.....

Life would have been just awesome.

All he would have to do was to hop from one book promotional event to the next, just like it happened for movie promotions. He would finish radio interviews, then magazine interviews, then newspaper interviews and maybe even head to various literary festivals to create some serious buzz for his novel for at least a month leading up to its release!

At the same time, the publisher at their end would also be super proactive in getting advance reviews published in various newspapers, magazines and in online portals for readers to get a sense of what to expect from the novel.

The pre-release promotion would then be followed by a grand book launch on the official day of release of the novel just like TB's book launch which he had attended several months ago.

To sustain the buzz after the launch, he would then have a well organized multiple city book tour in which he would have book reading sessions to interact with his enthusiastic readers.......

Maybe years later, if he became a bestselling author, he would have all those platforms to promote his book.

But right now things were different.

He was a debutant author.

The publishers at their end hadn't made any commitment with regard to holding a book launch or organizing at least a two to three city book tour. They had instead only made some feeble promises towards promoting the book at various book fairs etc. He got the feeling that the publishers felt that their job was done with only the publishing of the book as they anyway now had a whole new set of other authors' books to stay focused on. So the bottom line was that, whatever book promotion for *The Paperback Badshah* had to come at his end.

✳

Raghu spent a few hours doing some research to see how other hundred rupee published authors (especially the ones in the love/romance category) went about their book promotion. He noted that most of them promoted their books on social networks (primarily on Facebook by creating a FB page) to drum up some initial attention towards their writing. Most of the promotional activities came within five main categories-

Category 1: Corny 'love line' spewing content specialists-

In this category, 'the authors' promoted their books by posting love quotes taken exclusively from their own forthcoming release or from the 'romantic' creative portion of their brain or from a handbook of love or probably from some random site on the internet! The following kinds of status messages appeared on their FB page-

-Love is blind. But is it colour blind?

-Love isn't simple. It's complex.

-A love bite is better than a shoe bite.

Most of these corny love one-liners got positive reactions from readers. These reactions further motivated the author to churn out new love quotes which appeared as new updates, which in turn got further attention and reactions and resulted in creating some sort of buzz leading up to the release of their book.

Category 2: Self promotion and self display specialists-

In this category, 'the author' (mostly male) posted videos on their FB page in which random people spoke about the book and how it touched their 'soul' and 'impacted their lives' even before the release of the book! The promotional videos were then followed by 'fashion portfolio' type photos of the author, in which the author was busy pouting while looking straight into a camera!

Reactions from most readers were super positive!

Especially from love struck girls who went on an 'Awwww', 'Muahhhh', 'So cute', 'Cho chweet', 'Luv ya', 'Miss u' overdrive, which if saved in a specially created 'Comments' folder by the author could easily fill up a 32GB hard drive!

The author in this category also got jealous, pissed off reactions from some male readers who wrote comments such as-'Oye wannabe film hero…does your book even have a semi decent plot?', 'Attention seeker', 'Chutiya chirkut'!

The net result of all the promotional videos, photos, comments and reactions was that the author had generated sufficient interest for his/her new book leading up to its release.

Category 3: Recommendation seeking specialists-

In this category, 'the author' (or their publisher) somehow got hold of a more established writer to quote something positive about the book. Quotes such as- 'The book is a must read', 'A delightful read', 'A new voice in Indian fiction', 'A name to watch out for', 'The latest star on the block', 'Indian writing at its finest' etc.

Such positive recommendations made their way not only onto the cover of the new book but also onto the FB page of the author. Readers invariably reacted positively after reading these recommendations and ordered a copy of the book!

Category 4: Old school specialists-

In this category, 'the author' belonged to the old school of thought in which the author believed that only the sheer quality of their writing would do the talking. Even if they did do some Facebook promotion, it was only in the form of posting quotes, facts and meaningful 'writing related' information rather than clearly focusing on promoting their own book!

The net result of this approach was that there was a very lukewarm response from readers leading up to the release of the book.

Category 5: Contest specialists-

In this final category, 'the author' ran contests on their FB page to get a reader to purchase their book.

A book in this case was like a product (like a bar of soap or a tube of toothpaste) which had to be sold aggressively and quickly to a reader.

The contests came in various forms.

One author ran a contest which stated- 'You can win two autographed copies of my latest novel if you recommend my novel and FB page to fifty friends.'

Another ran a contest which stated- 'You can win a free pair of checked shorts if you order five copies of my new novel. Contest closing soon!'

While such a laughter inducing strategy in which a 'book' promotion was converted to a 'shorts' promotion would be ridiculed by most (especially by old school writers and readers), the strategy however seemed to pay dividends for the author.

It had served its purpose in generating interest among the target readers.

In a specific instance, a lady reader posted a series of questions as a comment- 'If I order ten copies, will I get two shorts or will it still be only one? What if the shorts don't fit? What all colours are you selling the shorts in? Please update.'

The author responded in detail to the various questions and also began new 'shorts', 'socks' and 'shirts' promotional contests to keep the readers interested! The net result was that with each passing day leading up to the book release, more readers joined the FB page!

Having made a note of these various ways of book promotion, Raghu realized that given the number of new releases each week, book promotion was an aspect a modern day author could ill afford to ignore, especially in the cluttered hundred rupee price point segment.

But he was also clear about the fact that a reader was very discerning.

While it was possible to initially entice a reader with the bait of free shorts, socks, shirts from a spring-summer or a fall-winter collection, *the bottom line was that a reader wanted a good story to read.* The writing at some level had to capture their attention. If it did…the chances were that they would recommend the book to their friends which in turn would create slow yet significant positive word of mouth publicity for a debutant author.

A few thoughts came to his mind.

Would the sheer quality of the writing in *The Paperback Badshah* do the talking?

Would he get at least eighty 'Awwww' and sixty 'Muahhhh' comments of love from readers?

Only time would tell.

The following day, he decided to start promoting his book on Facebook (on his own account wall and on a specifically created book page).

He decided that he was going to flood his timeline with successive book updates to grab the attention of his virtual friends!

He began by posting a series of corny love quotes which he had thought of, the previous night itself, which he felt would highlight the 'love' factor in *The Paperback Badshah*.

He posted the following ten love quotes-

-Love means never having to say sorry when you have eaten an extra idli.

-Love means never having to feel awkward when you feel the sensation while I overflow with perspiration.

-Love means never having to bid goodbye to a soulmate especially if she becomes your roommate.

-Love means you can cry without having to lie.

- Love is pure unlike the city water which is impure.

-Whether or not you have paisa in your pocket, always keep your girlfriend's picture in your trouser pocket.

-Whether or not you get dirty thoughts after watching porn, please ensure that your heart is always a clean, happy zone.

-Whether or not you have pimples, always ensure that the thoughts in your heart are clean and simple.

-It is better to be a love addict than a drug addict.

-In life you can choose to become a specialist or a generalist. But in love, please don't become a reluctant fundamentalist. Instead become a love scientist.

A few minutes later, he uploaded an image of his book cover along with the story blurb details. Ten minutes later, in a new update, he mentioned the various online links from where his book could be pre-ordered at a cool 30-35% deep discount! Twenty minutes later, in a new update, he uploaded a few baby photos of himself (as he didn't have any 'model' type photos!) to tug at the emotional heartstrings of a reader.

He was fairly satisfied with this blast of back to back updates. He was confident that word would quickly get around that he had written a book.

Ten minutes passed by, but there was still no feedback, likes or comments to any of his posts!

He found it really strange!

Maybe all his FB friends were busy at work. Maybe by evening, the reactions would pour in. But he couldn't help noticing that during this same time, a girl in his friend list had written the word 'BORED' on her wall and such a mundane update had already received forty likes and fifteen comments! One guy even cheekily commented that he could 'personally' visit her to help her get rid of the boredom! The guy's comment in turn got a further five likes from others!

The girl and the guy clearly seemed like born marketers from whom he could learn a strategy or two, and use it for his book promotion!

A few minutes later, he got a call from Suresh.

'Congrats Raghu! I just pre-ordered two copies on Flipkart,' Suresh told him.

'Wow! Thanks man. Long time!'

'I know, dude. I've been really busy on the work front. I'm telling you…*The Paperback Badshah* will become a bestseller.'

'Let's see. But will you read the book?'

'Dude, you know that I don't read books. Plus where's the time to read nowadays? I'm however planning to gift one copy to that chick Sarika in my colony. I will tell her that my friend is a writer. It will create a good impression. Then she'll think that even I'm cool.'

'Yeah do that. Boost my book sales!'

'By the way, I have an observation to make.'

'What?'

'In those baby photos you've uploaded…you look like a football! I'm pretty sure you were busy eating idlis even when you were small…ha ha! Ok dude…I've got to go for a client meeting now. Congrats once again! I'll spread the word in the office.'

'Sure man. Thanks a lot.'

He was happy that finally someone has read his status updates and had ordered his book!

During the afternoon, he got a call from Nandu.

'Congrats Raghu! Awesome achievement!'

'Thanks dude. What's going on?' he asked.

'The usual bullshit. Life is so hectic, work is so hectic and now I've to make time to read your book!'

'Yes, please make time!'

'I will. I want to tell you something.'

'What?'

'I don't know but I'm getting the feeling after reading the story blurb that your book is more of an "immature comedy" love story than a mature "bodies locked in full on passion" love story.'

'You read the book and decide.'

'I will read it and give you my feedback. Tell me one thing.'

'What?'

'Who's the character Alka based on? Is it based on Roma or that boob talker Sweety or anyone else I know?'

'First read the book and then let's discuss.'

'Ok fine. Am I there as inspiration for any of the characters in the book?'

'No dude.'

'Oh. Is my name at least there in the acknowledgements?'

'Oh dude...I forgot to put your name!'

'Are you serious?'

'Kidding man...of course it's there.'

'Oh cool. I'll pre-order ten copies right away and distribute it among my family and friends.'

'Awesome. Do that!'

'One final observation-'

'What?'

'-Those nonsensical love quotes which you've posted from

the non existent Raghu school of love are really hilarious...
especially the last one about the "love scientist"!'

As evening arrived, Raghu had managed to get more than
just a basic response for his various updates.

In fact, lots of comments, likes, and congratulatory
reactions poured in, which made him feel really happy.
Reactions such as-'Raghu! You actually wrote a book? Wow!',
'Congrats! Can't wait to read it', 'Catchy title', 'Interesting
story blurb', 'Nice cover design', 'Will pick up a copy for
sure', 'Way to go' etc.

His love quotes in particular were a big hit and got
entertaining reactions from his virtual friends. Reactions
such as- 'Raghu, are you seriously trying to be the new love
guru on the block? I think the world is coming to an end...
ha ha', 'Raghu, what do you even know about love? Are
you referring to ishq vala love or sex vala love or ishq-vishq
marriage garland mala-vala love? Waiting to read your book
to find out ☺'

The more he thought about it, the more he realized he had
no idea about the 'concept or definition' of love. He had just
written the book without thinking too much! Just as actors
played characters like army officers or sportsmen in reel
life with only a bit of real life research thrown in, similarly
even he had written a love story operating within an overall
framework of love as depicted in movies he had seen, without
ever having been in love!

A couple of additional thoughts came to his mind as he
received all this awesome feedback-

Were these positive reactions also going to translate into a
definite pre-order purchase of his book?

Or was it just a case of people 'liking and commenting' on

his updates in the same way they 'liked and commented' on hundreds of other posts each day on Facebook?

He had no way of finding out.

By the end of the day, a few of his other school friends, college friends and even some relatives gave him a call to congratulate him.

Even his irritating distant relative Gopi gave him a call to congratulate him.

'Congrats Raghu! I knew you had it in you to become an author. Do send me an autographed free copy. I would like to read it in my free time. Who knows? You might become very famous and forget all of us in Erode,' Gopi said, full of fake praise for him.

'Free copy, my ass!' he replied.

While he wanted to say that, what he actually did end up saying was, 'Sure Uncle. I will try to send you a free, autographed copy of my book.'

Over the next few days, he witnessed an unexpected demand for a 'free copy' of his book in the 'well-wisher' category of people! As supportive as they were of his creative endeavour, they were surprisingly cautious about putting their hand into their trouser pocket to whip out a hundred rupee note out of their wallet, to support a debutant author like him!

These same 'well-wishers' however never once hesitated in taking out a hundred rupee note while having an overpriced cup of coffee in a coffee shop!

He realized that this was the flipside of having an affordable price point of just hundred rupees for a novel! It was so cheap and affordable that people in this category thought that he would present them with a free copy and in return would be more than happy to receive their 'blessings'!

While he was more than happy to get their blessings, he really didn't want 'free copy' blessings!

He really had to filter through the 'free copy' requests!

In one case, a genuine 'well-wisher' had a valid concern-

'Raghu, I don't know how to order a copy of your book online. As you know, my knowledge in these matters is very poor. Each time my finger touches a computer keyboard, my hands tremble and get the equivalent of stage fright. My mobility is also restricted. It prevents me from walking to a bookstore. So please send me a copy.'

In this case, he was more than happy to send a free copy and get genuine blessings in return.

In another case, a not so genuine 'well-wisher', didn't seem to have a valid concern-

'Raghu, as you know I'm a voracious reader. I read four to five books at a time. Send me a copy of your book. I will read it and return it back to you in five days. Alternatively if possible, send me your manuscript in Word or as a PDF attachment by email right away!'

In this case the request for a free copy was rejected. *He was not a lending library! He was an author with a moderately sized ego who had slogged like a dog to write the book!*

Three days before release...

Raghu received an email from his publisher stating that the pre-order demand for the book from the various online sites had been pretty good over the past few days.

He was relieved.

So clearly, people were placing orders!

He was really thankful and humbled by this pre-release interest for his book.

In the email, it was also mentioned that his author copies (a free set of copies of the book which an author gets from the publisher) had already been dispatched by courier and would be reaching him in a day's time. Also copies of his book, fresh off the printing press were in transit to reach the various leading bookstores across the country.

After checking his email, he logged on to Facebook to check for new likes and comments for his various updates.

He noticed that he had received a rather strange FB message from Sweety which read:

Raghu, looks like some of us haven't bothered to stay in touch and have conveniently forgotten the people who prayed for them, who counselled them and wished the best for them.

And by the way, do you even know what true love is?

Isn't it easier to trivialize a beautiful feeling like love in the form of inane love quotes than actually feeling it in your heart?

Is it because you have never experienced it?

Many times, we fail to recognize the co-pilots who change the course of our life. They may be right in your vicinity but you may not even be aware…

He didn't know what to make of this cryptic message, especially the latter part of it.

He left the message unanswered.

He went to sleep.

Two days before release....

Raghu received the courier which contained his author copies.

He ripped open the cover. There were ten copies in all.

He held a copy of his own creation-*The Paperback Badshah* in his hands for the first time!

He felt emotional.

What a feeling!

He lovingly opened the book.

He first glanced at the acknowledgements page in which he had thanked his wonderful parents and friends. He then flipped quickly through the rest of the book. All in all, 65,500 odd words of *The Paperback Badshah* were nicely packed in 243 pages, in a very 'reader friendly' layout so that a reader could easily finish the book in three to four hours!

He told his mother about the arrival of the copies.

She sounded emotional and gave him a hug. He also called up his father who was at work and informed him about the arrival of the copies. His father sounded really excited on hearing this bit of news.

It was a happy family moment.

DISTRIBUTION

The D-Day arrived!

Raghu posted a new update on Facebook. It read:

The Paperback Badshah is out in the real world today. Those of you who have pre-ordered a copy, will be receiving your copy during the course of the day. Those of you who haven't yet purchased a copy, do place an order online right away or alternatively do visit a bookstore to grab your copy.

He also uploaded a few photos of his author copies.

Both updates got a lot of instant likes and comments.

The moment got to him. *He suddenly started feeling very nervous.*

A few questions came to his mind.

Would his book fly off the shelves in the various bookstores?

Would his email inbox explode with fan mail?

And most importantly…what would be the verdict on his writing?

Would it be a thumbs up or a thumbs down from a reader?

During the early part of the afternoon, he decided to visit a few bookstores.

Just as actors visited movie halls to gauge the audience reactions, similarly he wanted to observe first hand reactions to his book.

The adrenaline in him suddenly started to pump.

He was going to see his own book in a bookstore! How exciting!

He first went to the small bookshop near his home in Jayanagar itself from where he had purchased *The Girl with the Dragon Tattoo* for Roma.

Excitedly, he entered the bookshop and walked straight to the 'New Arrivals' section to see copies of *The Paperback Badshah. However, he couldn't spot any!*

He looked around again.

He still couldn't find any.

He then walked to the 'Indian Fiction Writing' section. His book wasn't even there!

Where the fuck was it then?

He walked up to an attendant who was arranging some books.

He made a polite enquiry about his book and proudly announced that he was the author.

The attendant looked at him with some sort of new found respect.

'So where's the book?' he asked the attendant.

'Sir, we don't stock Hindi titles.'

'Arrey...*The Paperback Badshah* is a book in English. Check your database.'

The attendant checked the database on his computer.

'Sir, the title is not reflecting.'

'Check again.'

'Sir, it is out of stock.'

'You just said it's not reflecting! Now you are saying it's out of stock? How can it be out of stock when today is the first day of release?'

The attendant made some weird 'I am confused' type faces at him, which reminded him of the kind of faces he also used to make during his management exams!

He realized that it didn't make sense spending any more time in the shop. He smiled, said a quick 'thanks' to the confused attendant and walked out of the bookshop.

He decided to go check out a bookstore in JP Nagar.

Half an hour later, he reached the bookstore in JP Nagar.

He entered cautiously and walked to the 'New Arrivals' section. His book wasn't there!

This was just too much!

This time he walked up to a store attendant, ready to download some angst and irritation.

'Where's *The Paperback Badshah*?' It was more of a command than a polite enquiry at his end.

The store attendant glared at him but surprisingly the query seemed to register.

The attendant started walking towards the 'Yoga Books' section!

He followed him.

In the 'Yoga Books' section, the attendant pointed at some books lying right at the bottom of a rack and then walked away for some other work.

Raghu felt bad seeing his book in this condition!

Four copies of *The Paperback Badshah* were located in what seemed like the lower most, back breaking corner of the bookstore! His book screamed out for his attention-'*Hi*

Raghu...look...look...look...I'm your book...at least you please give me a look...'

He walked down another aisle in the bookstore.

It was again the same story.

He spotted two copies of his book in the lower most rack of the 'Self-Help' section. In another corner, three copies were stocked in the 'Murder and Crime' section!

He walked to the 'Indian Fiction Writing' section.

No copies were there!

Copies of his book were located haphazardly in various sections except in the 'New Arrivals' and the 'Indian Fiction Writing' section, which were the most important sections!

If this was the strategic positioning of his book on the first day of release, he shuddered to even think about where his book would be located in the store, in the days to come, when new titles published by other authors would arrive!

Readers would never know about his book!

It would be a classic case of out of sight, out of mind!

He didn't want that to happen.

He decided to take charge.

He carried five copies of *The Paperback Badshah* and walked towards the store attendant who had earlier shown him the location of his book. He told the attendant that his book was a new arrival and had to be placed only in the 'New Arrivals' or in the 'Indian Fiction Writing' section but not in any other section.

The store attendant made a totally uninterested 'pissed off' face at him which seemed to suggest the following-'*Fuck off, man. Why are you making such an issue about the location of a stupid book? Get out of your dream world. No one except you-the stupid author...gives a damn about the location of the book. Let me give you a reality check instead. It's simple demand-supply economics at work. Successful authors get more coverage and front shelf display. You are a small time author. Deal with it. Your book will be placed in whatever little space is available, only after the more commercially successful books are placed! Such is life. So please don't feel bad. Take this "retail book location injustice" in your stride. And most importantly...please don't cry! At least not here! Go home and cry. Thanks. Bye.'*

Raghu vaguely understood the non-verbal message communicated to him by the attendant! He just left the copies of his book on the attendant's desk and walked out of the bookstore.

He felt really bad.

If this was the nature of the book distribution and availability in only two stores in Bangalore...what about the rest of the country? Maybe like Mr. Prasad, even he needed to carry a 'chaddi suitcase' loaded with copies of *The Paperback Badshah* and go door to door as a book salesman to promote and distribute the book! He even thought of a jingle he could sing while selling the book-*Ruk...ruk...ruk...hello dear reader... please give me a look...my name is Raghu...i'm the author of this book...please buy my book or at least please have a look.....!*

REACTION

Three days later.

It was just before noon.

Raghu pumped his fist in the air.

He had just finished reading an email sent by a reader about *The Paperback Badshah*!

It was his first reader reaction.

The email read as follows-

'Raghu....I frankly haven't laughed so much while reading a book as I did while reading *The Paperback Badshah*. The plot is simple to understand and is well organized. The best part of the book is the timepass humour which perfectly complements the beautiful love story. I hope it's read by one and all!'

He felt really happy reading this email!

He almost felt like he was levitating a few feet above ground level!

The book distribution and availability issues didn't matter anymore. *This sort of incredible feedback from a reader mattered much more.*

During the evening, while casually surfing the net, he came across a critical review of his book on a site. A reader had ripped his book apart totally. From being in a levitating state a while ago, he was now cut to size and brought back firmly to sweaty ground zero!

The detailed ripping by the reader read as follows-

I'm shocked by the alarming fall in the quality of Indian fiction writing in today's times. I'm generally a reader of serious, high quality literary fiction but a couple of days back, I happened to come across a link regarding a book called *The Paperback Badshah (TPB)* which appeared on a friend's Facebook wall. The link got me interested and I ended up buying the book given its affordable price point. Reading this book made me realize why the phrase 'toilet reading' came into existence! The book lacks a basic plot and fails to engage a reader intellectually. I'm sorry to say this but this is one of the worst books I have ever read.

Let me tell you why-

The plot of *TPB* is a story of two runaway lovers who face parental opposition and then eventually reunite with their families in the end. While this genre of runaway love stories have been done to death in sugary romantic novels as well as the movies, what makes *TPB* deserve special mention is its idiotic story line. The story line is worse than that of a B-grade Bollywood movie!

As a plot, it lacks depth and the expression of any real feelings between the runaway lovers, Alok and Alka. Their struggles as lovers through the various chapters in the book are poorly depicted. I get the feeling that the author, Raghu Balakrishnan spent little or no time at all in developing the characters. Also instead of trying to keep the plot from moving ahead, Raghu unnecessarily digresses to some random subplots. What makes matters worse is that he loads the book with a lot of juvenile humour which gets really irritating after a point.

Without giving away too many details from the non-existent plot, there are however specific parts of the book, which I certainly have to mention!

Let me begin with a poorly written love making scene right in the first part of *The Paperback Badshah*. This is how Raghu describes the scene:

"Alok and Alka were finally in the barn. Alok was hurriedly unfastening his pyjama strings while humming the song 'a aa e ee o o o mera dil na todo' from the superhit movie Raja Babu. Alka while undressing asks him, 'So are you all set to make the descent to the promised land?'

'Which land? Thailand, New Zealand or Switzerland?' he asks.

'I'm talking about my promised land...'

'Oh ok...that one. Let the descent begin...'

Minutes later, Alok's natural secretions finally find a comforting home in the confines of Alka's dense vegetation.

After the act, in the middle of the night, Alok mumbles gibberish to himself in his sleep: 'My kala cobra had got lost in a dense jungle...Hissss. Can someone please help me find a zebra?'

The next morning Alok is in high spirits.

'Alka my baby...my jaan...my jaanu, I don't want to stop. The next time I want to do "it" in a Maruti van and then in a slow moving caravan,' he tells her.

'Stop it you sex craving machine,' she replies.

'I'm not a sex craving machine. I'm a love machine. I don't think I will ever become a cricket run machine or a money machine. So maybe God has decided to make me a 24/7 love machine.'

'Ok fine. The next time we'll do "it" next to a washing machine.'

'Yes! Thank you, my zindagi…my love heera…my love jal jeera, my love tonic. You are simply the best! Can you please give me one more bosom jhappi and thanks again for the truly awesome night time masti! You are indeed a mahaan hasti. Maybe we should also consider doing "it" in a basti….'

'Alok, please stop! I want to discuss something important about our future together…'"

Is this seriously Raghu's imagination at work?-

Kala cobra-zebra? Love heera-love jal jeera? Bosom jhappi-night time masti-mahaan hasti-basti?

This is complete nonsense!

He has made a complete mockery of a tender love making moment of passion between the college lovers.

If you ask me, I want to flush him and his moronic imagination down a toilet. His description is frankly low quality trash which doesn't merit any further importance.

Moving on to other aspects of *TPB*.

Chapter after chapter in *TPB* is spent describing Chintu's (Alok and Alka's son) friendship with a small white tiger!

What is the relevance of this friendship to the main plot?

There is no relevance. It is complete nonsense!

Can the plot get anymore absurd?

In this book, it surely can!

Another chapter is devoted to how Alka loses her post pregnancy weight. In this chapter, Raghu describes a scene in which Alka tosses Alok in the air, like a chef tossing vegetables in the air!

I was completely 'mind fucked' reading this.

This by the way is just the tip of the iceberg! Another part of the book focuses on Alok securing a fifty book deal for a love story written by him! Is it even possible to bag a fifty book deal?

The chapters which follow are equally idiotic!

I however continued to read *TPB* till the very end, hoping for some sort of improvement and also hoping for some sort of logical conclusion to the story.

But I was proven wrong!

Raghu had kept his idiotic best for the very end of the book!

In this part of the book, it is about the family reunion. During the reunion, the white tiger (which believe it or not....has now transformed into a dog!) bites the arm of the caretaker who works in Alka's house.

And you know what happens next?

Chintu reattaches the arm right back into the caretaker's shoulder socket who then starts rotating his arm like a fast bowler! The caretaker then looks in the direction of the tiger and promises to give it a daily dose of tandoori chicken, chilli chicken and butter chicken!

Does this insult your intelligence?

It certainly insulted mine.

While Raghu may have the mental maturity and intelligence of a student in third standard, surely he can't be of the view that it matches that of a general reader?

The other (and more serious) issue I had while reading *TPB* is the number of glaring errors in the book. The idiotic plot line can be forgiven to some extent, given that it's a debutant author's work. But what certainly can't be forgotten or forgiven are the number of typos, grammatical errors and spelling errors in the book! The number of errors I counted were more than the number of pimples I had on my face when I was a teenager!

What were the editor, copy editor and proofreader assigned to this book doing? Didn't they see such glaring errors staring at them in the face?

Let me take the liberty of making a sweeping generalization.

Is this book reflective of the way publishers in the hundred rupee price point segment operate? Are publishers in this segment more interested in the 'quantity' of books they publish as opposed to being interested in the 'quality' of writing in the books they publish? Just because the book is affordable and as a result easily accessible to a reader at large, does it mean that it needn't be properly edited and proofread? You decide for yourselves.

Don't tell me later that I didn't warn you.

Reading *TPB* is guaranteed to lead you to a slow mental death. I would suggest you consume rat poison instead for faster results! ☺

As Raghu reflected on the various points in the scathing review, he was really curious to know the exact number of pimples the reader had on his face as a teenager!

He wanted to ignore the criticism like it didn't matter, but the truth of the matter was that it really did matter! *It stayed locked in his mind! He never ever had thought that his book could be ripped apart at so many levels!* He wanted to tell the reader that his editor himself had confessed that he had not been in a good space 'mentally' when the book was being edited! Maybe that had resulted in the various glaring errors!

He decided to go for a walk to clear his mind.

During the walk, he came across a signboard at the main road near his home.

The signboard had a message which read-

'Do not *drunk* and drive. Do not drive on the *footbath*.'

He smiled to himself as he thought about what the critic would have to say about this message!

*

A couple of days later.

Raghu was busy emailing various bloggers and professional book reviewers to check whether they would be interested in reviewing his book. He figured that by getting some sort of coverage from them, his book would definitely be able to reach out to a larger audience.

Just as he was about to draft an email to a blogger, he got a call from Nandu.

'You fucker, you call yourself a fiction writer?' Nandu asked him.

'Yes. Why?'

'When we spoke last, you said that no character in your book is based or inspired by me.'

'Yes, I said that. But why are you asking again?'

'I'm reading your book right now. It's pretty good. It's more comedy romance than actual love story as I had expected. But getting back to my point-'

'Thanks dude. What point?'

'-Remember I told you that after a fight I once had with Kavita, I made a tiger noise "Grrr..." in the bedroom?'

'I vaguely remember. So?'

'Is the character of the white tiger in your book based on me? Are you trying to make fun of me through your writing?'

'What? Are you crazy? How can the white tiger be based on your bedroom noise? It is not as if you have been under my creative surveillance! My book is a work of fiction. The various characters were created out of my imagination after months of creative perspiration!'

'You expect me to believe that? As if, you have so much of creativity to write a full fledged novel based entirely out of your imagination. Ok, just tell me one thing.'

'What?'

'Who's this attractive chick Alka in the book based on? As far as I can assess based on our conversations, I don't think it is based on Roma or Sweety.'

Before Raghu could even respond, Nandu very seriously listed the names of twelve girls they knew from their school days, as being the likely source of inspiration! Hilarious!

'Is it any of them?' Nandu asked him.

'Dude, I just told you right? My book is a work of fiction. All I have done is to create a world for my readers.'

'Fucker, first you make fun of me through your writing and then you give me this bullshit explanation.'

'No dude. I'm telling you the truth.'

'Ok man. Don't tell. In your future books, if you are using me as a point of reference for a character, at least please use me to create an interesting character of a double agent.'

'Sure. Why not? A double agent who works twelve-fourteen hours a day on weekdays and pays telephone and electricity bills on weekends!'

Raghu burst out laughing while Nandu muttered a few cuss words.

'Dude, this interesting thing happened,' he said a few minutes later.

'Raghu, wait! Let me guess. Each time we speak, some chick matter invariably crops up. This time did silicone implants fall out of a chick's upper body on top of your head like coconuts from a tree?'

'Dude, come on. Nothing of that sort happened.'

'Then what happened?'

'Sweety sent me a message on Facebook a few days ago. She asked me whether I knew the meaning of true love.'

He told Nandu the content of the message.

'Raghu, I think she likes you...or loves you!' Nandu stated excitedly. 'I think it is her way of dropping a love hint. It is a classic, time tested approach. Go for it!'

'Go for what?'

'Ask her out, you idiot! She is interested in you. Your luck seems to be really turning around. Good for you.'

'Sweety likes me? You really think so?'

'Yes, I think you also like her but you may not have realized it. This is the unexplained element in love.'

He thought about it.

Sweety was definitely a cool, good person. He remembered he had felt happy when she had told him that she had prayed for him.

But both of them as a 'couple'?

Was there really a 'love connection'?

How come he didn't get a whiff of it earlier?

What were the cool lines to communicate while asking her out?

'Raghu, you are feeling nervous, right?' Nandu asked him, interrupting his chain of thoughts.

'No…ok, yes. I'm nervous. How did you know?'

'We have been friends from our school days, boss. You have never been a chick magnet.'

'Nor have you.'

'You are right. But thankfully in my case, Kavita came along and I'm now in a happy place. The question to be asked right now is…do you have the killer moves to impress Sweety?'

'What moves?'

'Women like guys who can sweep them off their feet, pamper them and constantly spout deadly romantic lines to them. Can you do any of this?'

'I don't know. I've never done any of this before.'

'Exactly! That's my point. Just because you have written some "medium quality" romantic lines in your book, it doesn't make you a master of the "cool" moves which work in the real world. You don't want a Roma type flop show again.'

'That's a good point.'

'Even though you made fun of me in your book, I'm willing to help you out, if you want. Marriage has given me some good insight into the complex yet enjoyable world of relationships. If you are interested, I can conduct a quick "relationship readiness" quiz for you.'

'Really? You actually have something like that?'

'Yes, I do.'

'So is this what you really do when you keep grunting that you are always loaded with office work?'

Raghu burst out laughing again.

'Stop laughing you fucker. Let's meet for lunch tomorrow and I'll conduct the quiz. If you fail the quiz, the joke will be on you and I will be the one laughing.'

✳

The next day.

Raghu and Nandu were at Barbeque Nation in JP Nagar and had just begun a tasty buffet lunch.

'So Raghu, are you ready for the quiz? Are you ready to form the love connection with Sweety?' Nandu asked.

'I'm somewhat ready,' Raghu replied. 'But what do I have to do?'

'All you have to do is answer my questions. Your answers will determine whether or not you are relationship ready. So let's begin?'

'Cool.'

'Question number one for you- the *"how to prioritize"* question: An important cricket match is coming live on TV. Your parents are howling about something in the background. Sweety is calling you on your mobile. And you are getting irritated because you can't watch the match in silence. So what will you do?'

'I'll obviously give importance to the match.'

'You have spoken like a true cricket fan. May your tribe

increase! But that's the wrong answer…if you want to be in a relationship! The right thing to do is to pick up Sweety's phone call.'

'But…'

'Please don't argue with me! Moving on to question number two- the *"sacrifice and compromise"* question: In a healthy relationship, is love more about compromise or sacrifice?'

'A combination of both…I guess.'

'That's the correct answer, Raghu! Good going! Moving on to question three- the *"care"* question: If you are wearing a jacket because you are feeling cold and Sweety sitting next to you also suddenly starts feeling cold…what will you do?'

'Dude, she's built like a polar bear. She will never feel cold! But I will still ask her if she is feeling cold.'

'Is that your answer? That's a horribly insensitive answer! The right answer is to give her your jacket.'

'But if I do that, I will feel cold!'

'Once you are in a relationship, the focus is not on you. It is on Sweety and her needs and her interests. If you are feeling cold…you freeze! Who cares? You make noises out of your mouth like "Brrr…" or "Grrr…" or put your hands in your pocket and play pocket billiards.'

'That's pretty brutal.'

'It's meant to be. Moving on to question four- the *"together-together"* question: In a relationship, is giving space to each other more important or is doing activities "together-together" most of the time, more important?'

'Doing things "together-together", I guess? If I was doing everything all by myself, then why be in a relationship?'

'That's a fantastic answer, Raghu! You are correct. But remember as the relationship progresses with time, it is also very important to give space to one another. In yours and Sweety's case...I'm talking of not just emotional space but also physical space...given your respective big sizes...ha ha.'

'Hilarious! That's true!'

'Ok, back to the quiz. Moving on to question five- the *"relationship direction"* question: If Sweety asks you where do you see this relationship heading? What will you answer?'

'I'll tell her let's take it one romantic step at a time.'

'That's a fair answer. You guys should do combined emotional discussions before progressing to the next level. Moving on to question six- the *"comfort zone"* question: If Sweety asks you to relocate to her city of work, will you? Will you put her interests ten to twelve levels above your own interests?'

'Let me think.'

'Tick tock...tick tock. Bhaisaab, samay chala ja raha hai. Uttar dey dijiye. Keyboardji mein lock karna hai.'

'I thought in the quiz show on TV, it is computerji mein lock karna hai?'

'Raghu what the fuck is your problem? This is a quiz designed by me. In my quiz, it is keyboardji and not computerji. Now, just focus on my question and answer quickly!'

'I'll ask Sweety if we can both stay in Bangalore as I'm sure I'll miss home comforts. Or I'll speak to her if we can figure out a long distance solution.'

'It's an honest answer from you, but I'm afraid it's the wrong answer! Enough of sitting at home all the time! It's time for you to get out of your comfort zone! In Hindi movies, when the girl leaves her parents house, she always cries properly. I think you will be the first guy who will cry in an over the top manner when you leave your room, your house and your home comforts! Ha ha!'

'I guess you are right. But I've never understood why people always say it's necessary to leave one's comfort zone to discover one's true self, especially when, at the end of the day, the "home" is where the heart is!'

'Raghu, I've no time to listen to your philosophy. Focus on the quiz instead. Moving on to question seven- the *"sense of humour"* question. It has two parts. The first part: What will you do if Sweety finds your sense of humour very silly and keeps telling you repeatedly to grow up and behave like a mature adult? Will you clam up and stay quiet or continue with your nonsense whether or not she likes it?'

'Firstly, I think I have a decent sense of humour. Secondly, I don't think I speak too much of nonsense.'

'Really? That is what you think! Two incidents from the past just came to my mind.'

'What incidents?'

'Remember in 9th standard, during a class discussion that girl Pushpalata said that she was a *feminist* and you remarked out of context that you are an *optimist*? Remember in 10th standard, the discussion we had on religious beliefs and the presence of God in which Riya stated that she's an *atheist* to which you remarked, again out of context that you are a *love scientist*?'

'Oh dude. Those were deadly times! But what's the point you are trying to make?'

'The point I'm trying to make is that women find such juvenile comments, remarks, jokes highly annoying and frankly very stupid. We are now in our twenties but you still keep cracking these type of jokes. Even Roma called you a man-child. It's seriously time for you to grow up. The woman of today wants a guy who is suave, sophisticated, classy, well travelled, well informed, cultured and mature. Think it over.'

'Dude, I know I'm not the suave, classy or sophisticated kind. Speaking a little sense and a fair bit of nonsense has always been my natural style. You are asking me to curb my natural style. It's like asking Sehwag or Gayle to not belt sixes and only defend all day.'

'Ok fine. Don't listen to me. But don't blame me if things don't work out and don't feel bad if Sweety tells you the same things straight on your face.'

'Ok, I'll try to keep my mouth shut.'

'That's better. You have finally given the correct answer. Moving on to the second part of the question: What will you do if Sweety cracks a joke which you don't even find remotely funny?'

'I will not laugh especially if she hasn't laughed for any of my jokes.'

'Again a completely wrong answer! Whether or not she laughs for your jokes, you have to laugh for her jokes. Humour is a very important part in a relationship especially if it's the woman who is cracking the joke. That's my personal experience. The other day, Kavita cracked this really lame PJ and started laughing loudly. I didn't even find it funny but I still laughed along. She felt really happy.'

'What did she say?'

'Her PJ was: "Why do cricketers go to the cricket field?" I had no idea. Her answer was: "Because they don't go to office."'

'That's lame.'

'It is, but that's besides the point. The important thing is to laugh. Moving on to question eight- the *"honesty"* question:

Just imagine you and Sweety are playing that stupid "spin the bottle" or any of the other nonsense "truth or dare" type love games. Your turn comes and she asks you, "Raghu, which feature of mine, do you like best?" What will you answer?'

'Let me think.'

He started to think about Reema and Seema.

'Raghu, I'm getting the feeling that you are thinking of a feature which is highly inappropriate to be stated in public. So I guess, it is yet another wrong answer!'

'How did you know?'

'Why do you think I am coaching you?'

'Not bad, dude. Good observation skills. So what should I answer?'

'Restrict your answer to one among the following- "your smile", "your eyes", "your hairstyle" or your "personality".'

'So basically I have to give a fake answer. But isn't honesty the best policy?'

'No Raghu. LIC insurance policy is the best policy. Ha ha...ok, I'm sorry. Honesty is indeed the best policy but not in such matters. Being diplomatic is much more important. Do you want her to think of you as a horny human being who has only vulgar thoughts in his mind even though it fits in nicely with our existing depraved kalyug times?'

'No, I don't.'

'That's better. A quick example to illustrate further: Whenever Kavita asks me, "Nandu, am I looking fat? Have I put on weight?" I always reply, "Kavi, you have never looked better." She smiles. I smile. Both of us know it's a fake answer but still both of us feel happy! My fake answer has worked every single time. Touchwood. Imagine if I tell her, "You eat so much. I eat so much. Both of us don't exercise and to top it, we sit on our ass for over ten hours a day at work...then how the fuck will we ever lose weight?" If I give this honest answer...it will be game over.'

'Wow dude! This example did make a lot of sense. So the bottom line is to tell white lies in such matters.'

'Exactly. Moving on to question nine: the *"emotional"* question- Imagine Sweety feels emotional about something and then starts crying. When you ask her "what happened?" she sniffs a little and says "nothing happened" even though you know clearly that something has happened. So what will you do?'

'Crying for serious issues like someone's ill heath, death etc. or candy floss Hindi movie sniffing and crying?'

'I'm sure that on serious issues you will be genuinely supportive and understanding of the situation. But my question is more regarding issues which are typically perceived to be non serious for a guy.'

'Ok, in that case, I'll wait till she's ready to tell me what has happened.'

'That's again the wrong answer!'

'What! Why?'

'It is a good answer in a practical sense but it's the wrong answer under the circumstances.'

'So what the hell should I do?'

'You should sit in the corner of the room and say something like "don't worry...don't worry...it will all be ok" about twenty times to gently facilitate the download of the emotional problem.'

'Ok, I guess. But is it really necessary? Initially when I got my book rejections, no one even knew or cared. Even I was really sad. But I managed. Going forward, what if I get emotional and want to cry at the same time Sweety wants to cry? Who should be given more importance?'

'Who cares whether you want to cry or not? She is more important. If you want to cry, go put your head in the toilet or go sit on a park bench, talk to a butterfly and cry. No one wants to know.'

'Dude, that's rude.'

'Rude or crude, that's your problem, boss! Moving on to question ten: the *"big fight"* question-If you have just had a big fight with Sweety, will you apologize first?'

'But who started the fight?'

'Why should that be important?'

'Why should that *not be* important? If I've not started the fight… why should I apologize first?'

'Yet another wrong answer! A happy relationship is all about dissolving the "ego" and repeating the word "sorry" about 200 times in a year. Place it firmly in your memory bank.'

'But I thought there is "No sorry, no thank you" in love and friendship? I heard this awesome dialogue in *Maine Pyar Kiya*.'

'That was in a superhit movie. This is real life. Have you ever seen a pigeon deliver a love letter in real life?'

'Never.'

'Then it's better if you listen to me. By the way the song, *Kabootar ja ja ja* from the movie is really awesome.'

'It is. How many questions left?'

'You think I'm free all day or what to waste my time? Ten questions are more than enough.'

'Ok. I just hope I remember some of this gyaan when I meet Sweety.'

'That's your problem. Once you are a couple, the real fun begins. You will enjoy the beautiful realities of a healthy relationship with its glorious ups and downs.'

'Let's hope for the best. By the way, how did I do in the quiz?'

'You gave only 3.5 correct answers. So that means, you just passed with 35%!'

'So I guess I really have to improve on a lot of fronts.'

'Of course you have to. But for participating in this quiz, keyboardji will send you a cheque for ten rupees to your residential address…ha ha.'

'That's funny.'

'Raghu, jokes apart, I'm going to give a final bit of serious gyaan right now before we leave.'

'What?'

'My experience has taught me that a happy relationship is not about raw hot body lust but true tender love. Lust is short term and like rust. It complicates and corrodes the human mind. True love is long term. It calms the human mind. It is more important than lust and more precious and valuable than gold dust. I'm telling you…Sweety is a good, big built woman of today who really seems to care for you.'

'Dude! This is some intense stuff. Did you just make it up?'

'No, I'm dead serious. I believe in it 100%. And I do believe in spite of your really low quiz score, you are relationship ready.'

Just as Nandu said that, Raghu saw something *which he was not ready for.*

He saw Roma!

She looked as attractive as ever. She had just entered the restaurant with a guy whose appearance suggested that he was still in college! *A real man-child!* They seated themselves at a fair distance away from Raghu's table.

'Raghu, where are you lost? Who are you looking at?' Nandu asked him.

'Dude, that's her.'

'Who?'

'The woman over there,' Raghu said, pointing feebly in the direction of a table. 'That's Roma.'

'Roma's here? Let me see…let me see.'

'Control yourself, dude.'

'That's Roma? Wow! *She's hot.* Why don't you go say hi?'

'No dude. Can't you see she's busy with someone? It will be awkward. Plus there's nothing much to say after she threw me out of her house. More importantly, I want to now hang out with Sweety.'

'Ok. But Romaaaaaa…is damn hot.'

'You just gave me gyaan on love-lust, gold dust-rust and the way you are staring at her really puts your gyaan to test…'

Raghu stopped mid sentence as he noticed the man-child whisper something into Roma's ear which induced a giggly smile from her. The man-child then got up and started walking in the direction of the restroom.

Raghu's mind went into overdrive.

Roma had never mentioned a brother. It couldn't be her son! It certainly wasn't her buddah husband! Was the man-child a cousin, a friend or a new boyfriend?

He wanted to know even though it was none of his business.

'Nandu, I'll be back,' he remarked as he walked hurriedly towards the restroom.

In the restroom he saw the man-child at a urinal. He stood in the adjacent urinal, to the man-child's right.

'Hey, have we met before at Roma's party?' he asked the man-child point blank. He knew that such a direct question would definitely elicit a reaction out of the man-child.

'I've never been to any of Roma's parties. But how do you know Roma????' the man-child asked with a look of surprise on his face.

'We have common friends. I'm Karthik, by the way,' Raghu lied.

'I'm Murali,' the man-child mumbled while hurrying up.

'Are you her cousin? She's never mentioned you before.'

'No...no...I'm not her cousin. I'm her friend. I met her at a poetry workshop a couple of days ago.'

'Writing workshop or poetry workshop?'

'I said poetry workshop.'

'Oh ok. Roma is now into poetry? Nice. Is she around?'

'No...no...she isn't. She must be at her place. I've come for lunch here with my college friends.'

What a liar!

'Ah...ok. Carry on.'

Murali walked out of the restroom.

Raghu thought to himself.

Was Roma zeroing in on her Mr. Right from a younger age group?

If yes, good for her! Lage raho responsibly and enjoyably!

But strangely enough when she had thrown him out of her house, she had called him a man-child as she wanted a *real man* but now she was going around with Murali, a real 'college going' man-child!

As he came out of the washroom, he bumped into Nandu.

'Raghu, I've settled the bill. Let's leave.'

He nodded. With one final look in the direction of a table which seated an attractive woman and a man-child, he followed Nandu out of the restaurant.

Later that evening, he was checking his email.

He hadn't received any new book reactions but he had received a couple of emails from book reviewers he had written to. They were interested to read and review his book. He decided to send them a copy for a review.

After checking his email, he began checking updates of his various friends on Facebook. He noticed that Sweety was online on FB chat.

He decided to seize the moment.

Raghu: Hi Sweety. What's up?

There was no response.

A minute later, he got a reply.

Sweety: I'm here. It looks like some of us have been super busy of late.

Raghu: Look, I'm really sorry. I was genuinely tied up with my book related work. But I know that's no excuse. Can we meet? I've got things to discuss and express.

Sweety: What do you want to discuss and express? Tell me.

Raghu: Can't tell you over chat. Can we meet instead?

Sweety: Oh. It's not a good time. I'm leaving for Delhi tonight and then to Chandigarh. I've got three weddings to attend followed by a quick family holiday. I'll be back in a month's time. We can meet then.

Raghu: Ok ☹. By the way, have you picked up this book *The Paperback Badshah* written by this author, Raghu Balakrishnan? I was just wondering… ☺

Sweety: No, I haven't yet read it. Congrats though. I went to one store and it wasn't available. I went to another store and the attendant said it was sold out.

Raghu: Sold out? Wow!

Sweety: Don't get too excited. The store had stocked only two copies.

Raghu: Oh. Maybe you should order it online...wait, instead may I have the pleasure of gifting you a copy when we meet? ☺

Sweety: Sure, why not. By the way, what's happened to you? How come you are being so nice? Are you high or something after drinking a mug of beer? ☺ ☺

Raghu: No. It's just that I've had a moment of clarity. I'm a changed man. I'm thankful to you for having ignited the positive change in me.

Sweety: Whatever. I'll go finish my packing now. We'll meet once I'm back.

Raghu: We should and we will. Jai ho ☺

He smiled to himself as he logged out off Facebook. He had never used so many smilies in a single chat conversation, ever before! Thoughts about him and Sweety as a 'couple' slowly started to envelop his mind.

CELEBRATION

One month later.
It was around eleven in the morning.

Raghu was in his room.

The verdict was out!

He had just received an update from his publisher that *The Paperback Badshah* had sold over 10,000 copies! And in addition to the sales figures, the book also featured in the 'Top 5 bestselling books' list of three newspapers and in the 'Bestselling books' list of various online book sites!

This sort of commercial validation was beyond his wildest dreams.

The people of India had supported him.

Clearly despite the pockets of criticism, popular opinion seemed to suggest that readers were enjoying *The Paperback Badshah* as a quick, timepass read!

He felt truly overwhelmed. *As a writer, what more could he ask for?*

He ran out of his room to inform his mother about these fantastic book developments.

His mother gave him a hug. She certainly did feel proud of his achievement. He then called up his father who was at work. His father also felt super proud.

'Raghu, someone at work just sent me this inspiring quote as an email forward- *Remember in the rat race, even if you win, you are still a rat. So instead, always run with the lions. No matters even if you are defeated, you are still a lion.'*

He couldn't believe it!

What awesome father-son 'book sales' bonding on the phone!

Clearly the achievement had even made his father emotional and had finally made his father believe that he had done something cool with his life even though it wasn't job related!

The one other person he was excited about sharing this 'book sales' news to, was Sweety. She was back in Bangalore after her vacation. He was meeting her later in the day, in the same pub in Koramangala where they had met previously.

During the later part of the afternoon, he went to the bookstore in JP Nagar (the same store in which, copies of his book had been stacked haphazardly in the various corners) to check out the availability of his book.

This time he was in for a pleasant surprise.

He not only found his book in the 'New Arrivals' and in the 'Indian Fiction Writing' section, but also found it in the 'Top 5 books of the month' section!

Everything (including the retail book distribution) was finally falling in place!

'Look...Look...Look...that's my book!' he shouted to no one in particular.

The security guard gave him a quizzical look.

In the 'New Arrivals' section, he noticed that his book was in good company.

On its immediate left was a book on yoga in which a woman in hot pants was on the cover. On its immediate right was a book on cooking in which an attractive woman holding a saucepan in hand was on the cover.

He picked up a copy of his own book and admired it.

His book was now well and truly available in the public domain and competing fairly successfully with the other books for a reader's attention!

He moved away and then walked to the 'Top 5 books of the month' section.

His book was in the fifth position. In first position was TB's book *Hey politician...r u getting a hard-on when the legislative assembly is on?* which was still topping various bestseller lists, so many months after its release!

A few thoughts suddenly came to his mind.

Just as TB's books had played an important part in motivating him to write a novel, would *The Paperback Badshah* also motivate someone to write a book someday?

Just like TB, could he also envisage a bigger role for himself among the youth of this great nation?

Actually, he had ideas for a series of self-help books in mind which he felt would strike a chord with the youth. As he thought about his self-help book ideas, he noticed a guy and a girl walk to the 'New Arrivals' section, in the direction of his book!

They looked like they were in college or just out of college. The guy's arm was merrily wrapped around the girl's waist, which seemed to suggest that they were a couple.

The guy scanned the list of new arrivals on display and immediately picked up *The Paperback Badshah*! He seemed interested to buy the book after reading the story blurb but he wasn't able to arrive at a decision. Lost in thought, he first scratched an itch on his face. He then put a finger in his nose before finally arriving at a decision. He decided to consult his girlfriend. He removed the finger from his nose and poked her on her hip to get her attention!

She first gave him a quick two minute lecture on public manners. Then she listened to what he had to say. He handed the book to her. She read the story blurb on the back cover. The contents seemed to interest her. She nodded in approval.

The guy smiled. *The high command had given the approval!*

Raghu was really thrilled as he then saw the couple walk towards the billing counter, with his book in hand! This was the first time he was seeing someone purchase his book in front of his own eyes!

Half an hour later, he came out of the bookstore.

On the footpath, a few metres away from the bookstore, he spotted a roadside bookseller selling pirated books. He walked up to the bookseller who was proudly displaying the latest set of pirated books. He had a quick glance at the display and noticed that even *The Paperback Badshah* was very much in stock!

He picked up a copy and flipped through it.

Two chapters right in the middle of the book were missing! *Clearly even book piracy had a hierarchy!* Books written by the top authors were well pirated unlike books written by small time-first time authors!

He handed the book back to the bookseller.

He politely enquired about the price.

The bookseller told him that the book was selling 'decently' and was available for just sixty rupees!

He smiled and started to walk away.

As he walked away, he heard the bookseller scream in his direction and explain that he had 'monthly book sales targets' to meet and was willing to make a one time exception and sell the book at a revised price of fifty rupees!

Twenty minutes later, he reached home.

His mother was watching a beauty contest on TV.

In the beauty contest, he noticed that every contestant was winning an award for something or the other. One contestant was declared a winner for the 'best smile', one for 'best body', one for 'best teeth', one for 'best hairstyle', one for best 'underarms', one for best 'forearms', one for 'best set of legs', one for 'best look in western wear', one for 'best look in Indian ethnic wear', one for 'best look in a swimsuit' and so on...

A thought came to his mind.

Would he ever win an award for *The Paperback Badshah*? For instance-'The debutant author of the year award in the hundred rupee segment?'

An hour later, his father came home from work.

'Congratulations to one of India's rising literary stars!' his father told him, sounding really proud.

He nodded casually as he basked in this new found attention thanks to the successful completion of his creative endeavour.

'So Raghu, since you've finally achieved your big book dream, I'm sure you now have a new purpose....a new mission.'

'Yes, I do have a new mission.'

'That's good to know. So looks like you are *finally* excited about getting back to work?'

'Oh. Not really. Actually I was thinking about taking more time off to focus on my second book. After completing that, I shall get back to work.'

'WHAT!!!!!'

'What "WHAT"? You only told me to be a lion and run with the lions. You told me this in the morning!'

'RAGHU! YOU HAVE NO BRAINS OR WHAT? Are you an idiot? I praise you a little and you talk like this? A few copies of your book have sold and you want to write another book? Are you going to be sitting at home...again? This is too much!'

He was at a loss for words. *Was all that emotional father-son 'book sales' phone call bonding just for a moment?*

'So what's this new book going to be about? Is it going to be *The Paperback Badshah-part 2* or *The Paperback Badshah-part 555*?' his father asked sarcastically.

'No. I'm actually planning to write a series of self-help books for youngsters, to help them tackle their various problems in life. I have a few ideas which I want to work on.'

'Self-help books? Youngsters don't need your help. You need help! How can you guide them on life and career choices, when you yourself have no job?'

'The books aren't going to be just about career choices. It will cover many other topics. Let's discuss it later. Right now, I'm high on the success of *The Paperback Badshah*. I'll evaluate my options in the days to come.'

'What "options" will you evaluate? Unemployed people don't have options! Things cost money. You need to get out of the house and work....'

His father rightfully began highlighting the realities of life but thankfully the wax in his ear helped block out most of the gyaan!

'By the way, Raghu, I think there's an employment option which I think you should seriously consider,' his mother said, a few minutes later.

'What?' he asked.

'Why don't you become a personal assistant for any of these beauty contestants and carry their makeup kits, sunglasses, shoes and umbrellas? I think you will excel in such a profession,' she said, pointing at the TV screen.

Hearing this, his father burst out laughing.

This was unexpected.

Even he grinned.

It was roughly the 10,000[th] 'employment related' comment from his parents which nicely coincided with the 10k plus sales of his book! Maybe more 'employment related' comments from them would hopefully result in further book sales!

'Ok, I'm getting late. I'm going out right now,' he told his parents after the brief group laughter session for the day.

'Where are you going?' his father asked.

'Off to meet a friend.'

'Got a girlfriend or what?'

'Somewhat. It's in progress,' he replied sheepishly.

'What does that mean?'

'It's a long story.'

'Ok fine. What's her name?'

'Sweety.'

He saw his parents exchange glances and grin.

'What?' he asked his father.

'What we as parents couldn't do...a girlfriend will certainly do! Sweety will slowly but surely ensure that you *sweetly* take on lots of responsibility. All the best!'

'Let's see. I'm leaving in twenty minutes. I'll take a key. No need to stay up.'

He went to his room, had a quick shower and then wore the same white linen shirt, faded blue jeans and evening jacket which he had worn when he had gone out on his date with Roma. He then took out a packet from his wardrobe which contained two gifts for Sweety: A copy of his book and a small teddy bear which he had purchased the previous day to show his emotional, friendly and caring side.

He stepped out of his house with the packet in hand and left for Koramangala.

Half an hour later, he reached the pub in Koramangala.

He was feeling very nervous.

After all, he was now planning on expressing romantic dil ki baat matters to Sweety. But he had no clear idea of how he was going to do it. Nandu was right after all. While he had managed to write some romantic lines in *The Paperback Badshah*, in real life he just didn't know the 'cool' moves.

A few minutes later, Sweety arrived.

'Hi Sweety. How have you been?' he asked her.

'I'm good. How have you been?'

'All good. How was your trip?'

'My trip was awesome. As you can clearly see, I've put on a bit of holiday weight. I guess I need to spend more hours at my aerobics workout sessions.'

'Actually I think you have lost weight.'

He decided to follow Nandu's advice of being moderately dishonest in 'weight related' matters.

'Stop it, Raghu,' she replied smiling. 'But thanks for the compliment.'

'Wow! Nandu's relationship advice was actually working!' he thought to himself.

'So Raghu, tell me. How come we are meeting? What's the occasion?'

'I'll tell you. Shall we order something first?'

'Sure. I'll have a mug of beer. I guess you'll be having a glass of orange juice?'

He smiled. The same 'beer' comment repeated over and over again.

'No. Even I'll have a beer,' he replied.

Sweety ordered a pitcher of beer to start off along with some gobi manchurian and baby corn manchurian starters.

After the order was placed, he noticed that there was a bit of an awkward silence between them. He decided to take the initiative and come straight to the point.

'Sweety, I want to tell you something.'

'What?'

'Your Facebook message on love left me all confused. I like you. Do you also like or love me?'

'This question of yours just confirms that you are a total waste which should be eliminated at source.'

'Why?'

'Are you a child or what who needs to be explained everything? Can't you just realize some things on your own?'

'Realize what things?'

'Just forget it. Is this all one big joke for you, like those bullet points on love which you had posted on Facebook?'

'This is not a joke. But what did I do?'

'You did nothing! Now just cut your crap and listen to me. I like you.'

'Even I like you! I told you first.'

'Stop repeating like a parrot, "I like you, I like you"…'

'I'm serious. I really like you.'

'Raghu, don't try to silence me or interrupt me! I'm not a pre programmed talking doll. I'm a human being with thoughts and feelings unlike some of us, who reconnect at their own time and convenience.'

A waiter silenced them both by slamming their order on the table.

'Sweety, how was I supposed to know whether you liked or loved me?' he asked, once the waiter had left.

'Don't complicate things with your word play.'

'We can simplify things with foreplay,' he thought to himself.

'I heard that! That's totally inappropriate!'

'Can you please do me a favour?'

'What?'

'Can you please deactivate your mind reading and your talks with Seema and Reema? This is a humble request. The mind reading and boob talking gives you an unfair advantage. I can't mind read and my testicle twin brothers Ramu and Shamu down there aren't able to intercept and decode the messages which Reema and Seema keep sending you.'

'Ok fine. I promise I won't mind read anymore. But as I've told when we last met, Seema and Reema are my confidantes. They give me information which I think I'm entitled to. I don't want to end up with a Vikrant kind of loser again.'

'Fair enough. Thank God you have at least stopped the mind reading. I still think that you have the upper hand. I believe a human being should have only a right hand and a left hand.'

'Raghu, is that supposed to be funny?'

He grinned.

'Well it's not funny. It's stupid. Please don't make such immature comments.'

He stopped grinning.

Nandu was right again! Women didn't like immature jokes and comments!

'Ok Sweety. I'll try to not make such comments. Now let's get back to the topic of discussion. You were saying that you like me?'

'Yes, I do like you. In fact I've liked you since we spoke at the workshop. Then destiny distanced us. Then destiny reconnected us online when you were at your most vulnerable. Then destiny separated us again. And now destiny has brought us back together again. If these are not signals of liking and love for each other, then what is? Haven't you realized this?'

A few thoughts came to his mind.

The writing workshop seemed like a deadly *adda* for pyaar. Roma and Sweety had both noticed him there! But what was this destiny connection, reconnection and separation talk? Did destiny connect them or did a friend request on Facebook connect them? Was it really a kismet ka khel in progress?

He didn't want to bring any of this up for discussion.

'Thanks Sweety. I really had no idea. But now, I do know that I like you,' he replied eventually.

'Liking is one thing. But do you even know what "being in love" means?'

'"Love" is not meant to spoken about. It is meant to be demonstrated.'

'What an instant dialogue, Raghu sirji!' he mentally complimented himself.

'Raghu, do you mean it...or is this one of your jokes again?'

'I mean it. When I'm serious, you think it is a joke and when I joke you take it seriously.'

'Ok fine. So what does this mean?'

'This means that I'm planning to ask you out.'

'Are you serious? Oh Raghu...this is so sudden...so unexpected.'

He got up from his seat.

He shook his shoulders a bit. He then rotated his neck clockwise, anticlockwise and in an up-down manner. He then cleared his throat and started to sing '*Switty switty switty tera pyaar chaida...*' from the movie *Delhi Belly*.

'Raghu! Stop it! This is so embarrassing! People are staring at us. I thought you were going to ask me out?'

'That is what I am doing! Singing this song is my way of asking you, to be my girlfriend!'

'This is nonsense.'

'But it is genuine. I am genuine.'

'Hmm...Seema seems to approve. She just told me that your intentions seem genuine enough.'

'Of course, it is. Why would you doubt my intentions?'

'Unlike Seema, Reema thinks that you want to just do "it" with me and nothing else. I need to make certain things clear to you.'

'What?'

'I want a boyfriend who is emotionally available for me and who invests in building the relationship. Call me old school but I first want emotional connections. Not a fuck buddy as the "instant generation on the move" around us calls it. Are you ok with that?'

'I am.'

'Thanks for being understanding. I knew that you would agree. I see it in your eyes.'

'What do you see?'

'I see your dreamy eyes filled with only love and not raw lust for me.'

He suddenly thought of the gyaan Nandu had given him on love and lust.

'Sweety, love corrodes the human mind. Lust calms the human mind.'

'What?'

'Sorry…err…err…lust calms the gold dust, while rust calms the love over lust.'

'What are you blabbering?'

'I'm sorry. Let me try one final time: Love calms the mind. Lust corrodes the mind. Lust is like rust. Love is more precious than gold dust.'

'Ah! Beautiful Raghu! The writer in you is struggling to express words of love. Why couldn't you say all of this earlier? My woman instincts tell me that you seem possessive about me in a good way. I like that.'

'My manly instincts tell me that we have to forget our *basic instincts* for a while.'

He smiled. She also smiled and then slapped his hand which was on the table.

'Sweety, since you are smiling…does this mean we are now "officially" a couple?'

'Yes, we are one. You know what?'

'What?'

'I already feel that you complete me.'

'Really?'

'I feel that I don't have to act or pretend in your presence. I can just be myself. I think you really are that special someone for me, Raghu baby.'

Did he hear that correctly?

Did she just call him a baby?

What did he have to call her affectionately? Could he just call her by her name as it was 'sweet' enough?

Just then he remembered the packet which contained the gifts.

'Oh God...I completely forgot!' he exclaimed.

'What happened, baby?'

'One sec.'

He opened the packet and gave her the teddy bear.

He saw that she was getting emotional.

'Are you ok?' he asked sounding genuinely concerned.

'It's nothing.'

'What happened?' he asked again.

'It's nothing.'

He remembered Nandu's advice that when the woman is emotional, it is all about asking 'what happened' multiple times before the problem is finally downloaded. So he repeated 'what happened' a few more times.

'Ok fine. I'll tell you,' she finally said. 'This teddy reminds me of little Jimmy.'

'Oh. By the way, Jimmy had once come in my dream.'

'Raghu, don't you dare make fun of little Jimmy. I'm really attached to him emotionally.'

'I'm serious. I'm not making fun. He had come in a cricket dream of mine, when I was batting with VVS Laxman for India. He gave me his visiting card and motivated me to keep plugging away till I reach my goal.'

'How can little Jimmy come in your dream and motivate you, when you haven't ever met him? The little fellow must be drowning himself in whiskey.'

'In my dream, he was doing all right. He was enjoying himself with a model.'

'Raghu, please don't talk nonsense.'

'For a change, I'm not talking nonsense. I'm talking sense. But let's forget it. I've also got this for you,' he said, giving her a copy of *The Paperback Badshah*. 'I hope you like it.'

'Oh baby…of course I will like it.'

She flipped through the book.

'I'll read it and give you my feedback.'

'Please do. By the way, the book has sold over 10,000 copies.'

'That's really awesome! To actually write a book and for it to sell so many copies is indeed a commendable achievement. It makes you seem intellectual and all.'

'I'm no intellectual. I'm just a regular guy who has written a timepass, mass market, commercial fiction novel. Not some cutting edge, high quality literary fiction novel.'

'Awww…you are being so modest.'

'I'm not being modest. I'm being honest. The commercial success is all thanks to the wonderful readers and to that wonderful person who motivated me when I was facing my book rejections.'

'Thanks baby. I guess that would be me. Do you have any new book ideas in mind?'

'I've got quite a few ideas I want to work on.'

'That's awesome.'

He thought about it.

He wanted to write more books for his wonderful readers.

The self-help books which he had in mind were going to be a four part series which he had already titled as *The Relationship Badshah*, *The Bedroom Badshah*, *The Spiritual Badshah* and *The Boardroom Badshah*. He was itching to get cracking on *The Relationship Badshah*, in which he wanted to pass on tips to youngsters for them to be able to woo a woman of today by speaking 70% sense and 30% nonsense… the Raghu Balakrishnan way!

'Baby, give me your jacket. I'm feeling a little cold,' Sweety said, breaking his chain of thoughts.

'It's ok, Sweety. You are not that old. We are almost the same age.'

'What ok? I said, "I'm cold". Now just give me your jacket.'

'Oh.'

He gave his jacket. He remembered Nandu's relationship advice on this matter.

'Sweety, can I be honest?' he said a few minutes later.

'What?'

'Brrr….even I'm feeling cold. Maybe if we hug I'll feel warm.'

'Oh. I'm sorry, baby. Let me give you a special kissey. Maybe that'll help.'

'What's a special kissey?'

Sweety moved to the edge of her seat.

Seeing that, even he moved to the edge of his seat.

Their lips connected like a cricket ball connecting with the sweet spot of the cricket bat. It resulted in a fine, low decibel pleasurable sound which paved the way for what could only be described as a full on chumma dhamaka, which lasted for close to two minutes!

He felt triumphant!

While most guys and girls probably had their first kiss by the time they were in sixth standard and had humped by the time they were in college, he had finally had his first kiss as he was closing in on his 26th birthday! Woo-hoo! Better later than never! He was finally making some progress in the important aspects of life!

'Raghu you know something?'

'What?'

'You are a really good kisser.'

'Really? Me? Do you want me to become a serial kisser?'

'Stop! Why do you always talk nonsense and ruin a beautiful moment?'

'Ok, I'm sorry. I guess that's my natural style which I'm trying to keep in check. Can I come and sit next to you?'

'Yes, you can.'

He got up from his seat and sat next to her, to her right.

He bit his lips vulgarly and started humming the song (with additional lyrics of his own)- '*Ek aur chumma toh mujhko udhaar de de...aur badle mein...mera book royalty le le*' to signal his intent. Sweety however didn't notice and instead started whispering in a baby voice, a list of romantic things they could do as a couple in their 'together-together' time! Romantic things like:

Walking hand in hand on a rainy day; Cuddling up together on a cold day and sipping on cups of hot coffee and digging into plates of pakodas or samosas; Gazing at the stars while lying down on a mat in the balcony of her apartment; Playing hop scotch like oversized kids with the real kids in her complex and then rushing to her apartment to dig into a tub of calorie rich butterscotch; Standing in the famous *Titanic* pose with their arms stretched and feeling like the 'King and Queen' of Bangalore if not of the world!

After the romantic talk, she told him about some of her childhood stories, most of which featured her in the lead role as a 'tug of war' champion. She told him an incident in which she had single-handedly pulled six girls over the line, with just her sheer brute force! It was totally believable and he could visualize every bit of it!

Since he had been quiet for about ten minutes, he was beginning to get restless and was itching to tell her about the 'thermometer history' incident from his school days... the one in which his history teacher had pinched him and how his father had suggested that he could trap the teacher's finger under the armpit like a thermometer!

He mumbled the incident quickly and then decided to give her a live demonstration.

He stretched his left arm like an umpire signalling a no-ball and placed his forefinger of his left hand under her armpit.

'Sweety! Check this out! My finger is a thermometer!' he exclaimed with moronic glee.

'Raghu! Who cares about your bullshit school incident! What the hell are you doing?' she shouted.

'What am I doing? Look...my finger is a thermometer! Do you want to know your body temperature in Celsius or in Fahrenheit? My finger thermometer tells me that your body temperature is...'

Before he could complete, she interrupted.

'Apologize immediately, you sick pervert.'

'I'm not a pervert. I'm a moderately horny introvert who has fallen in love with a boob talking-mind reading-student counselling extrovert.'

'Just shut up and say sorry to Seema and Reema right now!!!!'

'Say sorry to them for what? What did I do?'

'Have a look.'

He looked to his left.

He realized what he had done.

It was something very inappropriate.

His left arm was merrily resting on Seema and Reema

while his forefinger was under Sweety's left armpit like a thermometer!

'Oh no...Sweety, I'm really sorry. It's not what you think.'

'Your apology is not accepted. You deserve this!'

'What? Another kissey?'

'No. This-'

Her fist rammed into his groin.

He yelped in pain.

'Sweety! What the hell is wrong with you? Why such extreme testicle torture at your end?' he asked after regaining a bit of composure.

'Every inappropriate action deserves a corresponding painful reaction. Reema had warned me all along that you are nothing but a South Indian tharki. I ignored her warning thinking that you are different. But I guess...all you men are just the same! You insert the love keeda by talking about love and romance but all that you really want is just some fucking action on the first date itself!'

'To begin with...I'm not a tharki. I also didn't insert any love keeda. I'm gullible and seedha. What happened was hugely inappropriate but it was certainly not deliberate at my end. But what you just did was deliberate. Why don't you ask your "great" confidantes Seema and Reema for their opinion?'

He meant the last bit sarcastically but he actually saw Sweety muttering something to her boobs! Unbelievable!

'I'm sorry, Raghu. Seema informed me that it was an accident at your end,' Sweety told him a few minutes later.

'Oh, she did?' he asked sarcastically.

'Yes, she did. Seema judged the matter in the Supreme Court of Love. After a thorough probe, she concluded the following: *While Raghu's thoughts are low quality, his actions are fairly high quality barring this one inappropriate action which happened by accident. He is a good human being and a thorough gentleman who deserves a second chance. Case dismissed!'*

He couldn't believe it!

Sweety had actually spoken to Seema and Seema had pronounced a verdict in an in house Supreme Court of Love? Hilarious!

'Raghu baby, promise me one thing.'

'Oh. I'm now back to being your baby?'

'Yes, you are my baby. Promise me that you will never hurt me.'

'You promise me that you will NEVER HURT ME!'

'C'mon baby. Don't overreact. It was just a gentle punch. Also promise me that you will always be fully honest with me.'

'I will be.'

He thought about it.

If he was fully honest and told her about his first impression of her during the workshop, her overdose of spirituality which irritated him back then and most importantly his time spent with Roma…he would definitely need to wear a helmet and an abdominal guard!

But he finally decided that he would tell her everything in bits and pieces in the days to come, so that a 'big love fight' could be averted and not have to be judged in the Supreme Court of Love!

'Are you lost in thought, my dreamy baby? I love you.'

'Yes, I was. I love you too. Right now, I'm feeling a tingling tak dhin dhin in my testicles and a romantic dhak dhak in my ventricles. I'm pretty sure this has never happened before. Maybe it's because I'm in love.'

'You know what?'

'What?'

'You should win some sort of award for your extraordinary ability to be able to blabber so much of nonsense.'

'And you should be the first person to win an award for having an in house Supreme Court of Love which gives "boob bhashans",' he muttered.

'You said something?'

'No, I didn't.'

He grinned to himself in his mind.

Would the 'nonsense generation' at his end exceed the 'boob bhashans' at Sweety's end during the course of their relationship?

He was surely going to find out in the days to come.

Later that night.

Raghu was back at home.

He was in his room, lying on his bed, tucked away comfortably under his blanket.

He was in deep sleep.

His mind had wandered to a chilled out beach in Goa.

It was the final destination he had wanted to reach.

A beach party was about to begin to celebrate the success of *The Paperback Badshah.*

The people at the party were waiting for his arrival.

He was currently parasailing.

He was in mid-air and was making a swift descent onto a specially constructed stage on the beach.

He finally landed onto the stage.

The people who had gathered started to clap excitedly.

He felt like a rock star.

He noticed that most of the audience comprised of people he had seen, met, interacted with or dreamt of, during his journey while writing *The Paperback Badshah*! They were all sitting in pairs with fellow humans, objects or animals and were holding copies of his book!

He noticed Shekhar sitting with chamcha-Mohan, Suresh with his client Mr. Singh, Nandu with Kavita, Mr. Prasad with his chaddi suitcase, David with his writing notebook, the shop assistant with the mannequin, TB with Biryani Begum, the old couple from the dinner date with Roma, Roma with her possessive buddah husband, the clichéd commentator with the balle balle commentator, the woman with her 'toy gaadi' loving son, Jimmy with the nude model, Chota Jadugar with his father, a baby faced leader with a goat, Digvijay with the HR manager, the religious baba with a cow, his editors- Sangeeta and Jasjeet, a faceless book critic with his irritating relative Gopi, Roma (again!) with man-child Murali and finally the bookstore couple who represented all the readers of *The Paperback Badshah* from across the country!

The party began in full swing.

He overheard a critic talk to another.

'....These hundred rupee type authors are only fame hungry. All they crave for is the media attention. No one wants to focus on the craft of writing. This guy Raghu, has written only one book but he is acting like a literary superstar! I still have no idea how his book sold so many copies. If his book can sell this much, then I'm sure that even if a monkey writes a book...it will sell.'

He noticed the critics throw copies of his book into the sea.

He felt bad.

But just then he noticed a woman lifeguard running along the length of the beach like she was straight out of *Baywatch*! She dived into the water. It wasn't to save a drowning human to but save a drowning copy of his book! Unbelievable! He couldn't believe that people cared about his book to such an extent!

He then saw Jimmy running towards him.

'Congrats Raghu on your bestselling book! Also congrats to you and Sweety on becoming a "together-together" couple! I'm really happy for you guys. By the way, I read your book.'

'You did? Seriously?' he asked Jimmy.

'Yes, I did. I however have some feedback for you- Your writing style and humour is really immature and infantile. When are you going to grow up? Will you spend your entire life writing books like this? How about some serious writing which can actually strike a genuine emotional chord with a reader? I know you will laugh as responsibility, maturity and other deeper, complex human emotions aren't keywords in your dictionary at the moment. But do give it a thought. You know I'm your well-wisher. By the way, I think your parents are proud of you. Have a look-'

He suddenly realized that he had seen almost everyone at the party except the most important people...HIS LOVING PARENTS! They were the ones who had put up with his nonsense and been instrumental in giving him the freedom to reach his goal!

He saw his mother enjoying the music and dancing merrily in a corner of a makeshift dance floor while his father standing a few feet away from her was imparting words of wisdom from his bank of life experiences to a few impressionable youngsters, who were listening quite keenly.

He couldn't believe it!

'Dude, your father still can't believe that you are planning to advise youngsters on how they should lead their lives by writing self-help books! Even I think this idea of yours is super funny! Your mother is however happy as she seems fairly confident that you are capable of at least getting a job as a beauty contestant's assistant. I will keep quiet now. But overall, you've done a good job. Adios my writer friend. Stay happy. Keep writing. I'm off.'

'Ok Jimmy. Take care.'

He noticed Jimmy run straight into the arms of the nude model!

He then noticed that rivals had turned friends.

Begum who never had a high opinion of TB's writing was sitting next to TB and was hugging him!

Seeing everyone around him having a good time with their respective companions, he suddenly realized that his companion *was missing*. He felt very lonely.

Where the hell was Sweety?

Just then he heard a loud clap of thunder and noticed a cloud of dust in the distance....

Two scootys were approaching him in full speed.

He noticed someone doing a full split on the bikes, like superstar Ajay Devgn had in *Phool Aur Kaante*.

He rubbed his eyes in disbelief at who it actually was. *It was none other than Sweety!*

What a delayed yet dramatic entry! Clearly her aerobics workout sessions for enhanced flexibility were paying off!

The scootys stopped exactly two feet in front of him.

Sweety got off and gave him a hug and then a quick kissey.

As they exchanged more kisses, it started to drizzle.

Everyone at the party started to run for cover to the nearby beach shacks.

Then an idea suddenly came to his mind.

Using a romantic move which he had always wanted to try since his school days, he used a copy of his book and covered Sweety's head against the drizzle!

She became emotional at this display of genuine care and affection.

She held his sweaty hand and they walked hand in hand towards a shack to get to know more about each other, to sip on a glass of feni and to hopefully share a plate of idli.

Another loud clap of thunder struck....

Raghu's alarm started ringing loudly.

He woke up with a start. What a dream!

He stretched a little and then looked around the room.

A new phase of life was about to begin. He was confident that he would take charge of his life in the days to come. *After all, he had confidently achieved his book dream.*

He had often heard authors say that writing a book for them was some sort of life changing experience.

He now knew why.

Writing *The Paperback Badshah* had been a journey of self introspection and self discovery which had made all the little struggles along the way totally worth it! It had been a journey which had given him a lot of personal happiness (but modest monetary happiness!) which years later, he would definitely reflect back upon with a lot of fondness.

He saw a copy of his book lying on the bed next to him.

He picked it up and gently patted the cover. He then mumbled a few affectionate words like a loving parent. The moment was an emotional, heartfelt one, which only a writer (whether or not published) would know for his work, far away from the critical, judgemental eyes of others.

THE END

Srishti's all time bestsellers ₹ 100 each

- A Dilli-Mumbai Love Story
- A Feeling Beyond Words
- A half baked love story
- A Life that you knew..
- A Little Bit of Love...
- A Little Love Incident
- And then it rained....
- Anyone Else but you
- A Roller Coaster Ride!
- As Long as I Love you...
- A thing beyond forever
- A Walk Down the Lane...
- Because you Loved me..
- Beep you! you BeepHole
- Belong
- Boundless Saga of Love
- By the River Pampa I...
- Careful what u Wish for
- Coming up on the show..
- Can't Cook a Love Story
- Corporate Atyaachaar
- Crazy Bloody Thing LOV
- Dancing with Maharaja
- Everything you Desire

- Few things left unsaid
- Forever in these pages
- From Cubicles 2 Cabins
- Heartbreaks & Dreams!
- Here Sat A Key Maker
- I am Broke....! Love me
- I am Still Committed..
- If God Had A Desk Job..
- If God went to B-School
- If I Pretend I am Sorry!
- It Happened that Night
- In Course of True Love
- I too had a love story..
- It's all About Love...
- It Should Be u!! My Love
- It wasn't Love at First
- I will Love Once Again!
- Jab se you have loved me
- Journey of two Hearts
- Just Like in the Movies
- Life is What you Make it
- Love Happens Like that
- Love, Life & A Beer Can!
- Love, Life and Dream on

- Love, Life and Lust...
- Love Life & all the Dots
- Love, me and Bullshit!
- Love Power Politics!!
- Love a Rather Bad Idea
- Love & Urban Melodrama
- LUV is a Dirty Business
- My Love Never Faked...
- Nothing for you my Dear
- Nothing Lasts Forever
- Of Tattoos and Taboos!
- Oops! 'I' fell in Love!
- Ouch! that 'Hearts'..
- Patyala Down De Throat
- Plz.. Kiss me or Kill me
- Reality Bytes 'Bites'
- She is Single I'm Taken
- Simple Things Make LUV
- Something in your Eyes
- Sumthing of a Mocktale
- 34 Bubblegums and Candies

- That Kiss in the Rain..
- The Dev-D Syndrome...
- The Equation of my Love
- The Funda of Mix-ology
- The Idiot-Dudes.....
- The India I Dream of
- The Journey of Rock...
- The Journey to Nowhere
- The Lost Scraps of Love
- The Off-Site Tamasha
- The Other way Round
- The Quest for Nothing!
- The Thing Between U & Me
- Those Small Lil Things
- Three Times Loser....
- To Whom it May Concern:
- When Life Tricked me..
- What... if not I.I.T.?
- Will you Marry Me Cupid
- Your Place or Mine?

◆

- Brain Building for achievement
  Herbert N. Casson

- Cheiro's : Language of the Hand

- Winning Personality:
  The Magic key to success
  F. Oss